DEATH IS A CLINGY EX

By

Randall J. Funk

Published in the United States by Ghost Light Press.

www.randalljfunk.com

ISBN 978-0-692-45798-6

Cover design by Ann McMan

First edition

Special thanks to:

Harold and Ann Snow, for their financial assistance and their faith in me.

Ellen Hart, for being a mentor and a friend.

Jessie Chandler, for all the help she provided, including introducing me to:

Ann McMan, for the fantastic cover art.

Matthew Glover, for his excellent website design.

Zach Curtis, for taking my author photo and doing great work with a faulty subject matter.

Mary Logue, for her helpful guidance during the writing phase.

Terese Pautz, for sharing her experiences with me.

John Nordling, for helping me polish up the book.

To all of my friends for their support and encouragement. Truly, it takes a village.

To Kris and Ben, for your patience and your love.

None of this is possible without you.

CHAPTER ONE

The most unfair part of a break-up is the timing. Here's what I mean:

At some point in the relationship (hereafter referred to as The Relationship), the Party of the First Part (hereafter referred to The Breaker) decides they want out of the arrangement. Now the end usually doesn't come suddenly—unless alcohol is involved—so The Breaker begins to work their way through all the emotional and intellectual baggage that surrounds the Big Event (hereafter referred to as The Break Up). However, the Breaker will do this while still being in The Relationship. The Breaker gets all the benefits of being with someone while slowly, secretly extricating themselves from said someone. Meanwhile, the Party of the Second Part (hereafter referred to as The Break-ee) goes along with a slaphappy grin on their face, clueless that the Doomsday Clock (hereafter referred to as, well, the Doomsday Clock) is getting closer and closer to midnight.

Finally, The Break Up occurs. And it takes a great amount of sensitivity on the part of the Breaker to realize that while The Break Up is weeks—or perhaps months—old to them, to the Break-ee it just happened. Failure to recognize this disparity can lead to recriminations and bitterness. And in some cases—usually involving alcohol—it can lead to restraining orders.

My name is Joe Davis. I get paid to write stuff like that.

That little passage comes to mind as I'm sitting in Glacier's Coffee House, waiting for an ex-girlfriend. I don't normally take meetings with exes. It's an invitation to a bad scene. But Tess said she was desperate, so I went against company policy.

Most of the time, I'm right at home in Glacier's. It's a converted café with checkerboard tile floors, straight-back chairs and picture windows. Said windows look out on Cathedral Hill, an old school brick-and-mortar neighborhood looming over downtown St. Paul. A stretch of retail along Selby Avenue buttresses the shady areas to the north from the upscale neighborhoods to the south. Glacier's draws the young and artistic denizens from the upscale side, meaning there's a lot of self-involvement and very little conversation. Perfect for writing. And on warm summer evenings such as this, it's walking distance from my place.

Tonight, though, I have a knot in my gut. It's been a few months, but the break up with Tess was an ugly one. She coolly asked for a point-by-point rundown of why I wished to terminate the relationship and when I was halfway through it, she started crying and threw a drink in my face. The entire bar was then treated to a point-by-point rundown of *my* faults, most of which revolved around me being a stinking piece of crap. She finished by punching me in the sternum and storming out.

I've avoided that place since then.

So, given that we left things on an I-wouldn't-piss-on-you-if-you-were-on-fire basis, I'm wondering why Tess would even bother contacting me. And this has me pondering, in my own shallow way, the nature of break-ups.

My laptop's open on the small round table. I write a blog for *The Daily Bugle*, a zine that began life as an indie rag before going digital. The blog (*Cup o' Joe*) covers all things humorous: relationships, politics, pop culture, daily living, etc. Essentially the same stuff I talked about at the lunch table in high school, but now get paid for it. I write three columns a week. It's not great money, but it's enough to pay the bills, keep the cats fed and have enough left over for some socializing. And hell, it beats working for a living.

The little gold bell over the front door jingles and Tess walks in, striking her usual stop-and-observe-the-place stance. Tess is an attractive woman and very well maintained. She's tall with raven-colored hair flowing perfectly to the nape of her neck and just enough make-up to show off her hazel eyes, high cheekbones and sculpted chin. A Bloomingdale's mannequin come to life.

Appearances, of course, were never the problem. As long as we were naked, things were clicking along fine. It was when we exposed our personalities that the disconnect arose. Tess sees herself as a powerful, driven, career woman. Others see her as an unpleasant, materialistic shrew. And by *others*, I mean me after I'd dated her for a few months.

I close the laptop and stand to greet her. She plants a not-quite-kiss on my right cheek. When we sit, the table suddenly seems smaller.

"How are you, Joe?" she says, situating the chair just so.

"I'm good."

"You always are." She waves a hand toward the slacks and dress shirt I'm wearing. "You didn't have to dress up."

"I'm going to a party later."

"Oh. Fine." Tess taps my laptop. "I read one of your columns last week."

"Which one?"

"The one about artificial butter flavoring." It was a column where I recalled working in a movie theater in college and how the butter topping was as easy to get off my hands as motor oil. "It was truly stunning work," Tess says.

Tess always made it clear that my fine brain was wasted on smallish topics. After all, I could be figuring out ways to make myself money or make others money or build research models into how to make money in the future. You know, stuff that's not remotely shallow.

"Glad you enjoyed it," I say.

"Can't wait to see what you come up with next."

"I've already got one in the can."

"And what's that?"

"A ten-point plan for peace in the Middle East."

Tess's perfectly trimmed eyebrows go up. "Really? What's the first point?"

"The total elimination of artificial butter flavoring on popcorn."

Her mouth tightens, pinching off whatever laugh might have escaped. "Okay, I walked into that one."

"Indeed you did." I drop the laptop into its bag and pull my mug of French Roast a little closer. "So, what's on your mind?"

Tess's right eye twitches a little. "Fine. Wouldn't want to keep you." She folds her hands on the table and fixes me with a placid look. "First, I'd like to apologize for my behavior when we last…talked."

"Well, it was a very sticky girl drink you threw at me."

"I know."

"And did you realize—because I didn't know this before—that the sternum is the *second* most painful place you can hit a guy?"

"I'm sorry."

"And it's dangerous. I think that's how Houdini died."

The pace of Tess's twitch picks up. "Are you finished?"

"I am."

"Good. Because I need your help."

This comes as no surprise. When Tess said she was desperate, I figured it meant something along these lines. What *does* surprise me is the look in Tess's eyes. It's not anger or disapproval. I've seen those often enough. This is fear.

"What's going on?" I ask.

"Someone's trying to kill me."

CHAPTER TWO

Now *there's* something you don't hear every day. Well, I suppose if you run a terrorist cell you do, but most of us are in the clear.

"Someone's trying to kill you?" I ask, "Maybe I need some more information here."

Tess's eyes brush the room. She lowers her voice. "A co-worker of mine is trying to kill me."

"Why?"

"It's a work-related thing."

"Something to do with stealing food out of the break room fridge? That kind of deal?"

There's a flare in Tess's cold eyes. "I'm asking for your help. Do you think you could be serious for five seconds?"

"I'm trying. But you work in an office that maintains insurance policies. How do things get intense enough for murder?"

The espresso machine fires up. Tess jumps. She puts a hand to her chest, catching her breath. She takes a bracing sip of my coffee.

"You need to know the person involved here," she says, "It's a co-worker named Nancy. She's pissed because I got a promotion."

"Ah. Sounds perfectly plausible."

"You don't understand. Work is Nancy's *life*. She doesn't date. She doesn't have friends. She works eighty hours a week, commutes and sleeps. That's *it*."

"What's the deal with the promotion?"

"Our boss, Tom, was promoted from Insurance Service team leader to Service Vice President. He's been doing both jobs for several months and he finally decided to name a replacement. I got the job."

"And this Nancy person thinks it should have been her?"

"Yes. She and I were the only in-house candidates and she wasn't remotely happy when I got it."

"Where do you get the idea she's trying to kill you?"

Tess's nails claw the table. "She's threatened me. Several times."

"How?"

Tess takes a folded piece of notebook paper from her purse and slides it over to me. It reads: *You know what you've done. You're dead. I'm watching you.*

I fold the letter up. "Lacks a certain touch of the poet."

"It's not a book report, asshole. It's a threatening note!"

The little bell over the door goes again. Tess turns an ugly face to a dude with a checked jacket and a lime tie. (Possibly a writer, but I'm going with poseur.) When she turns back, the fear is in her eyes again.

"There have been phone calls, too," she says, "Along the same line as that note."

"She's probably just trying to scare you."

"Well, it's working."

I slide the note back over to Tess. "Where do I come in?"

"I need you to go to an event with me."

Okay, this has entered my *Five Goofiest Conversations* list, and is rapidly moving up the charts. Someone's trying to kill Tess and she's asking me on a date? It's like getting a call from someone who's trapped upside down in a ditch, smells gasoline and wants you to pick up their dry cleaning.

"An event?" I ask.

"It's weird, I know. But it's a company thing and I think Nancy's going to try something."

"Why? Is it a guns and knives event?"

"No. It's an announcement of NewCo Mutual's charity drive. It's over at The Taft Hotel."

"Why would Nancy try something there?"

"Because one of the calls said I would be a dead woman by the end of the event. If somebody's going to get to me, this is a good spot. There's going to be a big crowd and not a ton of security. Plenty of chances for Nancy to do something."

"Why not go to the police?"

"With no proof?"

"You got a threatening note."

Tess tosses the note aside. "All the letters are cut from magazines. Anybody could have done this. *I* could have done this. It doesn't prove anything. I mean, *you* don't seem to believe me. Why should the police?"

Hmm, nice little twist of the Guilt Knife there. "Okay, fine," I say, "Why not skip the event?"

Tess looks at me like I'm a child who just wet himself. "Joe, there will be people there I need to talk to. And to be seen talking to. This is my career, after all."

Ah. Should have known better than to weigh Tess's career against her life. It's no contest. "Can't someone in the office help you out?" I ask.

"No."

"Why not?"

"Because I think Nancy has someone working with her."

I bite the inside of my cheek. "A co-conspirator? This *is* an insurance office, right? You didn't start running Covert Ops while I wasn't looking?"

Tess's manicured nails clack away on the Formica tabletop. "There have been times when I've been in meetings with Nancy and come back to find notes left on my desk. And I've heard a male voice during a few of the phone calls. She's not doing this alone. I can't trust anyone at the office."

Which brings up the Bonus Round Question. "Why me? As I recall, the last time we spoke I was the Anti-Christ with a piss poor attitude—"

"I apologized for that."

"On top of that, I'm not exactly the first guy you call in a situation like this. I'm a writer. Okay, journalist. All right, blogger. Still, I'm not a cop. I haven't thrown a punch in anger since the fifth grade. Hell, my favorite exercise is *running*. How much help can I be?"

Tess takes a long breath. "I don't have anyone else to ask. I talk about Nancy having no life outside of work, but I'm not any better. You're the closest thing I've got to a friend." She looks at me, eyes glistening. "Will you help me, Joe?"

I'd be a fool to do this. Tess is clearly blowing this thing out of proportion. It's an entanglement that won't come to anything but misery. I let out a long sigh and look her straight in the eyes.

"All right, when is this event?"

CHAPTER THREE

My big commitment for the evening is a birthday party for my friend Wheezer. No one's sure how old The Wheeze is (on a guess, early thirties, like most of our friends) or if, in fact, this is his birthday. And given the amount of creative pharmaceuticals Wheezie's consumed over the years, I doubt he knows, either. But every now and again, he throws a bash at Big Ben's Distillery, a kick-ass brew pub in downtown Minneapolis, and calls it his birthday party. While the event may be held anywhere from February to November, The Wheeze only holds one per year. His way of giving in to convention.

Though Big Ben's is cavernous, the pools of light from the hanging lamps give it a sense of intimacy. I'm at the bar, nursing a pint of Hefeweizen while my best friend Mike ignores his pint of India Pale Ale and goes on about his latest break-up.

"Everything is going great," Mike says, "I meet her parents. I'm charming. We have dinner. The conversation's wonderful. Coffee and dessert afterwards. Couldn't be cozier. Then they take the dishes into the kitchen and I'm left alone with her brother."

"Oh, you mean the one who's—"

"Retarded. Yes."

Our friend Carol is one stool over from Mike. She takes a hand away from her girly drink and waves it like she's erasing a blackboard. "Not retarded. Mentally challenged."

Mike spins toward her. "No, no. You don't know this kid. If anyone in that room was dealing with a challenge, it was me."

Against my better judgment, I encourage him to continue. "So what happened with the brother?"

"Ah, he starts in on me, telling me I'm ugly, I eat funny, his sister's only dating me because she feels sorry for me. Stuff like that. At first, I just ignore him. But he keeps going and I start getting pissed. So, I very politely tell him to shut the hell up. He doesn't. Then I tell him to go screw himself."

"And what did he do?"

"He punched me in the head."

Carol and I wince. Punching Mike in his big bulldog head is about the worst thing you can do. While his forehead doesn't look remarkable, it has a density that makes you think he's the product of a Cro-Magnon and a concrete block.

Carol asks, "How bad did he hurt his hand?"

"Pretty bad," Mike says, "He starts hopping around, screaming, 'My hand's busted! My hand's busted!' The family comes rushing in. I try to explain, but I know it's a lost cause. The mother's hysterical. The father throws me the hell out. I offer to drive Whitney home, but she wants no part of me." He finally takes a sip of his IPA. "Haven't heard from her since."

"That doesn't surprise you, does it?" I ask.

"Well, I could expect a little understanding! I'm the victim here. Who's prepared for a situation like that? You never hear about a special needs kid with an attitude problem!"

"What about Glenn Beck?" I say.

"Who?"

Should have known. Mike could probably follow politics if he wanted to, but he can't put down the comic books and grape soda long enough to pay attention.

He takes a long drink of the IPA, grimacing against the spicy bite of the hops. "To hell with it, right? Onward and upward."

"Into yet another quagmire," I say.

Mike's been my best friend since about five minutes after we got to college. He's like a big, ill-behaved Doberman: good-looking, charming, but very likely to eat your shoes or crap on the front porch.

He strokes his goatee. "Speaking of quagmires, how was coffee with Tess?"

Carol nearly spills her Cosmo on her sleeveless white blouse. "Tess? The woman who threw the drink at you? That Tess? Why would you have coffee with her?"

"She's needs my help. Someone's trying to kill her."

Since I've got their undivided attention, I give them the ADD version of Tess's likely paranoid fantasy. Carol brushes away the dark bangs framing her face and curls up against the bar, tapping her finger against her chin as she thinks. Mike, however, jumps in with the first opinion.

"You know what she's trying to do, don't you?" he says, "She's trying to get something started again."

"Kind of a weird way to go about it, isn't it?" I say.

"You said she's a little off the beam. A little power-mad. And she's been scorned. Women like her will try anything."

Carol rolls her large blue eyes. "How would you know?"

"Who's been scorned more than me? Believe me, Joe, you don't want anything do with this woman. She'll kick you to the curb first chance she gets. Revenge Break-Up. Classic Revenge Break-Up."

And the advice session ends because our friend Lars, his quasi-pompadour, his cheap suit and his orchestra, has burst into view. That's how Lars enters. He never saunters or ambles up. He just suddenly appears, a tangle of arms, legs, asshole and elbows, and hauls you into the middle of whatever he's doing right now. In this case, he swoops in, tosses a stuffed manila folder on the bar and orders an oatmeal stout.

"I'm giving you guys an opportunity," he says, as if this is what we'd been talking about for the last ten minutes, "It is a *sure fire* money-making investment." Lars fancies himself an entrepreneur. The rest of us fancy him a spectacular waster of other people's time and money.

"What is it?" I say, "Baby's First Ponzi Scheme?"

"No. Nothing like that." Then he gets a toothy grin and points at me. "Good one." Lars doesn't miss jokes. He just runs several seconds ahead of them. "It's an entertainment venture," he continues, "And I'm giving you guys a break. I've got all the investors I need for the overhead, but I want you guys to get in on the ground floor."

"Ground floor of what?" Mike asks.

Lars grandly flips open the folder. His gestures are always grand, if a bit jerky. The folder contains a detailed pencil drawing of a nightclub named Les Bos. Mike's big canine head hovers over the drawing.

"It's a nightclub?" he asks.

Lars casually slides in front of Carol. "Of sorts. You see, we're going to provide entertainment. For a discerning and bold type of male clientele."

Carol pokes her head out from behind Lars. "It's a strip joint?"

Lars wags a finger at her. "It's a gentleman's club."

"No," Carol says, "Gentleman's clubs are men sitting around a paneled room, smoking cigars and talking about stocks."

"And that's what we provide. That and some boobs."

Carol's severe eyebrows furrow. It's the thing about her: her smile can light up a room, but if she's not smiling, you best keep your distance. "The last thing the world needs is another strip joint."

Lars folds his bony arms in a stance of defiant superiority. "This isn't another strip joint. It's unique."

"What's unique about it?"

"The women strip each other."

For the first time, Mike takes his eyes off the folder. "Each other? Right up there on stage? Women taking off other women's clothes?"

"You got it. Sound good?"

"Are you hiring?"

"Sorry, my friend. Payroll's full up."

"Who said you had to pay me?"

Lars chuckles and lays a hand on Mike's shoulder. "I'm only in the market for investors."

"I'm in. Where the hell's my checkbook?"

The oatmeal stout arrives and Lars leaves his usual large tip. He sips the coal black ale and raises his eyebrows at me. "What about it, Joe? You in?"

I've got my cringe on. "I don't know. It's a little..."

"Daring?"

"Depraved."

He turns to Carol. "What about you, dear?"

"Yeah, I'm in."

Now *I* turn to Carol. "What?"

She shrugs. "Nobody ever lost money betting on the depravity of the American male."

Lars scoops up the folder and leans toward me, dropping his voice. "I'll keep a spot open for you. Think about it."

"Leave him alone," Carol says, "He's got a lot on his mind."

"Oh yeah, coffee with the ex. I'd steer clear of that one, brother." He pats me on the shoulder and he's off again.

I watch him go. "So, the nays have it?"

Mike stares into his beer. "It's your call." In my experience, that's a friend's way of saying *You're free to fuck this up seven ways to Sunday. I'll be at the bar if you need me.*

***

The party breaks up a few hours later. I'm not certain The Wheeze even showed up. He's not the kind of guy who does well with commitment.

I walk Carol back to her car. We're in the same ramp, a few blocks from Big Ben's. Mike and Lars were too caught up in planning their junior high fantasy/business venture to notice us leave.

"Joe?" Carol asks, "You still there?"

We're near Carol's car and I believe I've been staring at my shoes for the last few minutes. "Yeah, I'm fine."

"Thinking about Tess? This thing bothering you that much?"

I scratch my chin. "She's scared. Said I'm her only friend. Maybe I owe her."

Carol scrutinizes me with those big blue eyes. "A break-up is actually bothering you?"

"Is that odd?"

"Yeah. You break up with a girl every three or so weeks. Besides, you've never struck me as angst-ridden."

"I hang out with Mike. There's not a lot of angst left to go around."

"Tell me about it." Carol and Mike dated for about a year. Their break-up came as a real surprise. To Mike. "You really think she wants to get back together?" Carol asks.

"I don't know. Wouldn't make my dating life any worse."

"Yeah, I get that. I'm on a major losing streak myself." She twirls her keys on her finger as we reach her car. "So, you're going to help Tess?"

"I suppose. I mean, what's the worst that can happen?"

"She pulls your heart out, *Temple of Doom*-style, and eats it right before your eyes."

"Well, that would be a worst case scenario, yes. But I think I can brave it."

Carol spins away and flutters her fingers over her shoulder. "Your funeral."

My car is two levels up, and on the other side of the ramp. Fortunately, my cardio's in tip-top condition, so I jog most of the way. Coming up on my car, I see a folded piece of paper stuck under one of the windshield wipers. Probably a flyer for a pizza joint or something. I'm ready to toss it, but the little block letters catch my eye. They've been cut from a magazine. Several magazines, in fact. I open it up.

Do yourself a favor and stay out of this. Could be hazardous to your health. And *Could be* is circled in red marker.

I look around, as if the person who left the note is hanging out, watching me and giggling. I don't see anything, of course. The corners of the note are getting damp where it's touching my palms.

My funeral. Thanks for the good karma, Carol.

CHAPTER FOUR

I don't like big parties as a rule. Smaller gatherings like The Wheeze's faux-birthday party are fine, but large-scale blowouts turn me off. If I want to see people get liquored up, dance badly, vainly attempt to get laid and generally make asses of themselves, all I have to do is...well, all I have to do is go to a big party.

Corporate parties are the worst. They combine all the previous elements with the insular, sweat-the-small-stuff culture of your average office. Now imagine a guy who's spent his adult life religiously avoiding anything resembling office work being thrust into this atmosphere and you'll realize I'm in for a special kind of hell.

That's got me squirming as I drive my Saturn Ion through downtown Minneapolis. That and Tess's glare from the passenger seat. My black suit has apparently passed muster, but she hates the collarless white shirt. It sends the wrong message. ("F-you, I don't think enough of this deal to wear a tie.") That, of course, is exactly the message I wanted to send. For her part, Tess is resplendent in a low-cut black cocktail dress, high heels and gold jewelry. Like a less-crazy Vivien Leigh. A slightly-less-crazy Vivien Leigh.

Tess taps the folded threatening note on her leg. "You didn't see who left this?"

"No. If someone leaves a threatening note, they generally don't hang around. Sort of defeats the purpose of leaving a note."

"It had to be Nancy."

"Why would she threaten me? She doesn't even know me."

"She's probably tailing me. Remember what the one note said. She's watching me. She's probably trying to scare you off."

I'm tempted to tell her Nancy doesn't need to scare me off. For a sandwich and a bag of chips, I'd gladly drop this whole thing. But I stay quiet and we fall into tense silence, which is what we do best these days.

NewCo Mutual's gathering is at The Taft, a towering hotel on the west edge of downtown Minneapolis. The twelve floors are stacked around a sunken plaza; each floor with a walkway providing a view. Glass elevators shoot up and down on two sides. The plaza is surrounded by potted flora and crisscrossed with hanging lights. This is used for special events, such as the NewCo party. We arrive ten minutes before the party's six-thirty starting time. I leave the car with the valet while Tess tends to something at the front desk. She grabs my arm and yanks me across the carpeted lobby.

"Just stick close," she says, "Don't let me out of your sight."

"All night?"

"Of course. Is that a problem?"

"Well, I *was* banking heavily on standing at the bar, looking surly and chatting up the bartender."

"Sorry. I'm running the show. It's important. There's going to be people from both the home office and the field here."

"Okay, explain the difference to me again?"

Tess rolls her eyes, letting me know this has been explained to me before. "The field means our financial advisors who are working with clients. They sell our individual products: mutual funds, insurance policies, annuities, brokerage products, things like that. The home office works in support of the financial advisors. If they need to make adjustments or get information about their clients' accounts, they call us."

"Do the actual clients ever call you?"

"Sometimes. Or they write letters. Generally, we encourage them to talk to their advisors. Too many cooks spoiling the broth. That kind of thing."

Having been thus schooled, I'm content to let Tess run the show. Clearly, she's in her element. All the way through the lobby, she's like a lightweight contender pacing the corner before a big fight. As soon as we're past the velvet rope and into the party, her eyes light up and a huge smile blossoms. She moves from person to person, pressing the flesh, saying how glad she is to see them. Meantime, I get dragged around like a piece of luggage.

It doesn't take long to cover the whole territory. A long buffet table, set up with hors d'oeuvres, dominates the room. Tables devoted to each department are grouped around it. To one side, there's a long mahogany bar with three hustling bartenders and a large collection of booze. Insurance Service, Tess's department, is seated near the bar, which may be the only break I catch all night.

Suddenly, Tess fastens a death grip on my arm and whispers. "There she is."

Nancy matches up with the description Tess gave me: wavy hair pulled back into a severe ponytail, a plain blouse-and-slacks combo showing off nothing and no make up to be seen. Her skin is taut around the eyes and mouth, bringing to mind a Rottweiler ready to strike. She finds a place on the opposite side of the table and sits.

"Let's keep making the rounds," Tess says.

Thankfully, our next stop is the bar. Tess orders a Mojito and I get a vodka rocks. Let the games begin.

"I assume this is the cocktail hour?" I say.

"Yes. There's going to be a few words from Barry then dinner and a dance."

A dance. Wow, that's a depressing thought. "Who's Barry?"

"He's the CEO of the company."

"Do we have to stay for the dance?"

"No. But if you want to make an evening of it, I've got a room reserved for the night."

My drink stops just shy of my lips. "You reserved a room for us?"

"*I* didn't reserve it. The company has a block of rooms set aside and I said I'd take one. Better safe than sorry."

Yoinks. Somewhere, Mike is giggling. I know it.

I busy myself with following Tess around and keeping an eye out for Nancy. Tess spends her time talking to people I don't care about on topics that don't interest me. After a while, I'd actually take a bullet for her just to break the monotony. I'm contemplating the checked floor when Tess taps me on the arm.

"Joe, I'd like to you to meet my boss, Tom Reilly."

Tess par-whips me into a handshake with a burly, bald-headed guy who grips my hand like we're in the consolation bracket of a Tough Man contest.

"How you doing?" he says, flashing me a grin full of uneven teeth, "Tom Reilly, VP of Service."

"Joe Davis, Ayatollah of Rock and Rolla."

He laughs, more at my play on words than the inference I could care less about titles. Tom isn't in the boss mold as I would picture it. He's got piggy-eyes, a scraggly goatee and a suit he probably bought at Target just for this occasion. As he takes a big sip of his light beer, a pair of cufflinks, probably *not* purchased at Target, gleam in the low lighting.

"Quite a shindig, huh?" he asks.

"Quite a shindig, indeed," I say.

"Guess if you've gotta do these things, you want to do them in style. Waste of time as far as I'm concerned, but what are you doing to do?"

"You don't like parties, either?"

"The party? No, the party's great. I was talking about the charity drive."

I do a double take. "Not a big charity guy?"

"Ah, it's fine, if you're into that sort of thing and it's your money. I just figure company resources can be better spent."

"On what? Bonuses for overpaid executives?"

"Exactly, exactly. Give it to people who can do something with it."

"Like buy new cufflinks?"

He holds them up to the light. "You got it. Keeps the economy moving."

I've never been clear on which type of person I dislike more: those who willfully have bullshit points of views or those who simply don't know any better. Given his buddy-buddy variety of openness, I'm guessing Tom is one of the latter. Tess, her smile becoming more forced, tries laughing along.

"Business comes first," Tom says, his eyes dropping to Tess's cleavage, "You know why I hired Tess to take my place in Insurance Service?"

"A couple things present themselves," I say.

Tess giggles and hugs my arm, turning her chest away from Tom's gaze.

"Because she's focused," he says, his eyes returning to me, "Knows the business, doesn't let anything stop her." He waves his drink, indicating the entire party. "None of this dog-and-pony-show stuff." He turns to Tess. "You were the right choice to lead Insurance Service. Every day of the week and twice on Sundays."

Tess nods, suddenly shy. "I don't think everyone feels that way."

Tom's mouth curls into a little sneer. "Fuck 'em." With that bit of managerial wisdom, he turns to me. "So, Joe, right? What do you do for a living, Joe?"

Here's my issue: the conversations I have with nine-to-fivers usually go something like "What do you do?" "I'm a writer." "Oh, what do you write?" "A humor blog." Then I get a look saying it's too bad I'm thirty-three and live in my parents' basement.

"I'm in public relations," I say.

"Oh? Who do you work for?"

"The Irish Republican Army."

The piggy-eyes bore into me. "The IRA?"

"Erin-go-bragh, me boy-o."

Tom may have a vague idea he's being messed with, but he lets it go and turns to Tess. "You're doing good. Don't worry about what other people are saying. Stay true to who you are." Five bucks says he got that little nugget out of a motivational book about moving cheese or some shit.

Suddenly, Tom's face clouds and he stares across the room. I follow his gaze to a tall, steel-gray guy in a blue serge suit. The guy seems harmless enough, but the intensity of Tom's stare would indicate a fistfight is nigh. After a second, Tom again flashes his gnarly smile.

"I need to make the rounds," he says, "I'll drop by the Insurance Service table later on, talk to everyone. Nice meeting you, Joe. Be good to Tess. Hate to think she's banging a mick, but what are you going to do?" And he's off, his bald head bobbing over the top of the crowd.

"Great guy," I say, "Product of incest, I'm guessing?"

Tess finally stops forcing her smile. "He lacks a few social graces, yes."

"Doesn't exactly strike me as management material."

"Tom's got a lot of hidden talents. He's organized, he knows the business inside and out, he works well with people."

"Huh."

"And his father-in-law's the CEO."

"Ah."

One vodka rocks later, the cocktail hour ends and we find our seats at the Insurance Service table. Tess and Nancy glare at each other through the slightly-wilted salad course and into the rubber-chicken-and-overcooked-rice entrée. Meanwhile, by way of small talk, I keep getting asked the same stupid question by their co-workers.

"What do you do for a living, Joe?"

Leading to a bevy of answers.

"I'm a goat herder."

"I grub stumps."

"I sip cognac and kick ass."

Tess gives me an occasional dirty look, but is otherwise busy promoting herself like only a born politician can. After the entrée, things thin out a little bit at the table. I look mournfully toward the bar, craving another drink. Unfortunately, Tess shows no inclination of going that direction, so I'm forced to settle for a dessert of weak coffee and dry cake.

During one of my wistful glances toward the bar, I spot Tom and Nancy having a chat. I can't figure out if they're in an argument. Nancy's gestures are compact and forceful and she's speaking through her teeth. Tom holds his beer in front of him, glancing around. For a second, he leans in just as forcefully, the shock of it calming Nancy down. No one else seems to be paying attention.

I nudge Tess, getting an annoyed look in return. I nod toward the argument, but when Tess looks that direction, the participants are gone.

"What am I supposed to be looking at?" she asks.

"There was a, I saw a...you know what? Forget it."

Tess's look of disgust goes up to eleven. "How much have you had to drink?"

I politely sip my coffee, letting the *Not damn nearly enough* remain unspoken.

The program follows, hosted by a stiff-as-hell junior exec wearing a Hillary Clinton-esque pants suit. She introduces Barry, the CEO. Turns out, he's the guy with the steel gray hair that inspired Tom's earlier stink-eye. Unlike the MC, Barry actually commands the room, calmly and clearly stating the need to keep the community healthy and safe. He finishes to significant applause, leaving the MC to deliver some mind-numbing program notes. A short video follows, then the program is mercifully over and the staff starts setting the room up for the dance. I'm jostled by the crowd as the tables are cleared and the buffet is relocated to one side of the room. Then I realize Tess is gone.

Panic grips my chest. My head's on a swivel, searching the crowd. Son of a bitch. *One* job to do—stick close to Tess—and I've botched it. Mom always said I'd get in trouble by not paying attention to other people. (But hey, I'm the middle kid. We're supposed to be self-centered, aren't we?) I finally spot Tess near the bar. She's being guided into a back hallway by a guy just a step shy of being a gorilla.

The close-cropped black hair and the shoulders of his black suit stand out above the crowd. I get only a glimpse before they disappear through the door. I shoulder my way through the crowd. No idea what I'm going to do when I reach them. Getting beaten to death may be my only option. When I get through the door, the guy has Tess backed up against the wall, standing uncomfortably close.

"What's going on?" I say, trying to work an edge of authority into my voice.

Tess and the guy both sport wide smiles. "Hi, Joe," Tess says, "Meet my friend Brian."

Brian, the afore-mentioned gorilla, grabs my hand in a bone-crusher. "Brian Denton. How you doing?"

I'm about six feet tall myself, but Brian has half-a-head on me. Not that the head is impressive. It looks ridiculously small on the rest of his body. I'm guessing the health club is Brian's best friend. He's got the requisite jewelry, tan and cologne of your average metrosexual, but the simian quality of his face kills the effect. It's as if he was carved out of granite, assuming it was near the end of the day and the workman was anxious to get home.

Tess rushes to make things friendly. "Brian and I started in Service together."

He grins, his teeth obscenely white. "Same training class, same day."

"He was up for the promotion as well."

The grin fades a bit. "But Tess got the job. That's the important part."

"As long as it wasn't Nancy," Tess says.

Brian flinches like he's been kicked in the crotch. "Don't even think about that. Half the team would've left. We're all thrilled to have you on top." He makes a show of covering his imagined faux pas. "I mean on top of the department. The department. You got that, right?"

Tess playfully slaps him on the arm. "We'll talk later."

"Save me a dance." He gives me another crushing handshake. "Nice meeting you, Jeff."

"Joe."

"Him, too."

Brian disappears through the door. I wheel on Tess.

"You mind not disappearing on me?" I say.

"I was just talking to Brian. I was perfectly safe."

"Okay, fine. If you're perfectly safe with Brian, why am *I* here? I thought you didn't have a friend in the world."

"It's complicated. Just trust me. I *do* need you here."

Grudgingly, I let her lead me back to the party. The dance has started and music is provided by Stan Olsen and The Rhythm Kings; a combo so bland, they would have made Lawrence Welk puke. I'm anxious to leave, but Tess hasn't socialized with enough muckity-mucks. So, I get dragged around the room a little more. After a round of socializing, Tess almost walks right into Barry. Rather than rejoicing at another opportunity for social climbing, Tess freezes up. Barry regards her, coldly.

"Tess, right?" he asks.

For a second, Tess debates 'fessing up. She offers the forced smile and extends her hand. "Yes, I am. Pleased to see you, Barry."

He looks at the hand before giving it a half-hearted shake. "Things are going well in Insurance?"

"So far. Absolutely."

"Tom seems pleased."

If I didn't know better (and actually I don't), I'd swear Tess is about to hyperventilate. "I hope so," she says.

A slight smirk curls a corner of Barry's mouth. "I'm sure you do." He walks away without saying another word or offering a glance.

Tess looks ready to cry. "I need to talk to Tom. I'll be back."

I can only watch as she strolls to the bar and buttonholes Tom, dragging him into the back hallway. Huh. This security guard gig appears to be part-time work and a full-time pain-in-the-ass. On the bright side, Tess's leaving frees me up to grab a seat at the bar. I've just ordered another vodka rocks when someone taps me on the arm. I look over and, holy shit, it's Nancy.

There's a long moment where I wait for her to knife me. Fortunately, I'm just shit-faced enough not to care. I like to think Dean Martin went this way.

"Excuse me," Nancy says, "But you're Joe Davis, right? I mean, *the* Joe Davis?"

"*The* in what sense?"

"You write for *The Daily Bugle*."

Oh, *that*. "Yeah, I'm that Joe Davis."

"I thought so. My name's Nancy Balstrom. I just wanted to tell you—" She takes a deep breath. "I'm a huge fan of yours."

There's got to be a punch line here, right? But no, Nancy breaks into a wide smile, all trace of hardness disappearing.

"I, I think you're the funniest person around," she says, "I don't read much on the net, or anywhere else, but I never miss your column."

Well, this certainly beats getting knifed. "Oh. I...thanks. You really read my stuff?"

As if to back up her claim, Nancy runs down a list of my columns, including the ones about traffic cameras (and how to have fun with them), professional wrestling (and why it's under-appreciated), tennis (and why it attracts strictly douchebags) and Don Knotts (and why he was a better actor than Laurence Olivier).

"You're just amazing." Nancy chuckles and nervously tucks a strand of hair behind her ear. "I can't tell you how much I need a good laugh from time to time. That means everything to me."

"Thank you. It's, it's great to hear."

Nancy leans on the bar. "I *am* curious, though: why are you here with Tess?"

"Well, uh," How does a conversation that's two minutes old get this complicated? "We're, we're just friends."

"Oh. I'm surprised Tess needed a date. She doesn't lack for friends." There's a slight disapproval in how she says *friends*.

"I understand there's some tension there."

31

"She told you about that?" Nancy laughs and waves it off. "She likes the drama. It's really not that big a deal. Sooner or later, she'll sleep her way into another promotion and I'll have the Insurance Service job."

I officially feel foolish. I *am* being set up. Bet you anything. Tess has been stewing over our break-up and plotting this thing lo' these many weeks. Mike is right. I'm a gullible idiot.

The crowd jostles us a little. Nancy shoots them a hateful look. It's even more hateful look when her eyes come back to me. Because there's an arm draped around me and I know exactly who it belongs to.

"Having fun with my date?" Tess asks.

The hardness returns to Nancy's face. I turn to Tess. "This isn't a date," I say.

Now Tess's eyes get a little hateful. "Then what do you call it?"

"I thought I'm here for your protection."

Nancy's eyebrows go up slightly. "Protection? Protection from what?"

Tess picks up my drink and steps away. "Joseph? Can we talk?"

Swiping my drink is certainly the best carrot-and-stick operation she could run. I nod my apologies to Nancy and follow Tess through a knot of people. We find a spot at the end of the buffet table; the closest thing we can get to privacy.

I swipe my drink back. "Was that really necessary? The putting-an-arm-around-me thing?"

"I thought I'd remind you why you're here. You two seemed a little chummy."

"I don't know about chummy, but she doesn't seem like much of a threat."

"Get real. You can't see she's manipulating you?"

"She might not be the only one."

Well, it's out now. Tess puts her hands on her hips. "What is that supposed to mean?"

"Did you really need me here? Me and no one else? Because I've been here all night and I haven't seen anyone out to get you. Least of all Nancy."

There's a strong mix of hurt and anger in her eyes. "You have no idea how full of crap you are."

Now is my chance for the big *Frankly, my dear, I don't give a damn* exit. I knock back the rest of my drink and slam the glass on the white tablecloth. Before I can storm out, though, something catches my eye. A large, dark shape falling through space. I stare at it, slack-jawed. It's a person, but my mind can't quite grasp that. Like seeing a unicorn on your front lawn. It shouldn't be real, but there it is.

Tess follows my gaze. "What are you—?"

She turns in time to catch the impact. The buffet table explodes in a shower of glass, plastic flowers and splinters. We dive to the floor, recoiling from the explosion. All conversation, all noise of any kind in the place, stops, replaced by an eerie silence. Some people wander toward the ruined table, stiff-legged and stunned, like they just wandered off the set of *Night of the Living Dead.*

"What the fuck was that?" Tess asks, her voice a shocked whisper.

Then I see it. An arm and a leg extending from separate portions of what was once the table. There's a brand new pair of cufflinks on the arm.

So much for Tess sucking up to her boss.

CHAPTER FIVE

"So, this was Tess's boss?" Mike asks, settling into his chair.

"Yep," I say, "Guy named Tom Reilly."

"And he just crashed through the buffet table?"

"Right on through."

"From how high up?"

"They figure about eight floors."

"Is he…?"

"Alive?"

"Yes."

"No."

"Whoa." Then Mike sums it up with the expression guys use to cover every shocking, bewildering, upsetting thing we see: "Dude."

"Dude, indeed."

It's early afternoon and Mike and I are having coffee on what I call my front stoop. It's actually a small cement lip in front of the arch windows of my third floor apartment. A few months ago, I discovered said lip could hold two lawn chairs and leave enough room to kick your feet up, allowing enjoyment of the shade at the front of the converted brownstone I call home. Below us, joggers and bikers, decked out in fashionable sportswear, cruise up and down Summit Avenue, a rolling collection of mansions that F. Scott Fitzgerald once dubbed a "museum of architectural failures." Afternoon coffee is a ritual for me and Mike. Thanks to the nature of our jobs, we call our own shots. I write a blog and Mike sells real estate. His numbers are okay, but his real skills lie in finding excuses to get out of the office.

"Was it suicide?" Mike asks.

"The cops haven't said. I met the guy. He didn't seem the suicidal type."

"What's the suicidal type?"

"I don't know. Reads Sylvia Plath. Keeps a lot of rubber tubing in the garage. Trust me, it wasn't this guy."

"How close were you when he, y'know, hit the deck?"

"About four feet."

"Whoa. How did Tess take it?"

"Not at all well."

Not that I had been paying a hell of a lot of attention to her at that moment. Those few seconds of eerie silence gave way to all hell breaking loose once everyone realized what had happened. The place turned into a pocket riot. I sat with Tess in the lobby while she screamed and cried and hyperventilated. At one point, I realized I'd been repeating *Holy fuck* over and over again for about ten minutes.

Mike sits back in his chair and shoos Lenny, my alpha cat, away from the window. "You been talking to Tess a lot lately?"

"Too much."

Every time the phone rings, I'm never sure which Tess I'm going to get: Scared Tess, Sad Tess, Philosophical Tess, Angry Tess, Tess-Who-Wants-To-Come-Over-And-Just-Sleep-On-The-Couch-Because-She's-Too-Freaked-Out-To-Be-Alone-And-Don't-Read-Anything-Into-It-Because-She's-Just-Talking-About-Sleeping-On-

The-Couch-And-Why-Do-Men-Have-To-Turn-Everything-Into-Sex Tess.

Mike studies a woman in a sports bra and short-shorts jogging past the building. "You think it has anything to do with those threats she was getting?"

"I don't know. Maybe. I mean, Tom was the one who gave Tess the promotion. Maybe it has something to do with that."

Mike tugs at his power tie, sighing as the jogging woman disappears from view. "What about you? You feel safe?"

"What did I do?"

"I don't know. What did this Tom guy do? What do any of us do?"

"I know what *you* do. Frankly, I can't believe someone hasn't taken a shot at you already."

He gives it mock laughter, then bites his thumb at me. "Seriously, you should keep an eye on things around here."

"How would someone break in?"

The front of my building's protected by a security door (inasmuch as those things ever provide security). My backdoor can be accessed from the deck, but only after someone's walked through a parking lot in full view of every window in our building and every window in the two buildings around us. Besides, Summit Avenue, while not above the occasional crime, isn't the kind of street in which shady dudes stroll with impunity. I'm not invincible, but I'm not easily accessible.

I trace the lettering on my *Writers Do It Between The Covers* mug. "Hopefully, the police either catch someone or call it a suicide. I really want this thing with Tess to end so I can move on."

A sudden smile creases Mike's goatee. "Speaking of moving on, I took your advice."

"What advice?"

"Onward and upward. Remember? That's what you told me at The Wheeze's party?"

"I think you told yourself that."

Mike waves his hand, annoyed. He's not a detail guy. "Whatever. I got a date this weekend."

"Who's the luck—um, who's the girl?"

"You remember Carol's friend Jeannette?"

"Yeah." He's so casual about it, I don't get it right away. I stare at him. "Please tell me it's someone who looks a lot like her."

"No. It's her. It's Jeannette. We bumped into each other at Gully's the other night and there we are. Bingo."

"You told Carol about this?"

Mike's eyes are uneasy, but he thrusts his jaw out. "Why do I need to do that?"

"Because you know Carol doesn't want you dating her friends. It'll make things weird."

"Ah, that's just what she tells you. You know the real reason, don't you? It's because then she'll know I'm winning the break-up."

"Okay, if I go into my whole lecture about there being no such thing as winning a break-up, particularly when you've been broken up for two years, that's probably going to fall on deaf ears, isn't it?"

"You're damn skippy. Look, *she* broke up with *me*, remember? Hey, I'm fine with it, but it doesn't mean there's an etiquette I have to follow."

"Keep telling yourself that, sport."

Mike thinks it over, then snaps his fingers. "I won't tell her. Jeannette isn't going to want Carol to find out. I'll just swear her to secrecy."

"And while you're doing that, think about the inconvenience you're causing the rest of us. If you're going to sneak around with one of Carol's friends, I have to decide whether I'm going to cover for you."

His head swings around, his bulldog jowls following a moment later. "Why wouldn't you cover for me?"

"I'm Carol's friend, too. I didn't take sides when you broke up and I won't take sides now."

"You're taking the fun out of this whole thing, you know that?"

"I'll make sure that goes on your tombstone."

Back in the apartment, the front door opens and Lars bursts in, surfing across my hardwood floor. Lars lives right below me and except for the occasional blasting of African drums, screams of either pleasure or pain (I'm too afraid to ask) from his guests and his habit of dropping in unannounced, he's a pretty good neighbor. He's toting the overstuffed file for the strip club. His head pops through the open window.

Mike doesn't waste any time getting a second opinion. "Lars, I'm going on a date with one of Carol's friends."

"Congrats, dude. Go nuts. Hey Joe, can I borrow that candle-lighter thingie of yours?"

"It's on the shelf over the TV," I say, "What do you need it for?"

"I'm helping Old Man Albertson down in 1B."

"With what?"

"Getting him out of his apartment."

Much like everything Lars does, this sets off alarm bells. "Wait a minute, the guy's a recluse," I say, "Word on the street is that he hasn't left his apartment in, like, ten years."

"Yeah, I'm going to smoke him out."

Lars grabs the lighter off the shelf and turns in time to see me bum-rush the front door and block his exit. "You are *not* using my lighter to set fire to the building."

He pities my slowness. "I'm not going to set fire to the building. I'm going to set a fire *inside* the building."

"This is supposed to make a difference?"

"It's just a little fire inside a wastebasket. It won't even be in Old Man Albertson's apartment. It'll be out in the hall. I'll shout, 'Fire!' He'll have to get out to save himself. What's wrong with that?"

"You got six or seven hours? I'll clue you in."

I hold out my hand and after a moment of disgusted objection, Lars puts the lighter in it. He follows me as I return it to its resting place above the TV.

"This is how you treat your fellow man?" Lars says, waving his pipe cleaner arms about, "Old Man Albertson shouldn't be rotting in that crummy apartment. He should be out there seizing the day!"

"The guy is about a hundred-and-fifty-six years old. The day he could seize is way in the rearview mirror."

Lars claps his hands together and holds them out, pleading. "What is it? You don't trust me to control a little fire?"

"No, I don't. You never think these things out."

"What am I missing?"

"Okay, let's assume you don't set your beard on fire—and I'm really giving you the benefit of the doubt there—Old Man Albertson's been in that apartment forever. He opens the door, the old man stink hits the flames and next thing you know the whole building's a raging inferno."

"You're being ridiculous."

"I see. You're going to start a fake fire to drive a recluse out of his home and *I'm* being ridiculous."

Lars gives up the ghost and fades toward the door. "I'm going to get him out of that apartment. It's my mission in life."

Mike comes in through the open window. "What about the strip club? You're still doing that, right?"

"Yeah, of course," Lars says, "Everything's humming right along. Still time to get in on it, Joe."

"I'll keep my self-respect and my lighter. Thank you very much."

Lars shrugs and slides out the door. I walk to the breakfast bar, which separates my thin kitchen from the living room.

"Swell," I say, "Now I've got to keep an eye on Lars."

"Why don't you report him to the superintendent?" Mike asks.

"I can't. Lars is the superintendent."

"Seriously?"

"Yeah. He gets a break in his rent and he keeps up with all the gossip in the building. It's a win-win deal."

"If you don't count the building ownership and all the tenants."

"Exactly."

Mike makes his way to the breakfast bar. "Okay, about the situation with Jeannette—"

"You and I are going to pretend this conversation never happened. Do what you need to do with Jeannette, but refrain from further details. If Carol finds out and loses her shit, I need plausible deniability."

I set the coffee cups in the sink. Mike props his arms on the breakfast bar and drops his head on them.

"Been a hell of a week, one way and other," he says, "Watching a guy die right in front of you."

"Makes you think."

"Yeah."

"Wanna go play racquetball?"

"Sure."

Before I can even pack up, though, the phone on the breakfast bar rings. It's Tess, babbling away a mile a minute. I get in a series of *Yeah*s and *Of course*s before hanging up.

"Racquetball's out," I say, dropping the phone back into its cradle.

"What's up?"

"Someone's spying on Tess."

CHAPTER SIX

Tess lives in a high rise across the river from downtown Minneapolis. The whole drive over, I'm wondering how exactly I'm supposed to handle someone watching her. Is it a peeping Tom? A potential hit man? A process server? The only one I can really help her with is the process server and even that's an iffy prospect. Tess calls me on my cell just before I get there.

"Where are you?" she asks.

"About two minutes away."

"Okay, when you get here, I'm in my car. Just down the street from the building. Try not to be seen."

"By who?"

"By the guy watching my building."

"And how do I know who that is?"

Tess groans, tiring of this vaudeville routine as quickly as I am. "Just do what I ask. I'll explain when you get here."

Beyond simply turning around and going home, I've got no choice but to play this Tess's way. I maneuver over to the river parkway and follow directions. Tess's Audi is parked about half a block from the building. When I open the passenger door, a small cloud of smoke escapes. Tess is behind the wheel, chain-smoking to beat the band.

"I didn't know you smoked," I say, sliding into the passenger seat.

"I don't."

"Well, it's a hell of a mirage you got going there."

Tess stubs a cigarette into the rapidly-filling ashtray. "I mean, I don't anymore," she says, "I used to. Now I just do it whenever I'm stressed."

"Who's stressing you?"

Tess points to a blue Toyota on the other side of the street, directly across from the building. "That guy right there. He's been following me."

The guy in question looks like a really creepy insurance salesman. Even from a distance, you can feel an intensity in the way he stares at the building. The stare is interrupted only by an occasional sip of his to-go coffee.

"Who is he?" I ask.

"I don't know. Maybe he's Nancy's accomplice."

"I thought Nancy's accomplice worked at the office."

"I don't know! I didn't think anything would happen to Tom. I thought this thing would go away. What the hell do I know?"

Okay, this is Panicked Tess. I put a hand on her forearm. "How did you notice this guy was following you?"

"I saw him outside the NewCo building. He was on the sidewalk, pretending to wait for a bus."

"How do you know he was pretending?"

"Would you shut up and let me finish?" Tess tries lighting the cigarette with the lighter from the dash. She puffs on it about twenty times, still not getting a light. No wonder she gave up smoking. She's terrible at it. "I noticed the guy because he was looking at me," she says, "Kind of creepy-like. Then I saw him outside my building. That can't be a coincidence. The guy's following me. Nancy has something to do with this. I know she does."

"Well, there's only one way to find out."

I get out of Tess's car and walk over to the dude in the Toyota. Tess hisses at me a few times, but I ignore her. The guy slides out of the Toyota and stands with his hands on his hips.

"How you doing?" I ask, jerking a thumb over my shoulder, "My friend there thinks you're watching her. What's the story?"

The guy nods. "I *am* watching her."

Well, you got to appreciate him being forthright. All I need now is a confession of this guy murdering Tom and threatening Tess and we can wrap this whole thing up.

"May I ask why you're watching her?" I say.

The guy takes out what looks to be a small billfold and flips it open. Inside is a badge and an ID. Apparently, I'm being addressed by Sergeant Tim Hara, Minneapolis Homicide.

"Just keeping an eye on her," he says.

"And why is that?"

Hara doesn't answer right away. He regards me with a flat, expressionless face. The intensity of his stare gives me the willies. Hara's about medium height, with short, graying hair and slim build. If not for the hardness around the eyes, he really would pass for an insurance salesman.

"Your friend might have a few questions to answer," he says.

I glance toward Tess, who has one hand over her eyes. Smooth. I turn back toward Hara.

"What sort of questions?" I ask.

Hara stares at Tess as he considers his answer. "You two, um...?"

"We used to be. We stopped um-ing a few months ago."

"Okay. You heard about what happened to her boss?"

"I was there."

His focus is back on me. "You were there? When Tom Reilly was killed?"

"I was a couple feet away when he met the table."

"And was that was the only time you saw him?"

"No. We chatted at the bar earlier. Why?"

Hara rocks on the balls of his feet. "Nothing, really. Main thing I'm after is to ask your friend about her relationship with Mr. Reilly."

Got to admit, I'm not a fan of the way he says *relationship*. He draws it out ever-so-slightly, as if he'd add a nudge-nudge and a wink-wink if he could. "What about her relationship?" I ask.

"Maybe you ought to ask her. I'll chat with her soon enough."

With that, Hara slips back into his car and takes off, leaving me in the middle of the street. Slowly, I walk back to Tess and peek into the smoking chamber.

"You're probably safe to go back to your apartment," I say, "That was a cop."

Strangely, this doesn't relax Tess at all. Her eyes bug out and her mouth drops open. "A cop? What did he want?"

"Same thing I want right at the moment: to ask you about your relationship with Tom."

Tess stares at the steering wheel, a slight groan coming from somewhere deep in her throat. "Why don't we go up to my place and talk about it? I'd feel more comfortable up there."

That makes one of us. I never cared much for Tess's apartment. Yes, it has a fifteenth floor view of downtown Minneapolis, but that's its sole charm. You can't kick back at Tess's place. It's all white carpeting and tasteful artwork and glass furniture that leaps out and attempts to kneecap you. Also, one wall is nearly covered by a painting of an earl or a duke or some such douche whose eyes seem to follow you around the room. Unsettling, the lot of it.

Tess leads the way in and tosses her purse on the sofa. She runs a hand through her hair, sending stray strands in all directions.

"They think I killed Tom, don't they?" she asks.

"Why would they think that?"

"That's where it gets complicated."

"Start with something simple."

Tess lets out a long breath. "Tom and I had an affair."

"An affair?"

"Yes."

"Like a sexual affair?"

"Is there another kind?"

"I didn't think so, but one likes to hope." I feel like I've stepped into an acid trip. "When did this affair take place?"

"On and off for about a year. Don't worry. It was over before you and I met."

"I wasn't worried."

Tess grits her teeth. "You're a dick. Has anyone ever told you that?"

"Yes. You. Now, why don't you tell me the whole story?"

Tess walks to the drinks table and grabs a glass and a bottle of vodka. "Tom and I had a casual thing. No strings attached. But we had to break it off."

"Had to?"

"His wife found out. She threatened him with divorce, threatened to ruin his career, the whole ball of wax. He groveled his way back into her good graces. But he had to break it off with me, permanently. That was her asking price." A small flick of her hand. "So he did."

Tess pours a finger of vodka and downs it quickly. That air of vulnerability is back, but I can't tell if it's pain over the break up or embarrassment over the affair. Meantime, I'd swear that damn painting of the earl or duke is smirking at me.

"Okay," I say, "What in the blue hell did you see in Tom?"

"What do you mean?"

"I mean, he was a shithead. An enormous shithead. He was such a shithead, he made other shitheads go, 'Jesus, what a shithead.'"

Tess stares at me a second, then her mouth twists into a smile. "You're jealous."

"I am not."

"You are. You're jealous."

My head is filled with images of Tess rolling around with that blubbery moron and it pisses me off. That she doesn't have better judgment. That Tom carried on with a woman so clearly out of his league. That he…huh. Unless they've invented a new word for what I'm feeling, jealousy fits the bill. Fuck me.

I turn my back to both Tess and the douchebag painting. "Whatever," I say, "Fine. Why would the cops think you killed Tom?"

"I don't know. Maybe because Tom was waiting for me when he was killed."

"Excuse me?"

Tess pours another finger. "He had a few drinks and he wanted to talk about our relationship. I didn't really think it was necessary, but I didn't want to say no to him, either. If Barry had an issue with me because of the affair, I thought Tom could put in a good word for me."

"And that was all you guys were going to do?" My turn for the *nudge-nudge-wink-wink* tone of voice.

Tess's jaw tightens. "Yes. At least, that was all I wanted. Tom…might have had other ideas."

"Okay, so after he's been busted for having an affair, Tom still goes for a round of rumpy-pumpy at a company event with his father-in-law in the room?"

"Tom never did think a few steps ahead. Especially with a hard-on and a few drinks in him. Does that sound so unusual?"

No, it pretty much covers every guy I've ever known. "So, what was the master plan?" I ask, "He'd sneak up to the room, set out the candles and the Astroglide and hum Barry White tunes until you showed up?"

"Except for the snarky parts, yes, that was the plan. I seriously doubt anything would have happened. Tom was fun in bed—"

"Gross."

"But he was more trouble than he was worth. As far as I was concerned, I was going to leave with you. I figured after Tom sobered up, he'd realize what a mistake it would've been."

I stare at the beige carpeting, considering this. "Okay, speaking of me, where do I come in to all this?"

"What do you mean?"

"I mean, I was supposed to protect you at a party. I did that. Sure, Tom died, but that was outside my purview. So, I'm wondering what I'm supposed to do here?"

"Someone's still after me. Probably the same person who killed Tom. And now *I'm* a suspect."

I step over to her and take her hands. "Okay, let's dial it down a little. If you were a real suspect, you'd be in jail by now."

"And what about Nancy? She's still after me."

I'm getting an enormous headache in my eye. "Are you *really* sure she's a threat?"

Tess slips out of my grip. "Are you on this again? She kisses your ass for a minute and you think you know her?"

"Okay, fine, her exquisite, *exquisite* taste in humorists aside, you think she overpowered and tossed a guy twice her size off a balcony?"

"What about her partner? Maybe he did it."

"Or maybe it was a mafia hitman funded by the CIA and Castro and firing from the grassy knoll. Until I see one solid piece of evidence, I'm not going to believe Nancy's threatening you."

I start toward the exit, more than ready to call it a day. Halfway there, an envelope comes under the crack of the door. It brings me to a momentary halt.

"You expecting mail?" I ask.

Tess appears over my shoulder. "I get my mail downstairs."

I whip open the door. The hallway is completely empty. I scoop the envelope off the floor and hold it toward Tess. "I don't think it's addressed to me."

"You can certainly open it. I don't mind."

"No, I'd feel like I was intruding."

"Joe, will you just open the damn thing!"

I hold it away from me, hesitating. All that time in school and nobody ever taught me the tell-tale signs of a letter bomb. I knew college was a waste. I rip the thing open, hoping for the best. And I get it. No explosions, no acid, no anthrax. I can work with that. There's just a simple piece of notebook paper with some letters glued to it.

"What does it say?" Tess asks, still keeping her distance.

I read it to her. *You're next, bitch.*

Tess slumps down on the arm of the sofa. I look over the note again.

"Okay, that's pretty solid evidence," I say.

CHAPTER SEVEN

On one hand, I enjoy going downtown for lunch. There's a lot of movement and excitement, loads of nine-to-fivers hoping to scarf a quick meal before getting back to an afternoon of useless busy work. On the other hand, I don't tend to like people on an individual basis, let alone in a crowd. And I get the feeling everyone knows I'm not one of their number. Even with a cell phone clamped to my ear and a look of perpetual annoyance, I simply don't belong.

Adding to my sense of annoyance is Carol's obvious amusement at my predicament. An amusement so strong it comes right through my cell phone. "You're having lunch with your new number one fan?" she says.

"It's not recreation. It's research."

"Into what? A bold and daring expose of your one fan who's gainfully employed and doesn't live with their parents?"

"You think you're funny, but you are, in fact, snot."

She chuckles and there's the crinkle of the licorice bag on her end of the line. "Okay, so what are you really trying to get out of this? Other than a switchblade in the gut?"

"I don't know. Nancy's side of the story, maybe. Maybe a confession. Something that might help my investigation."

It takes Carol a few moments to work her reaction around a mouthful of red licorice. "Your investigation? Isn't that the sort of thing you're—what are the words I'm looking for—massively unqualified to do? Why not just hand the note over to the police and be done with it?"

"Because Tess doesn't trust the police. She thinks they're out to get her. I'm the only one who can really help."

Carol drops into a sing-song voice. "You still like her."

"It's not that."

"Joe and Tess, sittin' in a tree—"

"Don't you have a job to do?"

"I finished the ad. My time's my own."

Carol and I have that in common. Neither of us works in what you'd call a high-stress environment. I write humor blogs while a *Happy Days* DVD plays in the background. Carol writes ads while downing bags of red licorice. (The difference, of course, is that I don't have to spend an hour at the gym every night punishing myself for a *Happy Days* DVD.) But there *are* drawbacks. For example, I have free time to do moronic activities like investigating threats against an ex-girlfriend and Carol has time to listen to accounts of my moronic activities.

"Cut me some slack," I say, "I'm a man with limited brain capacity. I'm doing what I can."

Carol chuckles, but her voice suddenly takes on a serious edge. "Hey, speaking of limited brain capacity, is something going on with Mike?"

Ah crap, I'm not prepared for this turn in the conversation. "What do you mean?"

"I called him the other day and he sounded happy. I asked him about it, but he said he was just in a good mood."

"So?"

"So Mike's never in a good mood. Except when he's dating somebody. But when I asked him about *that*, he said he wasn't dating anyone."

"Well, you *are* his ex-girlfriend."

"No, that's why he *would* tell me. To remind me he's still in demand and moving on with his life. But this time he denies it. Isn't that weird?"

"Hum."

Carol speaks slowly. "*Is* he dating somebody?"

"Not that I know of."

"You're sure?"

I'll be sweating in another second. "Positive."

Thankfully, she's not right in front of me. If those eyes were scrutinizing me, Mike would be finished.

"Okay, I'll take your word on it," Carol says, "But if something *is* up, you'll tell me, right?"

"Of course."

We ring off and I begin hating myself. I have, by my actions and despite my better judgment, just decreed Mike a more important friend than Carol. But what can I do? It's right there in the Guys Rule Book, under Article Whatever, Subsection Something (guys aren't good at filing): No Guy shall rat out another Guy to a Chick. Unless there's Nookie in the deal. Nookie justifies everything.

Two minutes later, I'm out of the skyway and crossing a dirt parking lot. The NewCo Mutual Customer Service Center looms in view. It's a squat building covered with mirrored glass. Probably the designer's way of directing attention to everything in the neighborhood except his hideously ugly creation. I push through a revolving door and into a lobby dominated by a giant glass sculpture of a bass on a line; just the sort of thing any bass fisherman would love, assuming he was gay and had been kicked in the head eight times. Nancy's not in the lobby yet, so I'm forced to stand around and wait for her.

"Hey Joe, what's up?"

A large guy is passing through the turnstiles and heading my direction. It takes me a second to remember it's Brian, Tess's friend with the stellar pecs and the inferior intellect. He's dressed a lot like he was at the party: white shirt, open at the collar, gold necklace, black slacks. He smiles and treats me to another bone-crushing handshake.

"You look lost," he says.

"No. Just waiting for Nancy. We're having lunch."

He cocks his head to one side, not unlike a dog being shown a card trick. "Nancy? You're having lunch with Nancy?"

"That's the plan." And for some reason, I feel compelled to add: "Is that all right?"

He's quick to laugh it off. "That's fine. I just thought you'd be seeing Tess if you were going to see anyone."

"I found out at the party that Nancy's a fan of mine. She wants to chat about my column."

Brian nods, looking away. "Yeah, the party. Hell of a night that was, huh?"

"Especially for Tom."

"Hell of a thing. I didn't always get along with the guy, but damn, I didn't want something like that to happen to him."

"Where were you when it happened?"

The look in his blue eyes gets several degrees frostier. "What's that supposed to mean?"

"Just...curious. One of those questions, y'know? Like, where were you when Kennedy was assassinated?"

"I wasn't born when Kennedy was assassinated."

"Well, neither was I. I just—"

"Then why are you asking about it?"

"It's not important."

"Not important? It was a national tragedy."

If Brian was smart enough, I'd think he was fucking with me. But he seems genuinely pissed and I'm not sure if it's about Tom's death or Kennedy's. I hold my hands up in mock surrender.

"Just making conversation," I say, "Wondering how you're dealing with it."

He puffs up his cheeks and lets out a big breath. "Sorry, man. Under a lot of stress these days."

"Don't sweat it."

He runs a hand over his stubby black hair. "I was up in my room. On the eighth floor. Probably about three minutes from passing out. Then I hear this big fuckin' crash and everyone's running around, screaming. I get out to the balcony and look over and, shit, I don't have to tell you what I saw."

"No. I had a ringside seat."

Before I can ask anything else, Brian starts across the big marble floor, barely glancing back. "Good seeing you again, Joe. Have fun at lunch."

No sooner has Brian cleared out than Nancy slips through the turnstiles; a glare going out to everyone in the vicinity. Her outfit is not greatly than different than it was at the party, except the sensible shoes are white instead of black. Great. A lunch date with a hospice nurse. Still, she tries smiling and it brightens her face a bit. We greet each other with an awkward handshake.

"Where should we go?" she asks, skipping small talk as only the socially-awkward can.

"Well jeez, I was hoping there'd be a soup-and-sandwich place in the skyway. Do you think we'll find one?"

Her face crinkles. "Of course. They're all over the skyway."

"Um, yeah. That, that's where I was going with that, uh, that joke."

We stroll out of the lobby, catching a few *Is that Nancy with some dude?* looks that I do my best to ignore. Nancy keeps her eyes locked forward and her hands clutched to her purse strap. I could make try some small talk, but by its nature, the skyway prevents any talk of the weather or interesting sites.

"Busy," I say.

"Yep," Nancy says.

And that's the sum and total of the conversation until we get to the soup-and-sandwich place.

The place in question is cut from the same mold as the other skyway soup-and-sandwich joints: plastic booths, fluorescent lighting, little curlicue patterns on the walls to add a touch of class. We settle ourselves into a bright yellow booth. Nancy delicately (I'm guessing more delicately than normal) picks at her BLT. I take one bite of my Bacon-and-Cheddar Wrap and watch most of the contents escape the tortilla and swan dive into the paper wrapper. In short, the thing that happens every time I eat a wrap.

"I'm, uh, I'm sorry about what happened to your boss," I say, figuring a possible murder makes a decent icebreaker.

Nancy greets it with a small shrug. "Tom and I weren't close."

"Still, seeing someone killed like that—"

"I didn't see it. I was in my room by that time."

"It was a pretty wild scene," I say.

"How did Tess handle it?" And there's just a hint of nastiness around *Tess*.

"She was freaked out."

"I'm sure. Things seem to have worked out for her, though. They always do."

"What do you mean?"

"She got Tom's job. Didn't she tell you?"

My wrap—or what's left of it—stops just short of my lips. "No. I guess it slipped her mind."

Nancy keeps her scoff down to a dull roar. "I'm sure. Interesting little power vacuum Tess is caught up in. She barely gets comfortable at one job and she gets a brand new one." Nancy sets her sandwich aside. "If I may ask, what in the world did you ever see in her?"

This requires delicate handling. The first thing I saw in Tess was how that dress hugged her behind and accentuated her surprisingly prominent rack. And I have a weakness for cool, composed women who project a hint of sexual potential, even if said sexual potential is the only thing that's ever truly fulfilled. But how do I explain that to Nancy? How do I tell her a guy who makes his living specializing in fairly shallow observations is, in fact, even more shallow in life?

"Well," I say, giving a carefree little wave, "Not everybody's who they seem to be." That done, I quickly get back on track. "So, if Tess gets Tom's job, who gets her old Insurance Service leader's job?"

"It better be me," Nancy says, grabbing her sandwich again, "I should have gotten it last time. But I'm dealing with the same problem."

"How so?"

"My competition is sleeping with the boss."

Say what? "Wouldn't Brian be your only competition?"

"Yes."

"And he's sleeping with Tess?"

"Well, not now. But he used to."

Okay, how to put this casually? "How long ago was *used to*?"

"Way before you and Tess, I think. She threw him over for Tom. Typical of Tess."

"How did Brian handle getting thrown over for Tom?"

"I don't know. Not well, I would guess. But it was never an issue at the office, so I didn't think too much about it. My only concern is that Tess is going to feel guilty for screwing over Brian and give him the job to make things okay again."

Okay, my head is swimming. But I have to remember this is Nancy I'm talking to. In her world, Tess is skewed to look like Darth Vader crossed with Heather Locklear on *Melrose Place.* Come to think of it, this office is a lot closer to *Melrose Place* than I thought.

"I noticed you and Tom chatting at the party," I say, casually picking through the remains of my wrap, "Were you talking about the promotion?"

Nancy stares at her paper plate. "No. It was some other office business. Something he didn't want Tess to know about."

"Really? What was that?"

"Just a question about a client. Nothing that would interest you."

It does, in fact, interest me. But if I push it, Nancy will know I'm up to something. I've taken about as many chances, interrogation-wise, as I dare. We finish lunch by finally talking about my column, which puts Nancy in a chummier mood. She turns into a gushing fan and after about thirty seconds, I wish we were back to talking about Tess. Don't get me wrong. I love getting a compliment. But I can't take one for shit.

Post-lunch, I have a difficult decision. Do I walk Nancy back to the office or not? It would be going out of my way to do it, but would I come off as a heel if I just part from her here? Then again, if I walk her back, is that a gesture of intimacy, thus *really* giving her the wrong impression. (Given my general level of indecision in these matters, it's amazing I've ever dated anyone.)

As we step into the skyway, Nancy gives me a slight smile and says, "This was nice. Thank you."

Before we can move on to the awkward part, another bit of awkwardness presents itself. Tess comes around the corner of the sandwich shop and heads directly for us. And she doesn't look happy. Well, who's up for a little Something Blowing Up in Joe's Face?

Tess practically sticks her head between Nancy's and mine. "Having fun, kids?" She steps between us. "Joe, this better be about getting information from her."

Nancy's eyes narrow and betray a definite hurt. "That's why you wanted to have lunch?" she says, "To set me up?"

"I wasn't setting anything up."

"Bullshit!" And that draws a few interested looks from passers-by. "I should have known. Anyone with the bad taste to date her, you couldn't be what you appeared to be."

"No, I'm exactly what I appear to be." And I have no idea if that's a good thing.

Nancy sticks a bony finger in my face. "The two of you fucking deserve each other." She starts to push past me, but stops and lowers her voice, as if trying not to let Tess overhear us. "You think you have to protect her. You're making a huge mistake." She lets that linger a second or two, then stalks off. Thankfully, she doesn't punch me in the sternum.

"What was that all about?" Tess asks, "Are you two up to something?"

Angry glare-wise, I pick up where Nancy left off. "No, you actually read the situation perfectly," I say, "I *was* trying to get information out of her. Would have been nice to do that without making her hate me. Were you spying on us?"

Tess's face falls. "No, I was just going to lunch. I saw you two together, getting all chummy and I guess I freaked out. I'm sorry."

I let a breath out through my nose. Losing my temper isn't going to make the situation any better. "Don't worry about it. We were wrapping up anyway."

"Did you find out anything interesting?"

I did, of course, but it was all about Tess's fling with Brian and her promotion. This, however, is not the time or the place to ask about that. Instead, I give her a non-committal shrug.

"Nothing, really. We'll see."

Tess gives me a curious, but guarded look. "Okay. Fine. Walk me back to the office?"

Ugh. I just can't win today, can I?

CHAPTER EIGHT

"This is my part of the design," Lars says, walking down the runway leading from the stage, "I really want to bring the girls close to the customers."

"Of course," I say, "Anything to increase the odds of a drunk-and-disorderly."

This is dismissed with a laugh and a wave. "Always the worry wart."

For their part, Mike and Carol seem impressed with their investment. Les Bos is spacious and clean (at least for now), done up in a sleek black motif, as if everything were happening in a void. The wide stage features shiny silver stripper poles and a glossy runway bisecting the main floor. Mirrors adorn every wall and pillar, making sure the girls can be seen from all angles. Lars bounds through the guided tour, arms, legs and hair flying in all directions. Mike is pulled along in Lars's wake, looking like he's about to drool. Carol's arms are folded, fingers tapping her biceps, tongue clicking. I slouch along, wondering how I've arranged my life such that I don't have anything better to do.

Lars steps over a thick yellow line marking a sort of box at the end of the runway. "And this is where the best dancers do their stuff. It's the Stripatorium."

I stop short of the line. "Stripatorium?"

"Catchy, huh?"

"Sure. It's *what* I'd catch that concerns me."

"Oh, could be all sorts of stuff. A bra, a g-string, a—ah, you were making a joke, weren't you? Good one."

Carol grinds her teeth around a wad of chewing gum. "Stripatorium? You don't think that's a little degrading?"

Lars seems genuinely befuddled. "You think?"

"Yes," Carol says, "I do think."

"Huh. Then I probably shouldn't show you the Pudding Pit."

"Pudding Pit!"

Mike steps past Carol. "Forget working here. You got a room I could rent?"

Lars waves an arm toward the balcony overlooking the main floor. "Just the offices, my friend. And they're all occupied."

In spite of myself, I'm impressed. Unlike most of Lars's schemes, which fizzle at the first sign of practicality, this one seems ready to go.

"You and Chuck got this place up pretty fast," I say.

Lars nods. "Chuck knows his stuff. He got the idea at Tommy Sacco's bachelor party and knew he had a winner. Brought me on board and we were off to the races."

I neglect to remind Lars that past races with his buddy Chuck have included a combination coffee shop and taxi service, an urban Alpaca farm and a walking tour of old brothel sites. On those rare occasions when Chuck comes up with a halfway decent idea, such as his bus tour of haunted houses, it usually stumbles due to piss-poor planning; such as hiring a bus driver who turned out to be a raging alcoholic with a propensity for passing out while going down large hills.

"And you've got all your bases covered?" Carol asks, "Business plan, marketing plan, licenses, payroll, all that stuff?"

Lars proudly waves his folder, which now looks like the Federal Budget mated with a Gutenburg Bible in a hurricane. "All in here. Care to take a look?"

Carol holds a hand up. "I'll take your word on it."

"It's all good," Lars says, strolling toward a back hallway, "Take it to the bank. Got some girls trying out the Pudding Pit. You want to take a look?"

Naturally, Mike is the only one to take him up on that. They head to the Pudding Pit and I'm not sure if I'll ever see them again. Carol contemplatively circles a stripper pole until she realizes I'm watching her.

"Pudding Pit," she says, "Good grief."

"The man knows what he likes."

"Well, I *don't* like the direction this place is going."

"Yeah, it's sad when a strip joint specializing in quasi-lesbian activities for the benefit of drunken males can't stay classy."

She levels a look at me. "Do you just come up with that stuff off the top of your head?"

"No, I thought that one up a few days ago. I was just waiting for a chance to use it."

She leans against the stripper pole. "So, you're still not going to invest?"

"No. I've got better things to do with my time and money."

"Ah yes. Speaking of your precious time, how goes it with your investigation?" And she puts an amused little ring around the word *investigation*.

I slump down on the edge of the runway and tell Carol about my lunch with Nancy. She twitches up a corner of her mouth as I get to the end.

"Ah, women fighting over you. Do you ever get tired of it?"

"In this case, yes. It was creepy as all hell."

"You asked Tess about this Brian guy?"

"Haven't had a chance yet."

"But if Nancy's supposed to have a co-conspirator—"

I hold up a hand, trying to slow her down. "Hey, I don't know if this guy's in on it. In fact, from what I've seen, there's no hard feelings with he and Tess and no love lost with he and Nancy. And he and Nancy are aiming for the same job. Not exactly the way to keep a conspiracy together."

"But you don't know that for sure."

"I don't know anything for sure."

Mike and Lars do actually return from the Pudding Pit, stopping at the bar to draw mugs of beer. They find me staring at the floor.

"Problem?" Mike asks.

"His investigation," Carol says, doing the annoying air quotes thing.

"Caught anybody yet?" Lars asks.

I shake my head. "Not even close."

I quickly bring Mike and Lars up to speed. Mike stares into his beer while Lars nods gravely and stretches a finger toward me.

"Cherchez La Femme," Lars says, "Mark my words."

"What in the blue hell does that mean?" I say

"Beware the woman."

"I know the definition. I'm wondering how it applies."

"That? I leave up to you." Lars strolls away, ending things on a cryptic note. Lars always gets a mystical sage thing going when he's feigning interest.

I look at Mike and Carol. "Either of you function as a Lars interpreter?"

Mike raises his hand. "There's a woman behind all this. Simple as that."

"Thanks. That clears it right the hell up." I take a sip of Mike's beer. It's the cheap, watered down, mass market variety. Guess Lars figures no one comes to a strip joint for the quality of the beer. "Here's something that's bugging me…"

Carol snorts. "Oh God, you're what now? Columbo?"

"No, no, just think about it. Tom gets murdered over— what?—a promotion? Does that jibe with you?"

Mike shakes his head. "Jibe? No. It jibes not."

"That's what's been bugging me from the beginning. All this stuff is about what? Maybe a five thousand dollar-a-year bump in pay? Middle management is suddenly worth killing over?"

Mike slides his beer in circular patterns around the table. "Maybe it's not about a promotion at all. I mean, you said the guy was cheating on his wife, right?"

"Right."

"You talked to the wife at all?"

"No."

"There you go." Mike sits next to me on the runway. "Maybe the wife finds out about the affair. Decides to kill Tom and Tess."

"Then why is Tess still alive?"

"Well, that's probably something you should ask the wife, don't you think?"

Carol nods, a bit surprised. "Knock 'em dead, Kojak."

With that, we decide to call it a day. Lars is off tending to something and there's nothing left for us to see. As we head for the exit, Carol sidles up to Mike.

"I'm going to the movies on Friday night," she says, "You want to tag along?"

Mike's eyes race around the room. He tries to say something, but no sound comes out. Then he starts coughing up a lung. The man has a poker face like Lou Costello.

"Can't," he finally rasps.

"Why?" Carol asks, "You have...other plans?"

"No. Yes! Yes."

"What?"

"What? What what?"

"What are your plans on Friday night?"

"Oh, *that*. It's a...thing."

"A thing?"

"A whole thing. I don't want to get into it."

Carol offers Mike an opportunity to talk to the hand. "Well, good luck with that. Joe, do you want to go?"

"I might be in hot pursuit of an arch criminal," I say.

Carol takes it in stride. "Okay. I'll see what Jeannette's up to."

This sends Mike into a coughing fit so violent it would disgust an emphysema ward. I put a hand on Carol's arm.

"You know what?" I say, "Maybe I *will* go to the movies with you. All work and no play and you saw how that worked out for Nicholson in *The Shining*,"

Mike waves his encouragement as he struggles for breath. Carol and I set a meeting time and she leads the way out. Mike hangs back.

"Thanks," he wheezes, "You think she suspects?"

"You of sinking the Lusitania? No. Everything else is in play, though."

He shakes his head. "How do I get myself into this shit?"

Funny. I was wondering the same thing.

***

Much as I look forward to being grilled by Carol on Friday night, I've got some grilling of my own to do first. I send Tess a text message asking her to meet me at The Tav, my local watering hole of choice, and to bring Tom Reilly's address. I'm hoping she won't get too curious and ask me why I need it. Thankfully, she's either too busy or too trusting to ask questions. She simply sends me a text confirmation and we're off to the races.

The Tav is a combination pub and spiffed-up sports bar. It has just enough wood décor and low lighting to offset the multitude of video screens. My status as a neighborhood celebrity allows me to snag a high-top near the picture windows. Well, that and a party of four cleared out as I was walking in. I've just gotten a pint of Hefeweizen when Tess enters, wearing a tight-fitting black top and a loose black skirt. She gives the place the stink eye as she strides over. (The charms of The Tav were always lost on her.) She greets me with a nod, takes up a position on one stool opposite me and finds a home for her Prada bag on the other.

"Did you bring it?" I ask.

Tess frowns. "Always business with you."

"Funny. When we were dating, you complained I was never about business."

"Well, times change." The waiter interrupts this tete-a-tete and takes Tess's order for white wine. She takes a sticky note out of her bag, but makes no move to hand it to me. "Why do you need Tom's address?"

"I want to talk to Tom's wife."

"Why?"

"To make sure she isn't behind all this."

"She's not. Nancy is."

"We don't know that for sure, though, do we?"

"But we do know who Deena Reilly's father is. And I don't need you getting me in trouble."

"Oh, I see. You bang the big boss's son-in-law and *I* might get you in trouble?"

If the aim was to piss Tess off, I've scored a direct hit. Her face tightens to the point of implosion. Slowly and deliberately, she slaps the note on the table in front of me. I hesitate—the way one will before reaching into a bear trap—then snatch the note. It's an address in Northfield, a college town about an hour south of the Cities. I pocket the note as Tess's white wine arrives.

"You realize that's probably a waste of time?" she says.

"Wouldn't be my first." I take a bracing swallow of my Hefeweizen before moving on to even less pleasant subjects. "Since we're sharing information, can I ask you for some?"

"What do you need?"

"You and Brian. Tell me about that."

Tess's face doesn't crack. "What about us?"

"You were having an affair with him. Before you were having an affair with Tom."

"And before I was having an affair with you."

"Fine. But that doesn't concern me."

Tess takes a swallow of her wine and mutters something that closely resembles *Dickhead*. She asks, "Does it have any bearing on anything?"

"We're looking for someone who's killed Tom and is threatening you. Brian has a motive for both."

Tess gives this a single flip of her hand. "Brian and I are fine. It started. It ended. We're still friends. Nothing to it."

"You checked with Brian on that?"

"He's fine."

Given that Tess has known Brian for several years and I've had exactly two conversations with him—neither exceeding five minutes—I'm going to have to take her word on it. For now.

"All right," I say, "By the by, I understand congratulations are in order."

"You heard about my new promotion?"

"Nancy told me."

"Probably made some snide remark about how I'm moving up the corporate ladder."

"She did, in fact."

Tess throws a look toward the bar, ready to order another wine. "I was offered the Service Vice President's job. Was I supposed to turn it down?"

"I guess not."

"If people are going to talk, to hell with them. I can't help that." The wine arrives promptly, making me wonder if Tess has some psychic power over our waiter. She holds her glass close to her face and studies me. "I'll warn you now: Deena Reilly isn't a big fan of mine. And she's pals with Nancy."

"How do you know that?"

"Nancy's the one who ratted out me and Tom."

"And how do you know this?"

She leans close, as if there's anyone in The Tav who might care about office politics at NewCo Mutual. "Several months back, I saw Deena and Nancy having lunch, not far from where you and Nancy were eating. Before I knew it, Tom came to me and told me his wife found out about the affair and we had to cut it off. Didn't take a lot of effort to put two-and-two together."

"And Nancy knew for sure that you and Tom were carrying on?"

"I don't know. But she passed the suspicion along to Deena and I'm guessing that Tom caved when Deena confronted him with it."

Guess that will at least give me something to ask Deena about when I see her. We sit in silence and finish our drinks. I make no move to order another. Instead, I give the waiter an extended stare, hoping he gets the idea I want the check and not his phone number.

"Sounds like you got two candidates for your new old job as Insurance Service leader," I say, "Nancy and Brian. Who's it going to be?"

Tess rolls her glass around by its base. "It's going to be Nancy."

My eyebrows go up. "Really?"

"You're surprised?"

"No, not at all. You take every chance you get to remind me she's trying to kill you, get extremely hostile at any suggestions otherwise and now you're promoting her. Yeah, it all falls logically into place."

"First off, she's the most qualified. After me. That's hard to admit, because I like Brian. But maybe she won't be as pissed off if we work together."

"Keep your friends close and your enemies closer."

Tess points a finger of recognition at me. "That's right. That's exactly right. Where did you get that? Out of a book?"

"It's from *The Godfather, Part Two.*"

See, this is why Tess and I could never make it as a couple. What do you do with a woman who can't place the simplest of *Godfather* quotes?

***

So, my next bit of fun is talking with Deena Reilly, Tom's wife. Not only do I have to confess to her that I'm a rank amateur looking into her husband's murder, but I'm doing it to protect a woman he was sleeping with on the side. And I get to drive about ninety minutes through cow country for the pleasure. All the way down, I'm listening to a Men at Work Greatest Hits CD and wondering why the hell Tom would choose this kind of hellacious commute. Taking rush hour traffic into account, he was looking at a two-hour trip to and from work every day. And that's *before* you talk about the weather (which gets a little nasty between, say, November and April). I know people like the safety and quiet of the outlying areas, but there's convenience to be considered. If I had nine-to-five job, I'd live in a crack house if it was close to work.

Finding the place is a bit of an adventure. Thanks to retail and real estate development, Northfield sprawls across the local landscape. My GPS leads me to a development built into a hill just west of the town proper. I cruise rolling streets that look like all the other rolling streets before finally finding a two-story quasi-colonial, built from the same cookie cutter that created its neighbors. A black Chevy Blazer is parked in the sloping driveway. I ditch the Saturn on the curb out front and stroll up to the front door.

The woman who answers is a formidable brunette wearing sweats and a t-shirt. Her hair is pulled back in a ponytail, there's a towel around her neck and she's holding a glass of iced tea. Her thick eyebrows are arched, and her body language says, *Don't waste my time.* In another life, absent the adultery, she and Tess might have been friends. Or they might have grabbed Louisville sluggers and beaten each other to death. Who knows?

"Deena Reilly?" I ask.

"Yes?"

"My name's Joe Davis."

"Yes?"

If I did a bare ass slide across a hockey rink, I couldn't get a chillier reception. It's no fun knocking on doors when you're not welcomed. I don't know how Jehovah's Witnesses do it.

"I was wondering if we could talk about what happened your husband," I say.

The eyebrows draw together in a V. "Are you a police officer?"

"No."

"A reporter?"

"Of sorts. I write a humor blog."

"A *humor* blog? Why the hell are you interested in my husband?"

"It's, it's kind of a long story. Look, why don't I come in and tell it to you?"

"Why don't you tell me the story and *then* I'll decide if you're going to come in."

Yeah, this is going about as well as predicted. "For starters, I'm, uh, I'm a friend of Tess Lashley."

If this were an Elmer Fudd cartoon, you'd see the red rise up through Deena's face and the steam come out her ears. "You better make this a *real* good story."

I tell her everything I've got, from standing a few feet away from her husband's death to the various threats against Tess to the bits of office politics I've uncovered. Deena is unmoved by it all.

"Give me one good reason why I should answer any of your questions?" she says.

My eyes scan the room, searching out the vanilla walls and the glass trophy cases, as if the answer might be there. All I come up with is: "It was a *really* long drive down here."

"Goodbye."

She starts to close the door. I try to block it and wind up with the brass knob wedged between my nuts. My next appeal is through gritted teeth.

"Look, Tess is a former girlfriend of mine. She roped me into this and I'm not going to get a minute's peace until I figure out what the hell's going on. Or the police do it first. Either way, can you spare two minutes if it helps get rid of this pain in my ass?"

There's a pause. Then the door opens, giving my nads sweet, sweet relief. Deena throws out an arm, offering me entrance.

"That's the first thing you've said that's made any sense," she says, "Come in."

Deena leads me through the house and into the dining room. The place is immaculately kept. Dusted knick-knacks on wooden shelves, nice little pictures in gold frames. Even the kid's toys are in a little corral in one corner. It feels less like a residence and more like a museum. Deena checks herself out in various reflective surfaces. The dining room is dominated by a glass table and several straight-back chairs. A large deck is visible beyond the sliding door. Deena sits at the head of the table and pulls out a nearby chair for me. She arranges her iced tea precisely on a coaster. There's no offer of refreshment for me, lest I get ideas about staying.

"Thanks for letting me in," I say.

"I suggest you get to the point."

Fair enough. "Did Nancy Balstrom tell you about Tom cheating on you?"

Deena opens her mouth, but hesitates. The hesitation is all I need, and Deena knows it. "Yes. Are you really here about Tom or are you trying to get Nancy in trouble with her boss?"

"All due respect, but while I may not have much going on in my life, I *do* have better things to do than drive ninety minutes to be a corporate stooge."

She takes a sip of ice tea and sets the glass dead center on the coaster. "Fine. Yes, she told me. Nancy's a friend. She thought I had a right to know."

"I didn't realize you and Nancy were tight."

"We've seen each other at various company events. At least the ones I could stand to attend. She's a nice girl. Socially awkward. But someone I could talk to. And someone who's loyal. That's kind of a rare thing these days, don't you think?"

"I suppose. Speaking of loyalty, you stayed with Tom, even after you found out about the affair."

Deena waves toward a picture on a corner table. A studio portrait of a boy and a girl, roughly eight and six. Thankfully, they resemble her more than Tom. "My children need a father." She puts a few fingers to her forehead and takes a deep breath. "*Needed* a father. That's the only reason I let Tom stay."

I catch sight of another family photo on the wall: Barry Preston with his arm around Deena. "What did your father think of letting Tom stay?"

"He was opposed to it. But he said it was my decision."

"And nothing ever boomeranged back on Tom or Tess? At the office, I mean?"

"Business is business. That's what my father would tell you." She makes a show of checking her watch. I've got to hurry this along.

"Was the affair with Tess a one-time thing?" I ask, "Or were there others?"

"Well, aren't you Mr. Fucking Tact?"

"I'm sorry. Believe me, I find the notion of Tom having sex as gross as you do."

Deena's face brightens as she struggles not to smile. "I'm certain there were others," she says, "I never knew for sure, but I had my suspicions. He was always so careful about his cell phone, making sure I didn't see who was calling, deleting text messages right away. Plus, he'd get a hotel room up in the Cities whenever he had to work late or when the weather was bad. I don't know have any proof, but if I were a betting woman..." She waves her hand to finish the thought.

"And you still didn't leave him?" The question more or less slips out. I'm afraid Deena will throw something at me. Instead, she just shakes her head.

"Maybe I was protecting the kids. Or maybe I just like things simple. So much for that, huh?"

Deena sneaks a look at her reflection in the glass case, using it to straighten a few hairs. Hard to picture someone this careful about her appearance being married to Tom or even attracted to him.

My finger draws little figure eights a half-inch above the table. (Touching it would cause a riot.) "Was there anything bothering Tom? Anything he was worried about?"

"Anything that made me think he might be killed? No. And I told the police that. Now you know as much as they do."

"Probably less."

"So, you should leave this stuff to them."

Deena nods in the direction of the front door. Interview over. She walks me out, tugging at her t-shirt and sweats to arrange them. I turn to her once I hit the front walk.

"I suppose the police have asked you where you were the night of the murder," I say.

"Out to dinner with friends. The friends can testify to it. And so can the waitstaff at the restaurant. I'm sure the police have questioned them."

"It doesn't bother you that no one's caught the killer yet?"

She looks away, offended and maybe a little embarrassed. "I'm not *that* cold. Of course I want them to catch the killer. But I've got two kids to raise and a house to maintain and a shitload of paperwork to do. I don't have time to worry about it. You have the time, you worry about it."

The door closes heavily behind me as I leave.

***

Driving back through cow country gives me a lot of time to think. And not the fun thinking, like why Men at Work couldn't sustain their success and become the definitive band of the Eighties. Instead, I'm thinking about a murder, some threats and how they might fit together.

By the time I get home and run up the erector set of stairs to my deck, my head hurts too much to think about the case anymore. I need twenty minutes on the exercise bike at the club and a cold one at The Tav afterwards. Maybe I'll give Mike a call. We can plot strategy for keeping Carol at bay.

Two steps inside the back door, I realize something's out of sorts. Don't ask me why. Maybe it's a change of energy, maybe it's some brain function that recognizes things before putting a name to them. But if your apartment or car has ever been broken into, you sense it before you stumble across your first evidence to that effect. And my first evidence comes from the cats.

Two cats, litter-mates, run my household: Lenny, a handsome butterscotch tabby with the subtlety of a Sherman tank, and Squiggy, the nervous former runt of the litter whose black-and-white coloring and obsequious manner makes me think of a butler. Lenny's a classic bully, folding at the first sign of trouble. Therefore, it's no surprise when only Squiggy greets me in the back hallway.

"Sir," I picture him saying in his butler voice, "We have experienced a difficulty."

And quite a difficulty it is. My front door is wide open. My desk is trashed. Paperwork is spread all over the living room. My first concern is for Lenny, who turns up a few minutes later, wedged into his favorite hiding place: a small opening between the dishwasher and the refrigerator. (Somehow, for reasons defying my vacant knowledge of physics, he's thin enough to get into it but too fat to get out of it.) I close the front door and pull Lenny from his hiding place/trap. He thanks me by charging into the bedroom and sliding under the bed (his second favorite hiding place). Squiggy quickly follows, freeing me to assess the damage.

And that's the funny part. My stereo is still here. The laptop is where I left it. So is the DVD player and the TV. My collection of movies hasn't been touched. The iPad is fine. *Nothing* of value has been taken.

Something catches my attention: a large piece of notebook paper on the desk. Its message is in large printed block letters, scrawled in crayon. I stand over it and read without touching it.

Give it back or you're dead.

I try to catch my breath. I've been threatened on my blog a few times, but never taken it seriously. Most of the people who read my column are only threatening in the (relative) anonymity of cyberspace. This? This is not the work of your garden-variety pencil-neck geek. Squiggy pokes his head out of the bedroom.

"We have anything somebody would want?" I ask. Squiggy runs back into the bedroom and I reach for the phone. "I didn't think so."

CHAPTER NINE

Cops have always struck me as odd. They have this wariness about them, as if they've come down from Planet Cop and refuse to mix with the locals. Then again, they generally deal with the worst people and situations possible and the public view of them will go—without a hint of irony, mind you—from "Screw the pigs" to "Oh my God, where are the police?" in a heartbeat. Can't be a lot of laughs, being sworn to protect and defend a public to which you are deeply, deeply, deeply distrustful.

So, the barely concealed skepticism of the cop who responds to my call comes as no surprise. It's not as if St. Paul sent its finest. Officer Bukowski is a burly, balding guy in his mid-forties. He probably spends his shifts hitting fast food places, rousting teenagers and praying to God he doesn't wind up pursuing a suspect on foot.

"Nothing of value taken?" he asks, pausing over his little flip notebook.

"No."

"And no one was harmed?"

"Not physically."

He looks up from the flip pad. "So, why am I here?"

"Look at my apartment. It's trashed."

"Kinda looks like my first apartment. You sure you're not just messy?"

"Positive."

He steps over some scattered paperwork and examines the front door. I share the third floor landing with my neighbor across the hall. She peeked out a while ago and curious tenants from the lower floors have appeared on the landing below at various times. This is *not* how I like being the building celebrity.

Bukowski shakes his head. "No sign of forced entry."

"Excuse me?"

"Front door's clean. So's the backdoor and the windows. Whoever it was just waltzed in here. Did you remember to lock up?"

"I *always* remember to lock up. Sometimes I come back and double check."

He shrugs and tucks his bulging uniform shirt back into his pants. "I don't know what to tell you."

I gingerly move past a pile of books and collect the threatening note from the desk. "Here. The burglar left me a souvenir."

Bukowski's brow furrows. "Any idea who wrote this?"

"If I did, I'd know who broke into my apartment, wouldn't I?"

He gives me a *Don't tell me how to do my job* type of dirty look. "I'll ask around the building. See if anyone saw anything."

As if on cue, Lars appears in the doorway, hands in his back pockets. He takes a distracted look around the room as I steer Bukowski toward him.

"This is the building super," I say, "You should probably start with him."

Bukowski and Lars step into the hallway. I'm trying not to look at the mess. I can't wait for the cop to leave so I can get the apartment back in order. The cats apparently agree with me, refusing to come out from under the bed while the place is in this condition. Lars and Bukowski return. For some reason, Lars won't look at me.

"Well, we know one thing," Bukowski says, "We know how the guy got into your apartment." He nudges Lars with his shoulder. Lars looks remarkably how I must have looked when I was eight and had to explain to my father how I put his Cadillac in drive and crashed it into the house.

"I, uh, I left your door unlocked," Lars says.

I shake my head, as if trying to remove wax from my ears. "You left it unlocked?"

"I did."

"Meaning you were in here when I wasn't?"

"I was."

"And why is that?"

He makes a small gesture toward my mantle. "I was...borrowing your lighter."

My fists clench. "The lighter I wouldn't loan you?"

"Yes."

"Because I wouldn't help your jackass plan with Old Man Albertson?"

"Yes."

"So, you broke into my apartment and took it?"

"I didn't break in. I have the keys. I'm the super."

"Then why didn't you use those same keys to lock up on the way out?"

Lars rubs the back of his neck. "I forgot. I was so focused on helping Old Man Albertson, I just forgot about the door."

Bukowski scoffs. "You're lucky he remembered to close it."

In calmer circumstances, I could probably come up with a rational point-by-point breakdown of the idiocy involved in this, but at the moment, I'm so filled with rage that words pretty much fail me. All I get out is, "Lars...you...I...you...fucking...suck!"

Officer Bukowski clamps a beefy hand on Lars's bony shoulder. "You sure this isn't the guy who trashed your apartment?"

I'd love to see Lars hauled downtown and his rights—among other things—roundly violated. But I'm not a vengeful man. At least not when it comes to my friends.

"I'm sure he didn't," I say, "He's just an idiot with a stupid idea and no common sense."

Lars turns to Bukowski, palms up. "I'm a man of passion."

Bukowski steps toward me, probably to get away from Lars. "You think it was somebody in the building? You have an issue with any of your neighbors?"

"Not that I'm aware of. Most likely, somebody got in through the security door and caught a break when numnuts here left my place unlocked."

Bukowski holds up the threatening note. "I'll take this with me. Talk to the other tenants, see if they know anything. If I find something out, I'll let you know."

"You expect to find something out?"

"No."

He hands me his card and waddles out, pausing only to shake his head at Lars. Lars closes the door and springs over to me.

"I'm sorry," he says, "I thought I could get the lighter, smoke out Old Man Albertson and get it back here before you even noticed. How was I supposed to know someone was going to break into your place?"

"Well, the odds of it are sharply reduced *when my front door is locked!*"

"I know, I know. Look, I am going to make this right."

"Don't worry about it."

"No, no. It's my duty. As a super and a friend. I am going to catch the guy who broke in here. Bank on it."

"You're going to do this in addition to smoking out Old Man Albertson and opening a strip club where the women strip each other?"

"I'm a multi-tasker, Joe. Nothing's beyond my reach."

"Except, perhaps, the lock on my front door."

Lars, though, is wrapped up in a new task and beyond the range of my puny sideswipes. He whips open the front door and charges down the stairs. I lean out the doorway.

"By the way, how did it go?" I ask, "Did you smoke out Old Man Albertson?"

He stops on the landing, his enthusiasm momentarily stunted. "No such luck. I got the fire started okay, but he just opened the door and put it out with a fire extinguisher. Never even stepped into the hall."

"Well, good to know the ransacking of my apartment wasn't in vain."

"Oh, I'll get him out of there. Have no fear."

Actually, that—or the attempt toward it—is *exactly* my fear. I close my front door. And lock it.

***

As recently as yesterday, this whole thing was an annoyance; a favor to an ex-girlfriend as a way of getting rid of any residual guilt I felt over breaking up with her. Soon as I had done what I consider penance, I could walk away. But now there were assholes trashing my place, trying to find something-I-know-not-what. Now this is about saving my own ass as much as Tess's. So, it's time to talk to the person who got me involved in this in the first place.

Since our last tete-a-tete was on my turf, this meeting with Tess will be at her apartment. I get to her building early, so I'm forced to wait until she gets home from work. Turns out, Tom Petty was right. The waiting really is the hardest part. The lobby's nice enough; dark wood, low-lighting, tan carpeting. But the glare of the grizzled doorman makes the expected fifteen minutes feel like fifteen hours. I sit on a padded bench, looking for a comfortable position and trying not to be noticeable.

I make an attempt at being sociable. "See a lot of people come through here?"

"Yeah."

"Must be interesting work."

"It's not."

Back to silence. I glance at the clock on my cell phone for the seven-hundred-and-fifty-sixth time in the last ten minutes. The doorman scratches the bald spot in the middle of his rat's nest of graying hair and tugs at his worn, ill-fitting uniform.

"Thought you and Tess were quits," he says.

"We are. I'm just helping her out with something."

"What did you do?"

"Excuse me?"

"To mess things up with her. How did you get kicked to the curb?"

"Okay, not that it really matters, but I kicked her to the curb."

He sets the newspaper aside. "What are you? An idiot?"

"I've heard that said."

"That's a beautiful woman you hurt. Ain't you got no sense at all?" I stay quiet, hoping he'll go back to his newspaper. Instead, he keeps his watery, gray eyes focused on me. I feel compelled to offer a further defense. "I don't think she's lonely," I say, "I bet you see Tess come through here with a lot of guys."

He scratches his graying growth of beard. "Yeah, there's quite a few." For some reason, he decides to make peace, in his own way. "I guess you weren't the worst of 'em."

"Thanks." Then for some reason, I ask, "Who was the worst?"

"Oh, some fat, bald horse's ass, walked around like he was King Shit on Turd Island."

Now I only met Tom the one time, but that's about as good and as pungent a description of him as you'll find. "Was he here a lot?" I ask.

"Yeah. Thought they were quits, too, but then I seen him in here again."

"When was that?"

"About three weeks ago."

I sit up a little straighter, trying not to seem overly interested. "Three weeks?"

"Give or take."

"Do you know what it was about?"

"I don't know. And even if I could guess, it wouldn't be none of my business." With that, he makes of show going back to his newspaper.

Seconds later, Tess breezes through the lobby, gives the doorman a casual greeting and leads me to the elevators. "You two have a nice time?"

"Barrel of laughs."

"Don't take it personally. He doesn't like most guys. Women on the other hand? Whole different story."

"Yeah, he looks like a real ladies' man." Assuming the ladies in question are a collection of bearded circus freaks.

We don't say anything else until we're safely ensconced in her apartment. Since the break-in, I can't shake the feeling there's someone right behind me at all times, waiting to beat the stuffing out of me. That douchebag in the wall painting smirks at me, sensing my discomfort. Asshole.

Tess tosses her purse on the couch and heads for the bar. "Drink?"

"Maybe later. I've got to ask you something. Do I have anything somebody would want?"

"Well, you're good-looking, clean, funny within certain limits—"

"Not that. Is there any reason the person who's threatening you would be looking for something?"

Tess pauses while mixing a vodka tonic. "Maybe you better explain."

I tell her about the break-in at my apartment and the threatening note. She finishes making the drink and takes it down the hall to the bedroom. She half-closes the bedroom door and is visible changing out of her work clothes. I try to ignore it, but it takes effort. Finally, she emerges from the bedroom, wearing a black t-shirt and jeans.

"That is weird," she says, "Because I think someone broke in *here* a few weeks ago. I came home from work and found a notebook out of place."

"A notebook? That was it?"

"I know it sounds silly. But I know when something's out of place. And that notebook was definitely out of place."

I glance into the study, next to the bedroom. True to Tess's form, it's neat as a pin. Spotless black desk, gray filing cabinet, small futon. No sign of papers on the floor, no hint of dust, everything facing south. Very Feng Shui. Termite tracks would be visible in here.

"Maybe someone came in to work on the apartment," I say.

"Management would have let me know. And I double-checked with them. No one was in here."

"And nothing was taken?"

"No. Everything was right where it was supposed to be. Except the notebook."

"What was in it?"

"Nothing, really. I just used it for bills and my budget. Nothing was missing from it. But it was on the left side of the desk and I'm positive it was supposed to be on the right."

We head back to the living room. I sit on the arm of the cushy sofa while Tess glides around the bar, mixing me a vodka tonic. I'm not going to stop her.

"You think it was the same person?" she asks.

"Well, the break-ins don't exactly match. Someone comes in here and is so meticulous they only leave a notebook askew—" I love breaking that word out every now and again. "Then they come into my place, trash it beyond recognition and leave a threatening note."

Tess hands me the drink and sits on the sofa, tucking a foot under one leg. "So, there are two people in on this?"

"I don't know. Maybe. What was Tom doing here three weeks ago?"

Yeah, I could have made that transition a little more delicately, but stress gums up my self-editor. Tess freezes, as if someone hit a really big Pause button.

"How do you know he was here three weeks ago?" she asks.

"The doorman told me. We're tight now. What was up?"

She sits back on the sofa, not quite looking at me. "Tom showed up in my lobby after work one night. Completely unannounced. He followed me up here, stayed about twenty minutes and I could not give you a single reason why."

"Booty call?"

"Strangely, no. I mean, I thought that was the deal and I dreaded turning him down because he'd just promoted me." Dear Lord. "But all he did was spend time babbling about job pressures and doing the right thing and that was that. Then he left. Didn't even finish his beer."

"Was there *anything* you were able to make out? Did he even tell you why he was here?"

Tess stares at the glass coffee table as she recalls the conversation. She speaks slowly. "He said he was proud to have promoted me, but he thought he might have gotten me into some big trouble. Before I could ask him what it was about, he warned me to always do what I thought was right. To never put my career or material things in front of that. And he said he needed my help with something."

"What was that?"

Tess shakes her head. "I don't know. He just stood there for a second then he said he had to go. Put down his beer and walked out. Never brought it up at the office the next day. Never mentioned it again."

Swell. This would be so much easier if everyone just spelled out their motives and actions. I chit-chat with Tess as much as I dare while slowly downing the drink. I turn down the offer of another and call it a night, much, I sense, to Tess's chagrin. I make my way downstairs, drawing the doorman's glare as I stroll through the lobby. I resist the temptation to give him the finger. Just after I go through the glass double doors at the front, there's the screech of burning rubber to my right.

A red Lexus hauls ass out of a parking space just down the block. It runs a stop sign and disappears after taking a right hand turn. The windows are tinted, preventing me from getting any kind of clear look at the driver.

I stand on the sidewalk for several seconds. What the hell was that? Could be nothing. Could be a coincidence. But what if it's not? Maybe it's Sergeant Hara on another spy mission. But there's no way he's able to afford a car like that. Or am I just being paranoid? Yeah, that's probably the case.

Probably.

CHAPTER TEN

"You know what I worry about?" Mike says, "You ever reeled off a string of about six or seven sneezes and wondered if you might never stop? Y'know, you keep sneezing for thirty years, wind up one of those Discovery Channel oddballs? *The Man Who Couldn't Stop Sneezing?*"

"I don't worry about sneezing," I say, "I worry about hiccupping. I figure if you can't stop sneezing, you'll be dead inside three days."

"You think?"

"Oh yeah. Your entire body shuts down for a split second when you sneeze. You do that hour after hour, it won't be too long before your body just says, 'To hell with this' and stops working altogether."

"You got a point there," Mike says.

"And then of course there's, uh—"

"Dehydration?"

"Dehydration. Exactly. Your body can't lose that much mucus and hope to survive."

"Makes you think."

"Makes you think."

While Mike and I don't have an abundance of talent, we *are* good at stakeouts. That's not as easy as it sounds. You need two people who can talk for hours and say absolutely nothing. And that is right in our wheelhouse.

At the moment, our wheelhouse is the front seat of my car. We're parked by some row houses on an unassuming little street near Lake of the Isles, one of Minneapolis's Chain of Lakes. We're not far from the hustle and bustle of Uptown, the city's bar-centric hangout for urban hipsters. This street, though, has the feel of a neighborhood, the kind of place that almost makes me want to live in Minneapolis. Almost. We've got our collective eye on a brown row house with an oak door and gold lettering. Brian's place. We sip lattes and wonder—at least I do—how you do a bathroom break on a stake out.

"What time does this guy get home?" Mike asks.

"He should be on his way. According to Tess, he stops for one on the way home then gets ready for the evening."

"Well, he better get a move on. I meet Jeannette in an hour."

"And I meet Carol in an hour to cover the fact you're meeting Jeannette in an hour. So, maybe you can be a little patient and help me out."

Mike tries—and fails—not to pout. We're both dressed for an evening out. Both wearing black collared shirts and slacks; mine are tan, Mike's black. If someone doesn't think we're loitering, they'll certainly think we're on a date.

"How big, really, is this guy?" Mike asks.

"He looks like he's cornered the local steroid market."

"And how am I supposed to help?"

"Just back me up."

"How? We aren't fighters. Most of the time—no, *all* of the time—you just run away."

"And what do you do?"

"I fight dirty. Then I run away."

I wish there was another option, but ambushing Brian seems to be my only choice. I need to get him alone, thus ruling out work or most social occasions. And he's not going to let me into his home if he's got any kind of advanced warning.

"Why are we rattling this guy's cage?" Mike asks.

"Because he's on my suspect list. And he's got a past with Tess that I'd like to ask him about."

We go back to drinking our lattes and checking our cell phones. For me, all this is a preamble to dinner with Carol and her interrogation about Mike and *his* plans for the evening. Lucky me. A minute later, a car parallel parks about halfway up the street. A red Lexus. The driver's door flips open and Brian gets out.

"That's our guy," I say.

Mike shoves his oversized melon into my view, trying to get a look. "The troglodyte in the Lexus?"

"The same. Let's go."

"Go? Joe, that guy could pick me up and use me as a club against you."

"Get out of the car."

Before we can do that, though, something catches my eye, stopping me. Nancy's coming down the sidewalk, heading right for Brian. I put a hand on Mike's arm.

"Give it a minute," I say, "Some weird, wild stuff is going down."

They're directly in front of Brian's house. He suddenly slips a hand behind Nancy's head and grabs her hair. I scramble for my cell phone, thinking I'm watching an assault-and-battery. However, Brian does not assault Nancy. Unless you classify sticking his tongue halfway down her throat as assault. When it's done, he gives her a self-satisfied smile and extends a hand toward his door. She smiles back, coyly, and goes up the cements steps. Brian quickly follows her inside.

"What the hell was that?" I say.

"Well, when a man and a woman love each other very much, or when they've been drinking and have nothing better going on—"

"Shut up."

I stare at the wheel, trying to get a handle on what I've just seen. Brian and Nancy. In cahoots? Well, they're certainly on the road to cahooting.

Mike chuckles, a palpable relief in his voice. "Guess you're going to have talk to this guy some other time."

"Guess so."

"Meantime, I've got a date. Let's go, Jeeves."

He taps the ceiling like it's an old-time hansom cab. I'm too distracted to banter. I throw the car into drive and get the hell out of there.

"You remember what to tell Carol, right?" Mike asks, "I'm visiting with my aunt Corinne? That's what I'm doing tonight. Aunt Corinne's gout is acting up."

"Right. Gout. Got it."

"You're going to remember that, right?"

My mind is filled with the horror of Brian and Nancy making out. "No. No, I'm not going to forget that."

***

"So, you've got it figured out?" Carol says, picking at her Asian Chicken Salad.

"Got part of it figured out," I say, stabbing into my Penne Arrabiata, "I just need to put together the proof."

"And it *was* this Nancy person—"

"Working with Brian, the Office Bouncer. They both hate Tess. They both hate Tom. And by association, they both have a reason to hate me. Done and done."

Carol contemplates this while daintily picking at her food. This is how she eats in public. When dining in, she'll eat chocolate cake for dinner and beat herself up later in the gym. We're next to a picture window at the Stone Mill, giving us a view of the Uptown crowd; a mix of bar hounds, nouveau hippies and genuine oddballs. A few of the hipsters stare in at my dinner companion and she throws them the occasional friendly look in return.

"You're building all this based on one kiss in the street?" Carol asks.

"They fit the profile. Tess says it's both a man and a woman threatening her. Brian's strong enough to throw Tom over the balcony. It all fits."

"You just need, y'know, *proof*, right?" She's got an insufferable grin going.

I set my fork down. "I will get the details. For now, may I have my moment?"

Carol raises her hands in mock surrender. All this is disturbing my digestion. Unlike the hustle and bustle outside its windows, the Stone Mill is cozy, with its soft lighting, (faux) wood décor and large stone fireplace. Perfect for a nice, peaceful meal. Peaceful, that is, if you're not forced to cover for your idiot best friend.

"So, what's Mike doing tonight?" Carol asks, trying to appear nonchalant.

"Visiting his aunt."

"Which one?"

"Excuse me?"

"He's got three aunts. Which one's he visiting?"

Oops. This is what I get for being preoccupied with Nancy and Brian when I should have been listening to Mike's cover story. "Which aunt?" I ask.

"Yes. What's her name?"

Shit, the name, the name, the name. It was...yes! "Corinne. His aunt Corinne."

"Why's he doing that? He never visits his family."

"She's, uh, she's not feeling well."

"What's wrong with her?"

Okay, it was something starting with G. What was it? "She's got, uh, goiter."

"A goiter?"

Suddenly, that doesn't sound right, but I'm committed now. "Yes. A goiter."

"That lumpy thing on somebody's neck?"

Ah crap, *that's* what a goiter is? "Yup." My penne now has my undivided attention.

"So, his aunt Corinne, who was perfectly fine when I saw her a month ago, has now developed a massive goiter and only Mike can attend to her?"

"I could barely believe it myself."

Carol taps my plate with her fork, getting my attention. "Joe, you're bullshitting me. It's pretty obvious."

"Sorry. I was only going for mildly obvious."

"You're playing dumb ergo you're covering for him ergo he's dating somebody I don't approve of."

"That is an interesting piece of logic. And very well-reasoned." And I'll be in denial until we're both dead or quite mad.

Carol sets her plate aside. "How long have we been friends?"

"Since about ten minutes after you started dating Mike."

"And now you're choosing him over me. Is this how you treat your friends?"

She plays the guilt card well; I'll give her that. I glance up from my food.

"Look, there's you, there's Mike and there's this entity called You-and-Mike," I say, "I am your friend. I am Mike's friend. You-and-Mike are dead to me. And this is a You-and-Mike issue. I'm not getting involved."

With a small sense of triumph, I go back to my penne. Carol sips her wine and gives the restaurant a sour gaze. I'm not generally a fan of awkward silences, but this one seems to work in my favor.

Carol sets her empty glass down. "Which one of my friends is Mike dating?"

Fortunately, I've just swallowed the last of my penne or I might have choked on it. "What the hell do you mean?"

"The only person Mike could date that I wouldn't approve of is one of my friends. Which friend is it?"

"It doesn't have to be one of your friends. It could be a prostitute."

"Is he dating a prostitute?"

"Sure. Why not?"

One corner of Carol's mouth rises, half-annoyed, half-amused. "You're stonewalling."

I set my fork aside. "Okay, let's say Mike *is* dating one of your friends—and mind you, I'm confessing nothing, just speculating—why would it be a big deal? You guys have been broken up for a couple years now."

"Because when we broke up, we agreed to split everything, including our friends. We each kept the friends we had before we dated. If he's dating one of my friends, he's violating our agreement."

"Why did you get joint-custody of me and Lars? We were Mike's friends first."

"I don't know. I mean, I liked you and we got along great and it didn't seem fair to break up the group."

"What about Lars?"

"He lives in your building."

"Ah."

Carol toys with her empty wine glass. "He couldn't be dating Karen. She thinks he's gross. Michelle's been out of town on business. Stacey would actually tell me if Mike asked her out. I'm thinking it's got to be either Anna or Jeannette."

My eyes go back to my food. I can't look at her. My poker face is for shit. "Those are interesting choices."

"Okay, fine. Be that way. But I'm going to find out sooner or later. And when I do, I will remember you didn't 'fess up when you had the chance."

"I will lock my doors at night."

Carol gives that an amused little chuckle. "From what I hear, that doesn't do you a lot of good. The super will just leave your door open."

The check arrives, giving me a temporary reprieve. I take advantage by excusing myself and scurrying to the restroom.

The bathrooms are in a long hallway between the bar area and the restaurant. Coming out of the men's room, I nearly step into somebody. It's a tall, solidly-built guy with gray hair and a cheap dark suit. He stares at me with a pair of cold, steely eyes. Instantly, I've got the chills. I mumble an "Excuse me" and try to step around him. He doesn't move.

"You Joe Davis?" he asks.

"Um, sure."

"Somebody wants to talk to you."

I wince a little. The trials of being a celebrity. "I appreciate that. But I'm out with a friend and I'm always available to chat online."

Gray-Haired Guy grabs me by the throat and slams me up against the restroom door. He's quick and surprisingly strong. A second glance reveals a few scars among the crags and hard angles of the face. This is a dressed up thug.

"I don't give a fuck what you got going," he growls, "I say somebody needs to talk to you and that means you come with me. You got it?"

He lets go and takes a step back, gesturing down the hall. This whole thing gives me the same feeling I had in junior high when I was about to be stuffed in a locker. But this is probably going to be much worse. He grabs me by the shoulder and roughly moves me up the hallway toward the restaurant.

"Get moving. Don't make me ask again."

Carol is waiting out into the lobby, just at the end of the hall. Something bad might be in store for her, too. This isn't my specialty, but I've got to do something. I take a big step forward and mule-kick the guy in the thigh. It doesn't hurt him, but it knocks him off balance, giving me a running start. Carol smiles as I slip through the lobby crowd.

"I got the check," she says.

"'Preciate that. Now we gotta run for our lives."

Carol gets the fastest explanation possible as I drag her out of the restaurant and into the Friday night foot traffic. My first instinct is to get to my car, but it's parked several blocks away. There are more shadows that direction than people.

"We should find a cop," Carol says.

"You see one handy?"

Carol looks around, but of course, our need for a cop prevents one from being in the vicinity. "We should call 911," she says, "You have your phone?"

"Left it in the car. You have yours?"

"It's at home."

Swell. Death by stupidity. How did I not see this coming? We follow the crowd into the heart of Uptown, getting farther and farther from my car. The drunken and soon-to-be drunken foot traffic flows toward Chang O'Hara's, a nightclub kitty corner from The Stone Mill. It's early enough that no line has formed outside the place.

"We're going in there," I say, nodding toward Chang's, "We'll lose him in the crowd and sneak out. I know where the back door is."

"How do you know that?"

"I met a girl there once and we needed to get to the alley to—y'know, the hows and whys aren't important. Once we're out, we haul ass to the car."

We look back and sure enough, Gray-Haired Guy is still with us. Prickles of fear crawl up my spine. I've had nightmares like this. We follow the crowd right into the club.

And the place is practically fucking empty.

Carol stops. "Too early in the evening?"

"Or life taking another big shit on my head. Take your pick."

Chang's is, technically, a fusion joint, but it leans heavily on the Asian part for its décor. It's mostly hanging paper lamps, screens and swirling fans. The Irish part is restricted to graffiti on the tabletops and the occasional Celtic cross. The clientele, when they're actually in presence, could care less about the decor, as long as the booze is flowing and the bass is cranked. The upper level is a ring of large, loungy booths built around an opening to the lower level. The back hallway is just beyond the booths.

And as an added kick to the nuts, Mike and Jeannette are in the booth closest to the back hallway.

"Son of a bitch," I mumble.

Carol pulls me forward. "Don't worry about it. We'll stick to the plan. We can still get away."

"Yeah, sure. That's, that's a good thing."

She snaps a look at me, confused by my dawdling. "What's the matter?"

"Nothing, nothing. Maybe we should think about going with this guy. How bad could he really hurt us?"

"How bad does he need to?"

"Well, I think I could take a punch."

"When was the last time you had to find out?"

"Third grade."

"Oh for God's sake..."

"It was Deanne Stish. She was mean as a rattlesnake."

Carol drags me through the place. My heart sinks. Mike has no chance. Carol will spot them and there's nothing I can do about it. I can't text him a warning. Carol will notice any vocal clue before Mike does. Oh, and there's the small matter of the goon chasing us. All I can do is will a message to Mike, hoping somehow, cosmically, he gets the hint.

Not that he's earned it, but providence is on Mike's side. He catches a glimpse of Carol just as she's looking back for Gray-Haired Guy. His bug-eyed, open-mouthed, Don Knotts-esque reaction clues in Jeannette, a lovely blonde with a cute overbite. She follows his gaze and immediately goes pale. Mike grabs Jeannette and they drop under the table just before Carol can look into the booth.

We duck down the back hallway. There's a commotion behind us. I look back and see a tangle of bodies. Mike's and Jeannette's attempt to escape from under the table has brought them up close and personal with Gray-Haired Guy. Mike stumbles away from the wreck, one hand over Jeannette's face in the same creepy way John Huston pulled his illegitimate daughter from the sight of Faye Dunaway's corpse at the end of *Chinatown*. (I'd do a spoiler alert, but really? You haven't seen *Chinatown* yet?) Gray-Haired Guy rolls on the floor, holding his nuts and screaming in pain. I feel sorry for the poor bastard. He'd have been better off taking a low blow from a bowling ball rather than Mike's head.

"What happened back there?" Carol asks.

"The Gray-Haired Guy is, um, indisposed."

We reach the end of the hallway. In the time since my nocturnal adventure, the door has been outfitted with a large silver bar marked *Emergency Exit: Alarm Will Sound*. It's either to discourage burglaries or adventures like my own. Still, it's a bit of a pisser.

"We're screwed," I say, "The alarm's going to go off."

"You don't think I'm worried about that?"

Carol kicks the silver bar, opening the backdoor and unleashing a siren that's louder and slightly less annoying than Yoko Ono. We run around the building and back toward the street. We're near the mouth of the alley when it's filled by a guy with a bald head and a build like a city block. He holds up a hand.

"Gonna need you to come with me," he says. It's not a request.

Where the hell did this guy come from? Then I see the car parked illegally at the end of the alley and the large collection of keys in his hand. Ah, the wheelman.

Carol steps toward him. "You're with Gray-Haired Guy?"

He debates answering. "Yeah."

"I thought so." And Carol kicks him hard in the shin.

Mr. City Block is surprised, both by Carol's blow and just how much it hurts. He reaches for his shin and makes a swipe at us. We're just out of his reach. I need to appreciate Carol more. This is a girl who could have gone a few rounds with Deanne Stish.

We hustle away from Chang's. No sign of anyone following us. Within a few blocks, the bustle of Uptown dissolves into a regulation neighborhood. My car comes into view. We hightail it the last half-block.

I'm fumbling with the keys when Carol smacks her hand on the roof. "They're coming."

Sure enough, Gray-Haired Guy and City Block are both limping our direction. Now I'm power-fumbling.

"Christ Almighty, who *are* these guys?" I say, "You can't kill them."

"Move it before they kill *us*."

They've kicked up the pace. It resembles Quasimoto running a fifty-yard dash against a John Deere with a broken wheel. The sight is hilarious, but there's no time for that.

"C'mon!" Carol says, pounding the roof because that is *so* helpful.

Finally, I get the key in, on maybe my eighth try. We hop in the car and I struggle to get the key into the ignition. The guys are right up on us now. Carol grabs the keys away from me.

"Let me do it!"

And, of course, the damn thing goes right in. Good, too, because Mr. City Block raises a fist and crashes it down on the hood of the Saturn. I slip the car past him and hightail it the hell out there.

Carol looks back as I tear through Uptown, heading for the highway, St. Paul and home. "Who the hell were those guys?" she asks.

"I don't know, but they are *not* fans of mine."

We're quiet for several moments, letting the adrenaline wash out of us. I glance over at Carol, smiling in spite of the situation.

"Good work back there," I say.

Carol shrugs. "What are friends for?"

Yep. If it's between Mike and Carol, I think I know whose side I'm on now.

***

I didn't get drunk last night—my intake was just one glass of wine—but I actually wish I had. If I'm going to wake up tired, pissed off and suffering a headache, I should have at least had fun the night before.

I'm at the breakfast bar, cheering on my coffeemaker, when the phone rings. Phone calls aren't welcomed before my first cup of coffee, but I answer it anyway. I'm greeted by the irritatingly chipper voice of Lance, my editor at *The Daily Bugle*.

"Hey Joe, how you doing this morning?"

"What do you need, Lance?"

"Sound a little on the grumpy side, buddy."

"I'm not a little on the grumpy side. I've passed the Grumpy Side and am now residing in F.U. Valley. What do you need?"

"Okay, okay, that's cool. Just wondering when you're going to get this Monday's column to me."

Son of a bitch. I *completely* spaced that column. This investigation is now interrupting one of the few legitimate things I do with my day.

"Uh, sorry, Lance. Can I get it to you later this afternoon?"

"Sure thing, sure thing. Take your time. Don't mean to interrupt the process."

"You're really not. I just—"

"No, no. I know how you creative types work. Need your space, need to think things out. I understand."

"No, it's just that—"

"You rest yourself, get your head together and I'll see the column this afternoon. Take it easy, buddy."

It's not that I don't appreciate Lance's support. There's just something about mindless enthusiasm that turns me off. But if it buys me extra time, I'm not complaining. It takes ten minutes to shower, dress and get my laptop bag together. There's a full pot of coffee available, but writing up against a deadline should be done without distractions. That means a trip to Glacier's. I grab a cup of coffee for the walk over and dart down the stairs. Two steps out the front door, a hand drops on to my shoulder. Suddenly, a City Block is looking down at me. And he ain't happy. Shit, how did I not see this coming?

"We got a car over there," he says, "Get in."

"Um, I, I have a deadline."

Now there's a hand on my other shoulder. Gray-Haired Guy comes into view. He calmly throws a wicked right into my stomach.

I drop to my knees, seeing stars and gasping for breath. This has to be what dying feels like. My coffee cup has landed in the grass, but not before spilling enough to burn my hand. I'm yanked to my feet. As I'm being dragged to a car, I finally get my breath back.

"Okay," I say, "I'll miss the deadline."

CHAPTER ELEVEN

I was at a party in college once when someone got the bright idea to drive up to Duluth and watch the sunrise over Lake Superior. In the course of the three hour trip up there, Mike had a mini-pot-freak-out and started screaming about cops on our ass, Stoner puked down the (in)side of the car and Hondo and Freddie got into a fistfight over the proper way to calculate Earned Run Average. The upshot was a drive home under a glaring sun with a bunch of hungover, pissed off, paranoid guys in a car that reeked of vomit, urine and spent pot fumes.

And I still preferred that ride to this one.

Fortunately, these guys haven't put a bag over my head or thrown me in the trunk. And it's quiet. No conversation, not even a radio playing. Gray-Haired Guy does the driving, City Block stares out the window and I count the fat rolls on the back of City Block's neck. I'd ask where we're going, but I'm afraid they might tell me.

The trip takes us to a warehouse-turned-office-building by the river in downtown Minneapolis. It's nice enough, with the large wooden beams and the exposed brickwork. But being a prisoner makes it hard to fully appreciate the aesthetic. Gray-Haired Guy and City Block take up positions on either side of me as we ride the freight elevator up.

"We have an appointment?" I ask.

"Go fuck yourself," is the reply.

Once on the top floor, I'm led to a corner suite of unmarked offices and parked in front of a large oak door. City Block gives it a quick rap.

"Come," says the voice inside.

The door opens and I'm pushed into a huge corner office. Sunlight glares off the white décor, giving the place a sense of imperial majesty. No Roman pillars, but they'd fit right in. Way on the other side of the room, behind a dark-colored desk is a solidly-built guy with steel gray hair, chiseled features and a red power tie. Barry Preston, Deena Reilly's father and Tom's erstwhile father-in-law.

"Thank you," he says, cueing City Block to step out and close the door, "You're Joe Davis?"

"Depends. Does Joe Davis get to walk out of here when the conversation's over?"

"He does."

"Then I'm your man."

Barry thrusts an arm toward the chair opposite the desk. "Have a seat."

I walk across the tiled floor—half-expecting a trap door to open—and grab a seat in the chair. Barry steeples his fingers and studies me with cold blue eyes.

"Thank you for coming," he says.

"Didn't have much of a choice, did I?"

One corner of his mouth goes up, a crack in the ice. "We could have done this more peacefully last night. But I understand you became...belligerent."

I tamp down my age-old instinct to correct someone. There are goons stationed outside and the river is disconcertingly close.

"You could've just called me and asked to talk. Why send Hans and Franz out there?"

He ignores the question. The crack in the ice disappears. "You're not a detective, Mr. Davis."

"No."

"But you're conducting some sort of investigation into Tom's death."

"I wouldn't really call it a—"

"And it has brought you to my daughter's door."

"Well, it was just a—"

"Naturally, I'm curious as to why you feel the need to involve yourself in the business of my family. And my company."

Ah, now we're at the crux of it. I'm being muscled, told to mind my own business. And I have to admit: it's working. Any powerful guy who'll take time out of his Saturday morning to slap around a humor blogger is not to be trifled with. Especially if you're the aforementioned humor blogger. Panic buzzes through my chest. Sure, he said I'd walk out of here, but in what condition?

My mouth has gotten significantly drier. "I'm just helping out a friend."

"Yes. Tess Lashley. Is she paying you?"

"No."

"I understand you were once involved with her, but are no longer. Certainly, you can understand my curiosity about why you'd be involved on her behalf."

He speaks in a flat, business-like tone, with a light frosting of menace. I try to sound calm, but breath is in short supply.

"Tess is being threatened by someone," I say, "A couple someones, actually. And it might be the same someones who killed Tom. Don't ask me why. That's kind of what I'm trying to find out. And they're not only after Tess, they seem to be after me as well."

Barry gives that a barely perceptible nod. "And the reason you haven't turned this over to the police?"

"Tess doesn't trust the police—she thinks they're looking at her as a suspect—so she asked me to help out."

"And in turn you suspect Deena?"

I shrug. "I was looking for people who have a grudge against Tess. Deena has one."

"Do you still suspect Deena?"

"No. She was willing to stick with Tom, even after the affair, so there was no reason to kill him." That's not entirely true, but I don't want to let Barry in on that.

He studies the hunting trophies on the wall. "Then who *do* you suspect?"

"A few people. I don't have anything solid. Nothing I can prove."

"But let's imagine you find the proof. What are you going to do with it?"

"Hand it off to the police. Hope like hell this whole thing goes away."

"And that's it?"

The question throws me off. I go through my check list. Find evidence. Hand it over to the police. Life goes back to normal. The end. Is there something I'm missing?

"What else would happen?" I ask.

Barry stares at me, waiting for me to crack, have a nervous breakdown, whatever. Finally, he drops the finger-steeple.

"I believe you," he says, "You're doing this out of genuine concern for Miss Lashley, aren't you?"

"To start with, sure. Now? I'm trying to save my own ass as much as anything."

He holds up a cautioning hand. "Please understand, I have no animus toward you. I regard Miss Lashley as a dangerous person."

"Dangerous how?"

"She's ambitious. We live in an age of information. Give an ambitious person the right information..."

The light dawns. "You thought I was trying to dig up dirt for Tess?"

"Put yourself in my position. What conclusion would *you* draw?"

He's got me there. I'm inclined to give Tess the benefit of the doubt, but then again she never betrayed a member of my family.

Before I can say anything, though, Barry leans forward and folds his hands on the desk. "So, if Tom's murder and these threats to Miss Lashley are related, I imagine the threatening note Tom received is related as well?" My mouth opens, but I don't say anything. Barry's eyebrows lift slightly. "You didn't know?" he asks.

"Not at all. How did you know about it?"

"From my daughter. I'm surprised she didn't tell you."

Yeah, so am I. "I guess it didn't come up. When did Tom get a threatening note?"

"A few weeks before his death. It arrived in the office mail."

"Do you know what it said?"

"It accused him of conducting his business poorly—I'm euphemizing a bit there—and said he would pay for it."

"What did Tom do with the note?"

"As far as I know, he took my suggestion and turned it over to Corporate Security."

"Not the police?"

"I recommended he do that only in the event of further letters. I'm not aware of him receiving others. I believe the letter was turned over to the police after Tom's death."

Huh. Not only didn't Deena mention this letter, she denied Tom being under any kind of threat before he died. Was she covering for somebody? Nancy, maybe? Or was there another reason?

"If you don't mind," I ask, "I'm just curious. The night of the—"

"I was in the hotel bar having a drink when Tom was killed. I've told this to the police and it can be verified by any number of witnesses." He glances at his gold Movado watch. "I have a tee time."

"Fine. I have a deadline."

I hesitate, though, and don't rise to meet Barry. He sits at the corner of his desk, folds his hands on his lap and leans toward me. "Something you wish to ask me?"

I might as well dive in. "Just something that's been bugging me. More of a 'What's your opinion' type of thing."

"Okay."

"What was it Deena saw in Tom? I mean, she seems like she's on the ball and he was, well..."

"A half-witted primate?"

"I was going to say flaming dipshit, but you say potato..."

He chuckles, lightly. "Tom was the worst kind of weak man. The one who thinks himself strong but can't handle any kind of adversity. Men like that can be manipulated." He sighs. "Deena could manipulate him. She's my child and I love her, but I'm not blind to who she is. She has brains and ability. But she would rather have the trappings of success without putting any work in."

"Still, you helped Tom along."

Barry shrugs. "I let him be in charge of Insurance Service. It wasn't particularly challenging work. Deena pushed for him to get the Vice President's position and I backed him. If I'd have known his first act would be to promote his mistress, I might have reconsidered."

Barry walks me to the door. One hand goes to the doorknob and the other claps me on the shoulder. "A word of advice, Mr. Davis. People get nervous when their lives are looked at too closely. Whoever killed Tom must have expected the police to come after them. I imagine it's the price of doing that kind of business. But an amateur, even a well-intentioned amateur? Well, he can simply be removed. I'd caution you to remember that."

He opens the door and turns me over to the care of his goons. Yeah. Never had someone's concern for my health leave me with such an unsettled feeling.

***

"What the hell were you doing?" Mike says, pacing the floor of my apartment, "I was half-a-second away from getting caught. You have any idea what Carol will do to me if she finds out?"

"I do," I say, "And it's not going to be pretty."

"We had a plan, right? You distract her and I go on a date. It wasn't you distract her then drop her in my lap at Chang O'Hara's!"

"Okay, next time? Hang a sock on the door of the restaurant and if I'm running for my life, I'll know to come back later."

Mike lets out a disgusted sigh. I settle back on my couch, wondering if four-thirty is too early to crack my first beer. (I hope not. I cracked it ten minutes ago.) Meantime, the cats take up their usual positions on the windowsill, dozing in the sunlight. My apartment is back in order. My column on irritating bicyclists has been e-mailed out. If Mike wasn't stalking around, looking frazzled in his ratty black t-shirt and greasy jeans (his weekend wear) and I wasn't still recovering from the morning's creepiness, this would have all the ingredients of a lovely day.

Mike sits heavily on the arm of the futon. "For the record, you weren't running for your life."

"I didn't know that at the time."

"What about this morning? What was up with this Barry guy?"

I tell him about the chat, finishing up with the letter Tom received and Deena's failure to mention it. Mike gives it an interested, "Huh" and folds his arms.

"You think Tess knew anything about the letter?" he asks.

"No. She'd have said something. It *might* be what put Tom on tilt the night he showed up babbling at her place."

"Barry say anything else?"

"Not really. I couldn't decide if he was trying to pump me for information or intimidate me into backing off."

A shiver runs through Mike. "If you're smart, you'll drop this whole thing."

"If somebody's breaking in here and threatening me, I think the ship's sailed on that." I take a swig of beer. "How did things go with Jeannette? After the close call?"

A smile creeps—and *creeps* is the operative word—across his face. "Pretty good. It actually turned her on. Almost getting caught. When we got back to her place, she—"

"Why don't we leave it at *pretty good?*"

"What? You're a prude all of a sudden?"

"The less I know, the less I could reveal to Carol under torture."

"You got a point there."

Before we can settle into a decent awkward silence, Lars charges through the front door, bringing a decent awkward noise. In the few days since the break in, he's purchased a flip notebook. A pencil is lodged behind one oversized ear.

"All right, here's the idea I'm working on," he says, without preamble, "Someone strolls in, trashes the place and leaves a threatening note. So far, so good?"

I nod. "So far you have a perfect grasp of the obvious."

"Now, I've done some questioning around the building. And I've got three suspects."

"Only three?"

"There may be more. By the time I break this case open, I may be working on a vast conspiracy."

I pinch the bridge of my nose and mumble, "Oh dear God." Times like this, I envy depressives. They stay in bed and avoid these kinds of days. "Fine. Who are your suspects?"

Lars consults the list. "For starters, Judy Hein in 2A."

"Why her?"

"She's got a crush on you and you ignore her."

"You're kidding."

"Have you been leading her on?"

"She's sixty-nine years old."

"So that's a no?"

"That's a move on before I puke."

He thumbs through some pages in the flip notebook. "There's Mrs. Davenport in 6B."

"She's got a crush on me, too?"

"No, she's got a crush on Judy Hein. So, obviously..."

"Yeah."

Again with the notebook. "And there's Larry Murtaugh in 4C."

"Who's he got a crush on?"

"Nobody. He just thinks you're a creep."

"What did I do to him?"

Lars shakes his head. "Nothing. He just doesn't like the look of you."

"That's it?"

"That's it. But if I were you, I'd steer clear. Larry works for the post office."

I find this upsetting. Granted, I don't care for most of my neighbors, but that doesn't mean I want *them* disliking *me*. "All right, fine. Are you zeroing in on any of them?"

"Well, that's the catch," Lars says, "All of them have alibis for the time of the break-in."

"Did you verify the alibis?"

"How?"

"Witnesses. That's kind of standard practice with an alibi."

"You think?"

"I do. So do most detectives with a brain."

Lars scribbles in the notebook. "That's going to be a big help. Thanks."

An enormous headache is developing in my right eye. "Is that all you got?"

Lars flips the notebook shut. "Just about. Oh, and Mrs. Adams in 2C saw someone sneaking out around the time of the break-in."

"Excuse me?"

"She saw someone sneaking out around the time of the break-in."

Okay, relax, Joe. If you pick him up and throw him out the window, you won't get any useful information. "Did she happen to say what this guy looked like?"

"No. Mrs. Adams doesn't see too well. She heard the door open and close. Didn't recognize the big blob moving through it, though."

"Shit."

"Hey, hey, don't worry about it. The guy who did this wouldn't be *leaving* the building. I told you. This was an inside job the whole way." He taps the notebook with the pencil. "I'm getting to the bottom of this, brother. Have no fear." With that, he charges out of the room, whipping the door shut behind him.

Mike stands and stretches. "At least he's found something useful."

"Yeah, all I have to do is identify the big blob that wrecked my place."

"Okay, but I wouldn't try talking to any of your neighbors. Apparently, you're not real popular."

***

I will never, in this life, admit to taking a nap. They're the domain of very small children and very old people. If I lay on the futon with my comfiest pillow and perhaps an afghan, maybe some spa music on the CD player, and happen to fall asleep, hey, that's beyond my control. Doesn't mean I was trying to take a nap. I'm also, generally, a light sleeper, something exacerbated by recent burglaries and kidnappings in and around my once humble abode. Therefore, it comes as no surprise when a light scraping sound on the edge of my dream (the one where I'm riding bikes with Keira Knightley) wakes me up.

The usual assortment of confused thoughts greets me when I wake. *Where am I? The futon? Shit, I must have fallen asleep. What was that scraping? One of the cats? If it was Lenny again, I'll kick his butt. I should write a column on napping. Geez, I really need to brush my teeth. Are those footsteps on the stairs?*

The last thought brings things back into focus. Yes, those *are* footsteps on the stairs. Faint, closer to the first floor than to my place. And there's a note by the door. That explains the scraping sound. I slide off the futon and pick up the folded paper.

Your friend's an idiot. The guy you're looking for is big as hell and has short dark hair. I saw him going up there. He must have trashed your place. Believe me. A Friend (not the idiot one).

I whip open the front door and race down the stairs. Maybe I can catch up with my new Friend. Just when I get to the bottom, a door closes on the far end of the floor. There must be sleep in my eyes because I couldn't have seen that right. There's no way the person in that apartment left me the note. Is there? I wind up saying the name out loud.

"Old Man Albertson?"

CHAPTER TWELVE

Even on the most beautiful of days, I do wonder why I live in Minnesota. This afternoon, for example, is absolutely gorgeous. Low humidity, not a cloud in the sky; the kind of weather that feels like you're slipping into a warm bath as you walk out the door. Experience a day like that around here and you can't believe it could possibly be any other way.

But we have many other ways in Minnesota. The weather starts to get bitter sometime in November. Full-on winter begins shortly after and lasts until deep into April. After a month or so of rain, summer arrives around mid-May. It's great for a few weeks and then the humidity is cranked up to something resembling The Philippines and the bugs start their yearly assault. That fades in late September, leaving us with a few weeks of gorgeous Indian Summer before the temps start dropping again and winter is nigh. So, here I am. Thirty-three years of living in a state with maybe—maybe—five decent weeks of weather every year.

And for some reason I've never considered moving.

Still, I need to push aside these thoughts (after I've poured some of them into my laptop for future reference) and simply enjoy the day. The laptop and I are at a creaky wrought-iron table on the sidewalk in front of Glacier's. I get a wonderful view of the St. Paul Cathedral just down the street, as well as the traffic going past. This is, of course, only when I look up from the computer. But hey, at least I can say I'm working hard, right?

"Good afternoon, Mr. Davis."

There's a quality in the voice that makes me look up, suddenly. Deena Reilly stands next to my table, wearing a sleek black dress suit and giving herself a glance in the large window behind me.

"What are you doing here?" I ask.

"Nice to see you, too."

"Well, I just—"

She gives me a smile. "Don't worry about it. I imagine this is the last place you expected to see me."

"Pretty close. You want to sit down?"

Deena nods and pulls out a café chair, the legs grinding on the sidewalk. She situates herself in the chair and props an elbow on the table. I close the laptop and slip it into my bag.

"What brings you to the Cities?" I ask.

"Lunch with my father."

"Sounds like fun."

"It was what it was. I heard you paid him a visit."

"That's, um, one version of events."

She gives that a slight wince. "He sent his goons, didn't he?"

"Yup. I take it he's done this before?"

"Just be thankful you didn't meet me in high school."

For a second, I wonder what Deena was like in high school. Before the thoughts get too admiring, I snap back to reality. "How'd you find me?"

"I got your address. You didn't answer your buzzer, but while I was waiting, some tall, skinny guy came out of the building and told me I could find you over here."

I can always count on Lars to protect my privacy. "Why were you looking for me?"

"Guess I was curious about the meeting with my father."

Rather than give her some sort of *that's on a need-to-know-basis crap*, I come clean. "He wanted to know why I was poking around, what I was after, if I was working for someone. Y'know, the kind of things you'd normally ask a guy who writes a humor blog."

"If only said guy would stick to writing the humor blog."

"That's what your father was driving at. I take it you told him about my little visit to you?"

"Yes, but I certainly didn't ask him to send his goons and try to put a fright in you. I'm sorry for that."

I don't say anything, unwilling to let her off the hook that easily. Deena takes a pair of sunglasses from her purse and slips them on.

"I'm curious if you've found anything my father might be upset about?" she asks.

"Not really. Most everything I've turned up is stuff he already knew. I think he's more concerned with me poking around the company."

"Sounds like him."

I slide my cup of French Roast aside. "He did tell me something interesting, though. Apparently, Tom got a threatening note before he was killed."

Deena's face crinkles slightly. "I forgot to mention that to you. I'm sorry."

"Kind of a big oversight. Given that I asked you directly if Tom was under any kind of strain before he died. I'd say a threatening note qualifies."

She focuses the shades on me. "Makes you suspicious? That's fair. But there's no reason to be. It was just a case of me trying to protect myself."

"How so?"

"As you probably realize, my father's obsessed with keeping NewCo Mutual's name out of the papers, at least for the wrong reasons. He's not too thrilled about Tom being killed at a company event."

"Would it have been more convenient for him to get killed on his own time?"

"That's actually close to how my father thinks. He's helping my family through this whole thing. I can't afford to lose his support. If I didn't tell you about the threatening note, you'd have nothing to go on and you might lose interest in this whole thing. I'm sorry, but I have to think a bit like my father."

"Problem is, I'm not going anywhere."

"Doesn't look like that's the case. No."

We quietly sip our drinks. I like Deena. I can't help that. It's hard not to sympathize with what she's going through. Still, this woman had ample reason to kill her husband and threaten Tess. And she's tied into a fairly scary guy in her father. That creates a hell of a lot of possibilities.

"Seems like the only person he's really nervous about is Tess," I say.

"I'm not surprised. Tess is sneaky and she's ambitious. If you've got what she wants, you better have eyes in the back of your head."

"Seems like your dad can handle himself."

"But he likes to control things. I'll be honest, that's why *he* was mad about the affair. He thought he could control Tom. But Tess could control him better."

I rub my jaw. "Funny. He said something similar about you. The need to control, I mean. Thinks that's why you married Tom."

Deena stares at her reflection in the window. "I don't think it was that. Maybe it became that. At first it was just, I don't know, rebellion, I guess. The thrill of hooking up with one of Dad's employees; the kind of guy who would absolutely drive him nuts. I mean, Tom worked in security back then."

"Wow. From security guy to a vice-president. Nice."

"Not so hard if you marry well, right? At any rate, things with Tom were exciting in their own way. He wasn't smart, but he was devoted, and he liked to have a good time. You ever just found someone you had a good dynamic with right away?"

"Yeah. My cats."

Deena laughs. "Well, it was nice. And it was easy. Then we got married and it was both nice and easy. Then just easy. Then it wasn't even that."

I'll keep that in mind the next time my mother badgers me about getting married. "According to you, Tess is a manipulator," I say, "You sound like Nancy."

"Nancy and I pretty much see things the same way. Speaking of which, there was something else I wanted to ask you about."

"Feel free."

"Nancy called me yesterday and asked if Tom had mentioned anything about our family cabin. Do you have any idea what she's talking about?"

Huh. There's a new wrinkle. "No. Where is this family cabin?"

"It's up on the North Shore, not far from Duluth. I have absolutely no idea why she'd ask. I thought, I don't know, maybe you found out something. I'm sure you've dug up plenty of information about Nancy."

I have. Not that I'm willing to share much of it. "Haven't heard a thing about it."

Deena gets up, taking her drink with her. "I think I've bothered you long enough. It was good seeing you again. Good luck with Tess."

"Thanks."

"I get the feeling you're going to need it."

Before I can ask her about that little remark, Deena's sashaying down the sidewalk, drawing a few admiring looks. If I didn't get a sudden, wicked case of the willies, I might be giving her an admiring look as well.

***

After the chat with Deena, I call Tess and set up a meeting. Not entirely sure why, but I need to reassure myself about her. For purposes of avoiding her doorman and the douche in the painting, I talk her into getting together at a park just a few blocks from her building. The park isn't much to speak of, just a little patch of grass with a rock-lined running path, a few benches and a view of downtown Minneapolis. The parkway swings by the benches and right past the front door of Tess's building. We spent some time here when we were dating, so she was quick to agree to it. Hopefully, she realizes this is a business meeting and nothing else.

The beautiful day has turned into a beautiful evening. The air is surprisingly still. City lights are reflected in the river. I'm at one of the benches when Tess strolls up. The dying sunlight softens her features as she plasters on her most-winning smile and slides close.

"Like old times," Tess says.

"Kind of. Look, I've got a few questions to ask."

Her face falls a bit. "Okay, what's the deal?"

I start with the chase through Uptown on Friday night, followed by my kidnapping and meeting with Barry on Saturday morning. Tess stares at the grass, barely reacting.

"Barry actually thinks I'm trying to get blackmail information?" she says, "His opinion of me is *that* low?"

"You had an affair with his son-in-law. You think he's going to send you a gift basket?"

She waves this off. "Barry never liked Tom. Hell, I don't think *Deena* liked him much. The affair was just a blow to their egos."

"Did they ever threaten you?"

"No. Just a lot of dirty looks and cold attitudes. Tom probably got the worst of it."

"Did you know Tom got a threatening note? Just before he died?"

Tess looks at me, sharply. "You're kidding."

"I don't kid about stuff like that. I'm a dick joke man."

"I didn't hear anything about a threatening note."

"You think maybe that's why he came over to your place, the night he showed up babbling?"

"Maybe."

We're quiet for several seconds, watching birds glide near the water, joggers hustle along the trails, homeless people inspect the trash cans. Typical night in the city.

"You think Barry and Deena are behind this?" Tess asks, "Killing Tom, threatening me, the whole works?"

"I don't know," I say, "I'm more inclined to think it's Brian and Nancy."

"Brian and Nancy."

"Yeah."

"There's a Brian and Nancy now?"

I tell her the other part of my Friday night adventure. Tess shakes her head, as if she's just been sucker-punched.

"Whoa," she says, "Didn't see that coming."

"Join the club. You still think Brian's innocent?"

"I don't know. I should talk to him."

"Let me handle that. You know an easy way I can get a hold of him?"

"He goes to The Marquette Grill after work on Fridays. If I was looking to bump into him, that's where I'd go." Tess stares at the ground, shaking her head. "Nancy and Brian. Wow. I can't even put that image together. Maybe I ought to rethink Nancy's promotion."

"And then what? You give Brian the promotion and piss Nancy off further? Or you give it to somebody else and they're both still after you?"

Tess drops her head into her hand. "You're right. I'm screwed any way you cut it."

Despite my better judgment, I put an arm around her. Tess immediately puts her head in my chest and cries, softly. She's got my torso in a vice grip. Needy Tess. Or am I being manipulated? And why can't I shake these thoughts? Tess slides her face up closer to my collar bone.

"You feel like coming up?" she asks.

"I don't think that would be a good idea."

"I'm not asking for anything. We could have a drink. Watch a movie. Something like that."

"It always starts as something like that. I don't want it to turn into anything else."

Tess's head pops up, narrowly missing my face. "You can't even help me out? Just for a little while?"

"I *am* helping you out. You think I've got goons chasing me all over Uptown because I think it's a hoot?"

Tess scoffs and stands up. "Fine. Do what you like. Don't let me inconvenience you."

With that, she power-walks back toward her building. I run both hands through my hair, overcome with the desire to go back to bed and stay there through the winter. I've just stood to go when a red Lexus roars past me on the parkway. My Spidey Sense is tingling. By the time I turn around, the Lexus has half-a-block on me. And it's closing in on Tess. First instinct is to run to her, get her out of harm's way. But I'll never get there in time. Second instinct is to yell.

"Tess! Look out!"

She turns in time to see the Lexus jump the curb. She screams as the machine hurls itself right at her. All I can do is watch.

Tess dives out of the way.

The Lexus has to pull a quick left to avoid crashing into the building. It slips off the curb and stops, possibly contemplating another go-round. Third instinct kicks in. I scoop up a softball-sized rock from the trail and chuck it toward the Lexus.

As more than one Little League baseball and Pee Wee League football coach has pointed out: my throwing motion is for shit. I like throwing sidearm and off my back foot; the exact opposite of proper form. That's why I never get any real power on the ball. But I *can* throw accurately, assuming the ball ever reaches its target.

The rock seems to hover toward the Lexus for a long time. I have no feel for whether it's going to hit or fall short. So there's a large degree of satisfaction when it crashes through the back window.

I try to get a look at the driver, but he's ducking down. All I can make out is an enormous head, silhouetted against the dying sunlight. After a moment, the driver decides to take off, lest I chuck more rocks his direction. The Lexus hauls ass away from the building, disappearing down the street.

Tess gingerly pulls herself into a sitting position as I run up. She's got a few scrapes and bruises, but nothing more serious than that. Nothing as serious as it could have been. That realization seems to hit her suddenly. She buries her face in my neck, her body wracked with sobs. I stroke her hair and keep saying, "Shh" as if calming a child.

The Doorman pokes his head out. He stares at us for a second, stunned. Then his face curls into a sneer.

"Jesus, you two," he says, "Get a room!"

CHAPTER THIRTEEN

There's nothing more embarrassing than being unable to answer a simple question. (Okay, there's probably something more embarrassing, but it involves getting caught doinking your best friend's girlfriend in a tool shed at a college kegger. Not that I'd, y'know, know anything about that.) It's the kind of failure that casts doubt on your powers of observation, deduction and common sense. Like when I was eight and tried telling my father how I crashed his parked Cadillac into the house. (Or have I mentioned that already?)

That same feeling hits me as I talk to the cops about Tess nearly getting rundown. I had time to see the Lexus, warn Tess and huck a rock through the back window. But I didn't actually get the license plate number. Why? I really can't tell you. Or the police. Tess, of course, was too busy diving away from a speeding vehicle to take in a lot of detail. And the Doorman's recollection is confined to, "Some horse's ass trying to drive his sissy car into my building." There are no other witnesses.

The interviews take place in Tess's apartment, the first place she wanted to go once she was semi-coherent. She's on the couch, hair disheveled, a tear on the elbow of her blouse, a small scrape beneath it. I pace around, ready to dropkick the douche in the painting if he so much as looks at me funny. Over in a corner, the cops confer, probably debating the most diplomatic way to say, "You didn't give us shit so there isn't much we can do. Best of luck."

Sergeant Hara is also on the scene. He walks Tess through some routine questions. They're mostly about threats she may have received, if she's had a falling out with anyone, what have you. Tess plays deaf, dumb and blind, failing to mention either Nancy or Brian. Huh. Tossing away an opportunity to throw Nancy under the bus? What's up with that? When Hara's done with Tess, he invites me into the hallway for a little confab.

"What's your interest in this?" he asks.

"Tess was getting some threatening letters and phone calls at the office a while back. She asked me to come to a company party with her as, I don't know, protection I suppose. Then her boss got killed and another threat arrived and well, I got roped into hanging around."

Hara fixes an interested gaze on me. "You were at the party? As Tess's date? Did you ever get up to the eighth floor?"

"No. I was on the main floor the whole time."

"You sure?"

"I had a few vodkas, but I think I can remember my whereabouts."

"How about Tess? Was she up there at any time?"

"Not that I remember. She was with me, mostly."

"Mostly. So, she *was* out of your sight?"

"Just for a few minutes."

Hara's eyes flash a little. "When?"

"She and a co-worker went for a talk. But she was standing right next to me when the murder happened, if that's what you're driving at."

Hara locks his eyes on me. "Yeah, I'm wondering about your friend. She may not have thrown him off the balcony. But you see, we think Tom Reilly got beaten up by *two* people."

A jolt of electricity shoots through my gut. "Why do you think that?"

"Someone rifled through the drawers in the room. And I mean thoroughly. The place was completely trashed. Now, given the timeframe and the extent of the beating, it's hard to believe one person did all of it."

"One person mugs Tom while the other trashes the room?"

"That's the idea. Ring any bells with you?"

Could be Brian and Nancy, but I don't know that for sure. And I've got a thing about recklessly tossing people's names to the cops. Besides, much as I hate to admit it, I want to talk to them first.

"Not really," I say.

Hara scrutinizes me another second, then shrugs. "Okay. Let me give you some advice, though. You want to help her? Fine. But watch your back. She's a manipulator. Pulls that poor-little-me routine every time she senses trouble. She's nobody's victim, I'll tell you that much. You see anything you don't like, you come to me, okay? For your own good."

He emphasizes this with a lingering stare before strolling off down the hall.

Maybe Hara is on to something. Maybe I *do* need to watch my back. Maybe I've been looking at this whole thing wrong.

Crap.

***

The next step is fairly obvious: I need to talk to Brian. He owns a red Lexus and has connections to both Nancy and Tess. I decide to ambush him at his after-work hang out. Lars does me the favor of staking out NewCo Mutual and tailing Brian to The Marquette Grill. I'm hoping this will make us even and Lars will stop jackassing around the building, uncovering how much the neighbors hate me. Sadly, I don't think that's going to happen.

The Marquette Grill is a sports bar with picture windows looking out at the heart of downtown. It's the Happy Hour hangout for every nine-to-fiver in the vicinity. When I get there, Lars is at the bar, sipping a martini and giving off a James Bond air. Assuming James Bond was a tall, skinny doofus with an Elvis haircut.

I grab the stool next to Lars. "You have any trouble?" I ask.

"No. Well, one small incident. Don't worry yourself about it."

"What happened?"

"It was nothing. See, he almost spotted me, so I needed to create a diversion. I grabbed the first woman I could find and I planted one on her. It worked, too. He didn't spot me."

"There's a 'but' coming, isn't there?"

"But her boyfriend wasn't too thrilled. He tried to beat the hell out of me. I ran away. He got hit by a taxicab. See, what happened was—"

"You're right. I'm not going to worry myself about it."

Lars points me to a small table in the corner. Brian stares into a large beer and a plastic bowl of popcorn. He's bleary-eyed and unsteady. I leave Lars to pester the barflies while I approach Brian cautiously. He doesn't see me until I pull out a chair to join him.

"Good to see you, Brian," I say, sitting and propping an elbow on the clean wooden table, "How's tricks?"

Brian's face is flushed, dark circles under his eyes. Still, he puts on the usual slap-happy grin. "Hi, Joe. What brings you by?"

"Needed to talk to you about something."

"What's up?"

"I was hanging out with Tess last night and someone with a red Lexus tried to run her over."

"Shit. She okay?"

"Beyond being completely freaked out and terrified, she's just ducky. Here's what I'm wondering about, though: you own a red Lexus, right?"

"Yeah."

"Where were you last night? Right around dusk."

"I was at home. Why?"

Okay. Thought I was being direct enough. Let's try again. I give him a cold stare worthy of Ed Harris. "Like I said, you drive a red Lexus."

Slowly, ever so slowly, the light dawns. Brian throws himself forward, practically toppling the table. "Holy shit. You think I tried to run Tess down? Why the hell would I do that?"

"I know you two dated. I know it didn't end on good terms."

"So that means I run her over? Are you freakin' nuts?"

He's worked up about it, I'll give him that. And he seems desperate that I believe him. I switch from Ed Harris to a little Clint Eastwood cold aggression.

"Whoever it was, I hucked a rock through his back window. If I check your Lexus, or if the cops do it for me, it's going to be in perfect working order, right? No dings, no replacements to the back window, anything like that?"

Brian's eyes drop for a second. He shakes his head, vigorously. "No. Not at all. It's just fine."

Not sure I should believe him, but without actually checking the Lexus, I'm stuck. I let it go with a small wave of my hand. "Okay. Sorry I brought it up. It's just that, y'know, Tess has been getting threats and now this happens. I'm worried about her. Hope you understand."

"Sure, sure. Gotta, y'know, gotta look out for her."

The waiter swings by and I order a vodka rocks. Brian seems disappointed that I'm staying. I shift my gaze back to him, determined to keep him on tilt.

"I also want to talk to you about the thing with Nancy," I say.

One of Brian's eyes twitches. "What about me and Nancy?"

"You're sleeping with her."

The twitching hits DEFCON Four. Sweat forms on his upper lip. "What do you—?"

"I saw you guys making out last Friday night. Outside your place. Sorry about the invasion of privacy, but these things happen."

He gives his scalp a scratch that gets more vigorous by the second. "Well, that's fine. Nancy and I broke things off."

"That was quick."

"It's probably for the best. She said it was a mistake and, well, she's probably right." His face is bright red. I can't decide if he's sad or embarrassed.

"You and Nancy," I say, "I have a hard time putting that one together."

"Just a thing, I guess. We've worked together for a while. We got playful with the banter one day. I got an idea to try something and well, there we were."

"You got an idea to try something?"

Brian drops his voice to a confidential tone. "You ever wanted a woman who was a challenge? Someone who was going to fight her own sexuality at all turns? The kind that, even when you're doing it, you half-expect her to start slapping you on the ass and screaming, 'Stop fucking me!' You ever been with a woman like that?"

"No. But my friend Mike's probably had that experience."

"Well, it's a turn on. Believe me. I thought Nancy was going to be exactly like that. She gave off all the signals. So I gave it a shot."

"And was it like that?"

"No. Not even close. She just laid there the whole time, staring at the ceiling. When it was done, she just sort of sighed and said, 'All righty then.' We tried a second go-round, but it wasn't any better than the first. Worse, in some ways."

"So you guys broke it off?'

"Yeah. I mean, not right there on the spot. But she was supposed to call me over the weekend. Or I was supposed to call her. And we just never did. Let the whole thing go."

My vodka rocks arrives and I stir the olive stick around. "Got to be different. Moving from Tess to Nancy."

"Well, I didn't move there directly, but yeah, it's different. Tess is a great girl, man. She's smart, she's driven and she's wicked fucking hot. Wasn't happy when it ended, but that's how shit goes sometimes."

"Must have been rough, her taking up with Tom."

Brian pulverizes a handful of popcorn. "It was kind of rough, yeah. But what are you going to do? If Tess doesn't have any better taste than to take up with a fat ass circus monkey like Tom, what can you do about it?"

"Glad to see you're over it."

"Well, you live and learn."

He takes a large swallow of beer and slaps the mug back on the table. Suddenly, I'm hearing the *James Bond Theme*. It grows louder when Brian pulls his cell phone from his pocket. Cute ringtone. He shoots me a quick look just after he picks up. He doesn't, however, volunteer any information about who's on the line. Instead, he fires off a series of staccato answers.

"Uh-huh. Yep. Yeah. No, I'm not." Another look to me. "Yeah, it is. Okay, I'll be there." He slips the phone in his pocket and tosses a few bucks on the table. "Gotta run. Good seeing you again."

Brian bolts out of the restaurant. I want to follow him, but there's very little chance I can do it inconspicuously. Instead, I make a beeline to Lars, still sitting at the bar, and give him his marching orders. Lars hits the bricks, leaving me to pay for his drink.

While I wait for an update, I turn over the possibilities in my head. I spotted a red Lexus outside Tess's building one night. A red Lexus nearly ran Tess down. Brian owns a red Lexus. But he denies doing anything wrong. Still, the best theory is Brian and Nancy being in cahoots. But that's supposed to be over. If it's not Nancy that Brian's running to now, who is it? And if neither of them are behind this, who the hell is? I've just finished my second, and final, vodka rocks when the cell phone goes off. It's Lars.

"No dice," Lars says, "I followed him all through downtown, but he got on the freeway and lost me."

"How did you lose him on the freeway?"

"He was in a car. I was on foot."

"Why didn't you use your car?"

"I was having good luck on foot. I didn't want to break up my rhythm."

I want to freak out on Lars, but he was able to follow a car through downtown Minneapolis while on foot. That's amazing, if not necessarily commendable. I thank him for his efforts and hang up.

Back to the drawing board.

CHAPTER FOURTEEN

In times of crisis, it's good to have your friends around you. That is, of course, if your friends are any use in a crisis. Guy friends don't have the knack for comfort. Any problem that can't be solved by a well-timed fart is a little beyond us.

Lars and Mike are no exceptions. Fifteen minutes with them usually results in me having a screaming headache on top of any crisis.

"So, the question becomes," Lars says, pacing my hardwood floor, "Who was Brian rushing off to meet? And how does this person fit into the plot against Tess? How am I doing so far?"

I lean back against my breakfast bar. "Once again, you have grasped the obvious."

Mike, fresh from a date, stretches out on my futon. "What if Brian was rushing off to meet Tess? How does that fit in?"

Lars shakes a bony finger Mike's direction. "*That* is another good question."

I pinch the bridge of my nose, wondering if my growing headache is from the vodka or these two yahoos. "Okay, where was Brian headed?" I ask, "What highway did he jump off on?"

"Highway 94, heading toward St. Paul," Lars says.

I nod. "Okay, that rules out Tess. He'd take the Third Avenue Bridge over the river to get to her. And Nancy lives in South Minneapolis. He wouldn't use 94 to get there, either." I head to the sink for a glass of ice water. "I appreciate the help, Lars. Why don't you call it a night?"

"I'm not stopping now. I still haven't found out who broke into your apartment."

Mike looks over the back of the futon. "Shouldn't you be concentrating on the strip club?"

"I can't," Lars says, "I think I'm close to a break."

I sip the ice water. "In the case or your general sanity?"

"In the case. I think I've been looking at this thing—general sanity, that's a good one—I've been looking at this thing all wrong. I've been dealing with obvious suspects. I think it's deeper than that."

"Really? I was banking on it being much more shallow."

"No, no. I know who I have to focus on now: Old Man Albertson."

Yep, the pain is just spider-webbing out from my sinuses. "You think a shut-in broke into my apartment?"

"I think this shut-in business is a complete ruse. If I smoke him out of his apartment, we're all going to know him for the faker he is!"

"Lars, if he broke into my apartment, why would he write me a note telling me who actually broke in?"

Lars barks out a laugh, far louder than necessary. "That's what he *wants* you to think! He wants everyone to think he's a good-hearted shut-in, breaking his solitude to help out a shallow, unpopular neighbor. But it's all a lie. He's drowning in layers of deception, the likes of which you and I can only begin to imagine!"

I'd accuse Lars of being drunk, but he's actually calmer and less delusional when he's had a few. "Look, I appreciate this—" I say.

"Don't mention it, brother. It's a debt of honor."

"But I'm worried it's taking up too much of your time. I mean, Mike's right. The strip club is opening this week."

Lars contemplates this. "You got a point. Chuck needs a hand around the place. Okay, here's what I'm going to do: I'll spend the next few days concentrating on the club. Once that's open, I'm going full-out on this case. I don't care what it takes or who I have to haul down from their ivory towers, I'm getting justice for you and your stuff!"

With that, Lars gallantly strolls out the front door. Mike walks into the kitchen, fishes two beers out of the fridge and hands me one. I slump against the breakfast bar as I pop the top.

"What are you doing here anyway?" I ask, "Your date with Jeannette go badly?"

"No. She's got to work early."

"Ah. Thought there was trouble in paradise."

Mike leans against the fridge. "Well, she *was* asking me a lot about Carol tonight. Y'know, what it was like when we were dating. That sort of thing. I get the feeling she's jealous."

"Why would she be jealous after the fact? That doesn't make any sense."

"Since when does dating make sense?"

"True."

He settles back on the couch. I walk to the bookshelf and flick through my movie collection, figuring we might as well find some constructive way to pass the time. The phone rings.

"Maybe its Lars," Mike says, just before I pick up.

"Probably figured out a way to tie the break in to Al-Qaeda."

But it's not Lars, as Mike quickly figures out by the look on my face. After a few seconds of terse conversation, I hang up and start looking for my keys.

"What's going on?" Mike says, jumping to his feet.

"Nancy," I say, "She wants to meet me."

***

I've always loved spy novels. Double lives, hints of danger, clandestine meetings, secret agendas, the lot of it. Seems like a hell of a life. Thing is, it *is* a hell of a life, if you're not actually living it.

Still, I haven't completely given over to the John LeCarre/Len Deighton lifestyle. Instead of a coffee house with a sultry German singer crooning Marlene Dietrich tunes, I get a parking lot next to a dumpy playground. It's in South Minneapolis, not far from the river. The neighborhood seems quiet enough, but still, it's after dark in a large city. Mike and I sit in my Saturn, keeping an eye out for Nancy.

"You sure I should be here?" Mike asks, "I mean, I'm not jeopardizing this thing, am I?"

"She didn't tell me to come alone. I assume you're fine."

"You sure? Because if you need me to, I'll take off right now. It's not a problem."

"Don't worry about it."

"You sure?"

I let out a breath and look over at Mike. "Do you want to leave?"

Mike holds up his hands. "No, no. It's cool. I'm just, y'know, I'm just thinking of your concerns."

"Really? Were you thinking of my concerns the time I caught you banging my girlfriend in the woodshed at that kegger?"

"Hey, I've apologized a hundred times for that. And she seduced me. And I actually saved you because Jill turned out to be an evil snake woman. And shut up."

Truth be told, I don't *need* Mike here. There wasn't anything threatening in Nancy's phone call. She just said she had information I might be interested in and would I like to meet someplace? I suggested a bar, but she shrugged that off. Suggesting her house got me the same reaction. She proposed a park not far from her place. Guess the park is familiar enough without being the ultimate familiarity of meeting at her house. Or she's setting me up for something. And if Nancy's going to try an ambush, I feel better having Mike here. Not that he'd actually save me, but he'd at least be a witness at Nancy's murder trial. An anonymous witness, but still…

A few minutes later, a green Toyota Corolla pulls into the lot, parking on the opposite side from us. Nancy emerges and gives her car a long look, as if ready to admonish it for something. A few seconds later, she shrugs and steps away, looking toward me.

"Guess that's my cue," I say, reaching for the door handle.

"Good luck." Mike's nice enough to leave the *You're going to need it* unspoken.

I slip out of the car and cautiously approach Nancy. We meet in a cracked pavement No Man's Land between the cars. The pale light gives the hard angles of Nancy's face a ghostly pallor. Can't help but notice a chill in the air.

"Thank you for coming," she says.

"Curiosity got the better of me. So, what brings me by?"

Nancy takes a breath. "I need you to know I'm not the enemy. I've been angry with you lately, but I think we're on the same side. More than you know."

"Really? How would that be?"

Nancy steps close, as if someone's going to hear us in the middle of an empty park. "Does the name Fran Mahoney mean anything to you?"

"No. Should it?"

"Tess hasn't mentioned it?"

"No. Who the hell's Fran Mahoney?"

Nancy stares at the empty swings blowing in the breeze. You can practically hear the computer humming in her head, wondering exactly how much she can trust me. Finally, she looks at me again. "There's something going on. Something that killed Tom."

"And is threatening Tess?"

Nancy scoffs. "Tess. Tess might be in on it."

There's an irritated prickling just inside my skull. I've been getting it a lot lately. It's either perpetual annoyance or a brain tumor. I'm not sure which I'm rooting for. "Might be in on what?" I ask.

Nancy waves a hand, trying to regain control of herself and the situation. "Tom pulled me aside at the party and said there was something going on. Something very big and very corrupt. And he needed my help with it."

"Did he say what it was?"

"No. We were supposed to meet later on that night, but well, you saw what happened."

"Vividly. Did he give you any clue as to what was going on?"

Nancy shakes her head. "No. Just that he was scared. He mentioned Fran Mahoney and then said something about the family cabin. That's as far as he got. I'm wondering if Tess knows anything."

"If she does, she hasn't said anything to me."

The wind blows a few strands of hair across Nancy's face. They look like cracks against her pale skin. "I need your help," she says, "If Tess knows something about Fran Mahoney, I need you to find out about it."

"Really? Last time I looked, I'm supposed to be *helping* Tess. Now you want me to work against her. How do I know I can trust you?"

For a second, that vaguely hurt look comes into her eyes. "Because you can. Look, you know how much Tom liked Tess. Well, he came to *me* for help. And he said he didn't want Tess to know anything about it. So, who do you think you can trust?"

Things devolve into a staring contest, both of us trying not to shiver in the cold breeze. "I'll be honest," I say, "Most of this time,

I've been thinking you're behind all this. Trusting you isn't going to be easy."

Nancy folds her arms tight, practically hugging herself. "Come to the office tomorrow. I've got some information about Fran Mahoney on my computer. Then you can decide if you want to talk to Tess about it. Fair enough?"

"Fair enough."

"Good. If you show up, I'll know I can trust you. If not, well, then you're stuck with Tess. And you're beyond help."

With that, Nancy spins on her sensible heel and walks back toward her car. I head back to the Saturn and slide in next to Mike.

"What was that all about?" he asks. I give him the quick version and he shakes his head. "You sure you're not being set up?"

Before we can consider that, a gigantic roar shakes every window on the block, including the ones in the Saturn. I slam my head into the steering wheel and cover it with my arms. Mike drops below the dash. For a few disorienting seconds, we have no idea what the sound is or where it's coming from; if it's a meteor, a plane crash, World War III. All we know for sure is that we're still alive. That's good. We can build on that.

I look around, ears ringing, trying to find the source of the roar. Through the front window, I see what looks to be a giant bonfire across the parking lot. The pavement is scorched. The leaves in the trees are smoldering. My stomach drops. I hear my voice far away, saying the only words that come to mind.

"Nancy's car blew up."

CHAPTER FIFTEEN

"You were in the parking lot?" the cop asks.

"Yeah," I say, slumped on the curb.

"You see anybody around? Anyone near the car?"

"No. It was totally clear."

"You're not supposed to be in the playground after dusk. What were you doing here?"

Yeah, that's a good question, isn't it? What in the blue hell have I been doing? Getting people killed? Or were they already doomed and I just get to witness it? How did coffee with an ex-girlfriend turn into this shit? These questions clam me up, forcing Mike to do the lying.

"We were going to Uptown," he says, without missing a beat, "Trying to grab a drink before bar close. We wanted to make sure we were going to the right place, so we pulled in here to use the payphone."

"Why not use your cell phone?"

"Low battery."

"Looks fine to me."

"That's what I said: poor reception."

The cop stares at Mike and makes a note of it on a little notepad. "This friend you were meeting in Uptown," he says, "What's their name?"

"His name?" Mike asks.

"Yes."

"The name of my friend?"

"Yes."

"It's Gordon."

"Gordon what?"

"Excuse me?"

"Gordon's last name. What is it?"

"His last name. I'm sorry. Yeah, I was distracted by a thing. Anyway, his last name is Sumner."

The cop scribbles it down. "Gordon Sumner?"

"That's correct."

I hang my head, wondering if either the cop or Mike realizes that Gordon Sumner is the real name of Sting; the lead singer of The Police. Oh well, Mike could have chosen Sting the wrestler or Sting the Shawnee Warrior or Gordon Shumway, the real name of TV's *ALF*. Guess I should be thankful for the small things.

To Mike's credit, he's recovered nicely. Right after Nancy's car blew up, all he could do for several minutes was scream *Holy shit* at varying volumes. By the time he got it together, the people in the neighborhood were on their front lawns and the cops were on their way.

The cops do their best to screen off the smoldering remnant of the car. Not an easy task, given the level of damage. The cop dealing with us asks a few more routine questions and Mike provides a few more routine lies. But the interrogation's just getting started. Sergeant Hara is on the scene and, after consulting with the first responders, he's directed over to us.

"Let's chat," he says, hoisting the crime scene tape.

We step away from the crowd, the cops and the flaming vehicle. Hara stands with his hands on his hips and his head cocked to one side. Even in the dark, the cop eyes bore into me.

"What happened here?" he asks.

I don't bullshit him. He'd see through it and I'm still too shell-shocked to make up a decent story. I tell him about the meeting with Nancy and what we discussed, down to Fran Mahoney and the suspicions of Tess. Hara doesn't so much as blink. He eyes Mike.

"All this true?" Hara asks.

Mike sticks his hands in his pockets and shrinks into himself. "Absolutely. Then again, I might be confused. I confuse easy. I can't confirm or deny anything."

Hara looks to me again. "Nancy suspected Tess of something? And now she's dead. Interesting."

I nod toward the hulk of the car. "I don't suppose Nancy thinks so. Then again, she doesn't think much of anything anymore, does she?"

Hara works a piece of chewing gum. At least I think he's got gum in there. "If Nancy was after Tess, you'd want to protect Tess, right?"

"Not at those prices. You got an issue with Tess, why don't you talk to her?"

Hara glares a hole in my forehead. "Believe me, I will. And I'll be talking to *you* soon."

Hara slips under the crime tape and back to the crime scene. Mike and I stumble through the crowd. I try not to make eye contact with anyone, try to get my head together.

And figure out what to do next.

***

While I've never claimed to be a deep thinker, I'm at least a focused one. If I'm off on a particular train of thought, a building could come down around me and I wouldn't notice it until I had to use the restroom that no longer existed. And witnessing somebody's fiery death does nothing to alter that.

Right now, I'm lurching like a zombie through the Minneapolis skyway, ducking past one busybody after another, all while juggling two Styrofoam to-go boxes of food. I become vaguely aware of someone's cell phone ringing. Then I realize it's mine. I dig the damn thing out of my pocket and answer Carol's call.

"Where are you?" she asks.

"Downtown Minneapolis."

"Twice in one lifetime? What's the occasion?"

"I'm having lunch with Tess."

There's a slight pause on Carol's end. "Lunch? You two are on lunch terms again?"

I'd like to tell her I'm running behind schedule and can't talk, but the soup-and-sandwich place was damnably efficient and the NewCo Mutual Service Center is already visible through the skyway windows. Sadly, I have time.

"Lunch is a cover story," I say, "I'm trying to get some information."

"From Tess?"

"Despite Tess, actually." I tell her about Nancy's invitation to come to the office and get some info. That, of course, was taken off the docket when Nancy was taken off the docket. "So, the only way I can get up to the office is if Tess lets me in."

Carol hums over this for a second. "Just be careful."

"Yeah, that would be a first." I slide through a tangle of middle-management types without losing my grip on the boxes. There's a moment of preoccupied silence before Carol's voice breaks in again.

"Are you all right?" she asks, "I mean, after the Nancy thing?"

"I'm fine. I was on the other side of the parking lot when it happened."

"No, I don't mean that. I mean, well, emotionally. Are you okay? That was a hell of a thing to see."

I stop and lean against the wall, not far from a busker playing a clarinet. "I didn't sleep much last night. I didn't want to close my eyes because I was afraid I'd have nightmares. Then I finally fell asleep and had the nightmares."

"Well, if you need to talk—"

"My weed dealer's just a phone call away."

Carol lets out a breath; could be a laugh, could be a scoff. "Okay, fine. Have it your way. On a lighter note, at least one of our dating slumps is over."

"You're speaking only for yourself?"

"Yep. Got a date tonight. I'm meeting him at The Stone Mill."

"Cool. I'd ask about the young fella, but it's taking all my concentration to get through the skyway."

"Fine. I'll let you get back to your lunch date."

"It's not a—" But she's hung up before I can get that out.

My winning streak carrying the box lunches continues all the way over to the NewCo Mutual Service Center. Tess is waiting for me in the lobby. She gives the to-go boxes a looksee.

"Cobb Salad?" she asks.

"Yes."

"Dressing on the side?"

"Of course."

"Lite French and Ranch?"

"As always."

"Good work." I half-expect her to throw me a Scooby Snack.

We stop at the security desk so I can get a visitor's pass pinned to my shirt like a damn trainee badge. Then it's past the turnstiles, through a commons area of glass and soothing beige and up eight floors of elevator music (the aural equivalent of waterboarding). We come out on a floor filled with gray cubicles and, of course, more glass and beige. Can't let the workers get any inspiration, I guess. As Service Vice President, Tess rates an office, even if it *is* only slightly larger than a bathroom stall. I set the food on the desk while she closes the door.

"This is nice," Tess says, popping open the dressing containers, "You never brought me lunch before."

"No one was trying to kill you before."

She shakes her head as she tosses the salad with a plastic fork and spoon. "Always about business with you."

"Yeah, you know me. Mr. Laser Focus himself."

I bite into my wrap and watch it spill all over the napkins in the box. (I never do learn my lesson.) I set the mess down and prepare to tackle it with a knife and fork, all under Tess's disapproving glare.

"How's the office holding up?" I ask, "I mean, after what happened to Nancy?"

"Fine, I guess. I mean, there's a state of shock there. I've got to hire a new Insurance Service team leader."

"Inconveniences all around."

Tess narrows her eyes. "Is that a shot at me?"

"No. Sorry. Have you talked to Brian?"

"Not yet. We're having drinks tonight at The Stone Mill."

I pause in picking at my wrap. "Drinks with Brian?"

"Are you jealous?"

"No, just…it's fine."

Tess shakes her head. "A car bomb. That's incredible. How did she even get as far as the playground?"

"Police think it was either on a timer or was a remote-operated thing. My guess would be a remote control. I mean, why even take a chance on the thing going off with Nancy not in the car?"

"Any idea who could have done it?"

"They might have a few people in mind. Haven't heard anything, though."

"Huh. Good."

I glance back toward the outer office. "Was Nancy at her new job long enough to even move into her office?"

"Yeah. It was my old—well, new old—office on the opposite corner."

I do the mental geography to figure out where Nancy's corner office is located. I concentrate on my food, trying to keep my tone casual. "You ever heard of someone named Fran Mahoney?"

"Fran Mahoney? No. Who is she?"

"Just a friend. She's a client of NewCo's. I was wondering if you ever came across her."

Tess stares at the wall as she tries to place the name. She shakes her head. "I have no idea. Sorry."

Huh. I threw that out there, hoping to get a reaction. Tess gave me nothing. Either she's genuinely never heard of Fran Mahoney or she's a hell of an actress. I wonder why Nancy thought the name was so significant?

We small talk our way through the remainder of lunch. I need to get free of Tess to look around the office. And for that, I've put my best man on it. And by best man, I mean, my worst man. Two steps out of the office, Tess's cell rings. She leans into the office as she answers. I'm close enough to hear both ends of the conversation.

"This is Tess Lashley."

Mike makes an effort to drop his voice an octave. "Ms. Lashley, this is Sergeant Terrance John Hooker of the Minneapolis Police Department." Oh for God's sake, Mike. "May I have a moment of your time?"

"Um, sure." Tess shakes the phone toward me. "I need to take this. Can you find your way out?"

"One set of elevators in the place. I should be okay."

Tess blows me a kiss and disappears back into the office. Once I'm far enough out of view, I cut toward Nancy's office. Two things could go wrong here: either I'm spotted, or the door is locked. Fortunately, everyone has their eyes on their computers and their phones, so I'm in the clear there. And the door pops right open. Done and done.

The office is neat as a pin. Apparently, Nancy didn't get much chance to unpack. A single laptop sits in the middle of the desk. I turn it on and after an eternity, the main screen comes up. It's an introductory page, requiring a password. Shit. I rifle through the desk drawers and find a sticky note with the words "fucktess" scrawled across it. I punch it in. Sure enough, it's Nancy's password.

I don't know how to negotiate my way through the computer. There's no file marked *Fran Mahoney*. I find a page that allows me to look up client accounts. Fortunately, only one Fran Mahoney comes up, a woman with a Duluth address and a birth date that goes back several decades. There's an open correspondence case, but nothing in it and no explanation of what a correspondence case is. I grab a stray piece of paper and scribble down both the address and the name of her financial advisor: Wayne Donovan. After pocketing the info, I dig through a few of the boxes. Just office supplies. Dead end. Again.

"I'll give you a hint. That's not the elevator."

Tess is standing in the doorway; her face is frozen in a mask of cold fury. "What are you doing in here?"

For lack of a better explanation, I say, "Looking around."

"Oh great. Thank you. I couldn't have figured that out on my own. Is this why you had your friend Mike distract me with some bullshit phone call?"

"Oh. You, you figured that out, huh?"

"Right about the time he asked me to come down to police headquarters and consent to a strip search."

I roll my eyes. Mike, you fucking idiot. "I just needed a second to—"

"Get me out of the way? Why do you need to dig up information without me knowing about it? And why do you need information on Nancy anyway? She's gone, Joe. That's the end of people threatening me. That's who killed Tom. That's the end of it."

"What about her supposed partner?"

"Nancy had to be the brains behind everything. With her gone, it's over."

"You really believe that?"

"Yes. Now, do you want to let me walk you to the elevator or should I get security to do it?"

I walk to the door and am practically shoved toward the elevator bank. When we get there, I turn to Tess.

"This isn't over," I tell her, "There's more to this than Nancy supposedly threatening you. I can't let this go."

Tess tosses her head and looks away. "Sorry, Joe. But I can. I guess this is it for us."

I step past her and into the elevator. The doors slowly close between us. This is it for us? Not hardly, Tess. Not hardly.

CHAPTER SIXTEEN

I almost never get writer's block. It's not in my make-up. If you walk around this planet with a general disdain for its inhabitants, you usually find something to write about. When I'm blocked, though, that general frustration with life has no safety valve. I become a truly miserable bastard; angry, hateful, unable to laugh off life's little foibles. In a sense, I'm The Unabomber with a better creative outlet.

I have a file on my desktop called *Holding Pen*. It's stocked with lesser columns, usually on subjects vague enough to apply to any time and place. A sort of insurance policy. If I'm up against a deadline and can't get anything going, I dip into the *Holding Pen* and fill column space until I'm more inspired. At the moment, the only thing worth sending off is some half-assed thoughts on my childhood fear of clowns. Not my greatest column, but thankfully, not my worst. (That would be the one about the time I wrecked my old man's lawn mower and, well, let's just say it's the last time I write anything after four glasses of wine.)

Recent events have put me on tilt. When you keep picturing exploding cars and charred bodies, it's a little hard to write glorified dick jokes. And now I've managed to alienate Tess, all to get information that I'm not sure is worth anything. I've tried Fran Mahoney's number several times, but so far all I've gotten is a voice mail and no return phone call. I hate dead ends. And now I'm spending more time staring at the keyboard than actually putting my fingers on it.

Mike, on the other hand, has recovered beautifully from Nancy's death; able once again to embrace the smallness of his own existence. He's sitting on my futon, feet propped up on my coffee table (even though I've told him a hundred times not to do that) drinking my beer and eating my potato chips.

"I think I was wrong about Jeannette," he says, "I don't think she's jealous of Carol. I think it's something else."

"Like what?"

"I think she's interested in a threesome."

I spin my chair toward Mike. "You, Jeannette and Carol? Are you insane?"

"Look, there's no chance it will happen. Doesn't mean I can't indulge the fantasy."

"And you have?"

"In the shower this morning and in a gas station bathroom last night."

I've repeatedly asked Mike not to share these sorts of details with me, but he can't control himself. It's like he's got Tourette's Etiquette. I turn back to the computer screen.

"Problem?" Mike asks, "You've been a little edgy lately."

"Well, excuse me. I just saw someone get blown up two nights ago. It's a touch upsetting."

"Maybe it's time to—"

"And I'm too obsessed to walk away from it. Either I get some answers or I don't get another moment's peace and I can't write any more columns and I get fired and wind up living in my parents' basement."

Mike stops crunching a potato chip. He spits crumbs as he speaks. "Developing a bit of a dark side, aren't you?"

"I've always had one."

"Yeah, but a funny dark side. This? This is just shitty."

I stalk into the kitchen, looking for the chocolate-covered raisins. I always need chocolate-covered raisins when ideas aren't coming. Mike's cell phone beeps (far louder than necessary) as he steps over to the breakfast bar.

"Text message from Lars," he says, "Everything's going great with Les Bos."

"I'm very happy for the two of you."

"You going to the opening?"

Suddenly, my head feels heavy, like it wants to crash into the counter repeatedly. "This is one of those need-to-be-there-to-support-a-friend situations, isn't it?"

"I'm using it as a stare-at-naked-chicks situation, but to each their own, I guess."

I try going back to the computer, but I've got Restless Brain Syndrome. Instead, I pace the floor while Mike ignores me and slugs his drink. Finally, I grab my keys off the desk.

"I can't hang around here," I say, "I've got to do something."

"And what will that be?"

"Tess is meeting Brian for drinks at The Stone Mill. I want to go see what that's all about."

Mike follows me toward the door. "How are you going to do that?"

"I don't know. Spy on them. See how cozy they are. Something like that."

"This'll be a mistake. I'm telling you."

"Noted. Are you coming?"

"Of course," he says, drily, "What would you do if someone got killed and I wasn't around to see it?"

***

The bar area at The Stone Mill is, like the restaurant portion, quiet and dimly-lit; an immediate contrast to the hustle-and-bustle outside. The bar itself is shaped like a big horseshoe, ringed by tables and booths. Mike and I grab drinks and find a spot in the corner.

"You see them?" Mike asks.

"Yeah. Opposite corner from us."

I hunker down over my Hefeweizen and keep an eye on things. Tess and Brian are visible through a little sliver of an opening in the bar. From here, I can keep an eye on them and duck out of sight fairly easily if they happen to glance my direction. They don't appear to be particularly intimate; sharing drinks and not a lot of conversation.

"Why do we care about this again?" Mike asks, swirling the whiskey in his glass. (Frankly, I wish he hadn't ordered a whiskey. He forgets that it makes him mean as a rattlesnake until he wakes up with multiple bruises or in Detox. Or both.)

"Because Brian is still on the suspect list. Particularly now that Nancy's dead."

"You really think this guy could hook up a sophisticated car bomb?"

I groan and shake my head. "I don't know. You ever get the feeling that all the information is in front of you, but you just can't figure out how to put it all together?"

"Yeah, you pretty much described my time in college."

Things don't get friendlier or more interesting at Tess's table. Mike aimlessly looks around the place. Suddenly, he grabs my arm.

"Carol's here with a date," he says.

Oh shit. I completely forgot Carol was going to be here. She's at a booth on the far side of the bar, sharing a laugh with a guy who, if I was to venture a guess, works in financial services, has a gym membership and has never once peed in the shower. Mike's assessment is probably different. He still doesn't do well seeing Carol with other guys. And he really doesn't do well when he's been drinking whiskey. My cover, as well as most of the glassware in the bar, is in serious trouble.

"It's no big deal," I say, knowing it sounds lame as it comes out.

"No big deal? This guy could be an ax murderer for all we know. I can't believe Carol is this careless."

"Mike—"

"I'm going over there."

Before I can stop him, Mike's off, lumbering through the crowd. I abandon my position and catch up just as he arrives at Carol's booth. She's laughing at some witticism when she suddenly notices us looming over the table. The laugh disappears.

"Hi guys," she says, weakly, "What brings you by?"

Mike starts to lean over the table, but I shove him back and slip into the booth next to Carol. Mike is forced to sit next to her date.

"We were just hanging out," I say, "Having a few beers. Thought we'd say hi."

Carol has one hand poised on her Cosmo glass while Mike glares at her date, practically bearing his fangs. The date looks around, possibly wondering if he's being punk'd.

"Well, that's, that's great," Carol says, "Guys, this is Ted. Ted, this is Joe and, um, Mike."

Ted, up close, is your typical metrosexual; perfectly gelled brown hair, moisturized skin, tanning bed complexion. His feeble smile displays a set of perfectly white, perfectly straight teeth. He offers a hand to Mike, who shows no inclination to take it until I kick him under the table. Mike puts on a grin (or grimace) and grabs Ted's hand harder than necessary.

"Ted works out at my club," Carol says.

"In finance, are you?" I ask.

Ted looks at me, surprised. "Yes. Did Carol mention me?"

Mike raps his knuckles on the table. "No. Carol's never mentioned you." Then he winces after another kick under the table.

Ted toys with his whiskey sour. "And what do you guys do?"

"I write a humor blog."

Mike tries cracking his knuckles. "I'm in waste management. Disposal, really." He bends one of his fingers back too far, causing him to yip in pain.

While her date is distracted by Mike's antics, Carol leans toward me. "What is *really* going on?"

"Tess is having drinks with Brian. I was spying on them when Fredo over there spotted you."

Carol grabs my forearm. "You're the reason Mike's here?"

"It was an accident. I forgot you were going to be here."

"That's too bad. Because you're going to be having a lot of accidents in the very near future."

We break our little huddle. Mike is leaning uncomfortably close to Ted.

"We've known Carol a long time," he says, "We're tight. She watches out for us. We watch out for her. Some creep messes with her, he's messing with all of us. You got me?"

Carol grips my leg and whispers through gritted teeth. "Get him the hell out of here."

I slide out of my chair and grab Mike by his shirt. "Okay, Fredo, we've paid our respects. Say good night to the nice people."

Mike shows no inclination to leave, but one look from Carol changes his mind. He points to his eyes and then to Ted's: the *I'm watching you* gesture. I drag him back to our table.

"You will do me one favor," I say, "You will not go over there again."

"Hey, if this guy gets out of line—"

"Look again, junior, you're the only one getting out of line. Now stay put."

He slouches, resentful. "Yes, mother."

I go back to watching Tess and Brian. In my absence, things have picked up a little. They're in the midst of an intense conversation. And not a particularly friendly one, by the look of it. Things start to escalate. Brian grabs Tess's wrist. She winces and tries to pull away, but he's not letting go. Suddenly, I'm on my feet and heading around the bar. Somewhere in the distance, Mike says, "What's going on?" But I don't stop to explain. Tess's eyes widen as I walk up. Brian, though, isn't paying attention.

"Let go of her arm," I say, trying—and failing—to drop my voice an octave.

Brian looks up, bleary-eyed. "What the hell? I can't leave the house without you showing up?"

"What can I say? I'm a victim of your deafening awesomeness. Now, let go of her arm."

"I'm making a point. And mind your own business. And fuck off."

This distracts him just enough for Tess to boot him in the shin. Brian lets go of her arm and pops up, ready to go across the table. I step in his way, pretty much throwing myself in front of a bulldozer. Brian, however, becomes aware of his surroundings and takes a deep cleansing breath.

"I'm going to hit the pisser," he says, "And when I get back, your ass better be gone."

Brian limps past, bumping me harder than necessary. Mike arrives, glaring after Brian.

"What's that asshole think he's doing?" Mike asks.

"Take it down a notch," I say.

"Bullshit. Nobody shoves my friends around like that."

This is a dicey situation. Mike is not, by nature, a fighter. However, he is, by alcohol, a fighter. Mix that with the anger of seeing Carol on a date and this could get ugly.

I turn to Tess. "Everything okay?"

She's unfazed. "He's just drunk. What are you doing here?"

Yeah, what *am* I doing here? Despite Mike's best efforts, *I'm* the one who blew our cover. Left with no options, I do the time-honored guy thing: I ignore the question and glance toward the restrooms.

"I should talk to Brian," I say.

Mike hunches his shoulders, a crazy aggressive look in his eyes. "Let's kick his ass."

"No. We're going to talk. If you behave yourself, I'll let you beat up somebody on the way home."

Mike follows me down the tiled hall to the men's room. I push open the dark wood door and discover Brian alone, desperately trying to hit the urinal. His head lolls my direction.

"Fuck you," he says, "Get out of here."

While I try to think up a diplomatic approach, Mike stalks over to the urinal, grabs Brian's underwear and jacks them halfway to the ozone layer. Then he puts a forearm against Brian's head and slams it into the white tile wall. So much for diplomacy.

"I would suggest you talk to us," Mike says, "Or you and your balls will be getting separate checks."

Brian tries a few backswings, but they can't reach Mike. And with every miss, Mike tightens the wedgie. Brian speaks through gritted teeth. "What the hell do you guys want?"

"You got a little aggressive with Tess out there," I say, "Something on your mind?"

"No, no. It's just…she knows about me and Nancy. I'm trying to tell her that I'm loyal. To her. The Nancy thing was a mistake."

"Which part? The affair or you blowing her up?"

"Me? Jesus, are you crazy? I had nothing against Nancy."

"Not even her getting the promotion?"

"No. Shit, blow somebody up over a promotion? That's nuts. And besides, a car bomb? I wouldn't even know how to put one together!"

I'm tempted to remind him there are kids in the Middle East and Northern Ireland who can improvise an explosive device and aren't yet potty-trained. But then, y'know, why bring something ugly into this mugging?

"Where were you the other night?" I ask, "After you left the bar?"

"I got a call from Nancy. I met her at a bar over in St. Paul. We talked. I went home. That was that."

"What did you talk about?"

He hesitates and Mike ratchets up the pressure. Brian waves his hands. "Fine, fine. She wanted my help with something."

"And what was that?"

"She wanted to check out a cabin."

My eyes search the beige walls, as if the answer might be amid the graffiti. Then it hits me. "Tom's family cabin?"

"Yeah, that was it, I think. She wanted to look for something up there. Something that Tom might have been into. She didn't want to go by herself, so she asked me to come along."

"What was she looking for?"

"I don't know. In fact, I don't think *she* actually knew. She just said she'd know it when she found it. That was it, man. That was the last time I saw her. Now, do you guys mind? My wang's hanging out and my face is getting kind of cold."

Mike looks at me, waiting for my order. Great. Now I'm Michael Corleone calling off the dogs. Before I can do anything, though, the door opens and Carol's date, Ted, strolls in. He freezes in the doorway.

"What are you guys doing?" he asks.

I say: "It isn't what it looks like." And realize how completely stupid that sounds.

"So, you're not beating and raping a man in here?"

Mike, unfortunately, takes over the conversation. "You got it, brother. This is what we do. Beating and ass-raping. We are bad motherfuckers and we hang around Carol all the time. Do wrong by her and your ass is next!"

Ted disappears from the bathroom, practically leaving a Road Runner-esque cloud of dust behind him. Mike cracks a smile.

"That was fun," he says, "Can we do this more often?"

"I'll take it up with my staff. Now, would you let Brian and his wang go free?"

Mike backs off and quickly grabs a wastebasket. I slide to the door and crack it open. We're half-expecting Brian to zip up and go crazy. Thankfully, though, he concentrates on separating his underwear from the crack of his ass. Then he storms past me, bowlegged, and disappears down the hall.

Mike sets the wastebasket down. "You believe what he said?"

"I don't know. But if he didn't blow up the car, who did?"

We step out of the restroom, only to find Carol waiting in the deserted hallway. Her hands are on her hips and there's a murderous glint in her eye. Great. Out of the frying pan and into the Seventh Ring of Hell.

"What did you guys do?" she asks.

I play dumb. "What's wrong?"

"Ted came back to the table, slammed his drink and left. That's it. Date's a complete disaster. What happened?"

Mike tries to do the Clint Eastwood squint. "We did what we had to do." Carol punches him in the stomach. He falls back against the wall. "Hey, hey, no fair hitting," Mike says.

Carol puts a finger in my face. "You two can run around playing Starsky and Hutch all you want. But if you ever—ever!—screw up a date of mine again, I will dropkick your balls into another state!"

With that, she turns on her heel, ready to storm off. Tess, though, winds up blocking her path.

"What did you guys do?" Tess says, "Brian walked by the table, said his asshole hurt and he was going home."

Carol and Tess look at us, disgusted and confused. I turn to Mike, who shrugs.

"I don't get it," he says, "When did we become the bad guys?"

CHAPTER SEVENTEEN

I've never been good under pressure. It's why I never succeeded in Little League. Perfect example is the time I got in at shortstop late in a game, under the league's Everyone Plays When The Outcome Can't Possibly Be Affected *rule.*

I came in with two outs and our team leading by eight runs in the bottom of the sixth. Nine batters and a hell of a lot of missed grounders and fly balls later, the lead was one and the tying run was on third. A grounder came my direction. Instinct took over. I glided to my right, got my glove down and the ball rolled right in. When I straightened up, the batter was fumbling down the first base line. I had time. Just needed to get the throw in there clean. I cocked my arm and promptly fired the damn ball into the bleachers, killing Mrs. Odegaard's Pekinese.

I quit Little League shortly after that. (And my father suspects Rip Odegaard's the one who comes over every now and again to slash his tires.)

As you can see, my brief bout with writer's block has passed. Good thing, too. If I don't crank out at least three of these columns a week, the bills pile up fast. I click *Send*, giving the column up to the world and my annoying editor. I kick back in the café chair, enjoying the last of my Glacier's Sumatra. I'm waiting on Tess. No matter where I go with this nonsense, it leads me back to her.

Tess walks in a minute later, looking not at all like the woman I dated, or even the one I met here a few weeks ago. Her gait is slightly stooped, there are dark circles under her eyes and she can't quite get her hair under control. She marches straight to the table, avoiding eye contact with the rest of the place and sits, heavily.

"How's Brian?" I ask.

"I wouldn't know. He doesn't appear to be speaking to me."

"Take it he's not going to get the promotion?"

"I wouldn't go that far. I don't know. I have a lot of things to sort out. Barry said I don't have to find a replacement right away. Just like Tom, I can do both jobs until things settle down."

My eyebrows go up. "Chatting with Barry, are we?"

"Just business. He's not the only one I've talked to lately. I had to talk to Sergeant Hara. He asked me a lot of insinuating questions about where I was the night Nancy was killed; if I had any issue with her, stuff like that."

"What did you tell him?"

"I denied everything, of course. I didn't have anything to do with what happened to Nancy."

"But you certainly weren't crying the blues, right?"

Now Tess regards me with full-on suspicion. And I'm certainly returning the favor. It was a different story when I suspected Nancy and Brian. Now, since Nancy died, everything's out of whack.

"Is something on your mind, Joe?"

I try to affect nonchalance, casually sipping my coffee. "Fran Mahoney."

"Okay, again with that name. Who is she really?"

"It was a name Nancy mentioned to me before she died. Somebody she was concerned about. That's why I was in her office the other day. Trying to find some information on her."

"And what did you find out?"

"Not a whole lot. She lives in Duluth and Nancy had a correspondence case open on her."

"What did the case say?"

"It didn't say anything. And this is probably a good time to ask: what in the hell is a correspondence case?"

Tess sighs, trying to stay patient with my utter ignorance of her business. "Okay, you know insurance service maintains NewCo Mutual insurance policies. Well, the way we do that is through cases that are generated. Some are generated automatically, by the computer. Some are generated by a phone call from the financial advisor. Some are generated by direct correspondence from the clients."

"And the last one is what the Fran Mahoney case would be?"

"Exactly."

"But we don't know what the correspondence is all about?"

Again, Tess sighs, burdened with both the weight of the world and the moron across the table from her. She takes her laptop out and sets it on the table, spending a few minutes looking something up. I spend the time sipping coffee and watching her type with purpose. Finally, Tess sees something that captures her attention. She looks confused for a moment, then shrugs.

"It still doesn't say anything," Tess says, "That's weird. Normally, the letter has to be scanned in and a summary written as soon as the case is opened."

"Maybe Nancy didn't get to it before she was killed."

"Maybe. Strange, though. It wasn't like Nancy to not follow through on something like that."

"So, we have no idea what the correspondence is about?"

"No. We'd have to ask the client."

"I've tried calling her. No answer."

"The advisor might know." Tess swings the laptop shut and drops it into her bag. "Joe, I'm going to ask you, nicely, not to contact this woman or her advisor. This is a company matter."

"Really? People are getting killed and you think this should still be handled internally? You think Sergeant Hara sees it that way?"

"It's Sergeant Hara's job to investigate this stuff. The only reason *you* are involved is because I asked you to be. And now I'm asking you to let it go. Nancy was a threat and now she's gone."

"It's not like she went to fucking Aruba. She was killed. Right in front of me. You think I can let this go?"

Tess grits her teeth and draws herself up, throwing her laptop bag over her shoulder. "I hope you'll come to your senses. Before someone gets hurt."

Some statements are so preposterous, they crash my brain's smart-ass hard drive. All I can do is fumble for words while Tess strolls out. So much for the woman who got me involved in all this nonsense. Guess I'm on my own.

***

"I can die now," Mike says, gazing over the railing, "I'm completely serious about that. I could have an aneurysm or stroke out or something right here and they'll find me in my coffin with the slap-happy grin to end all slap-happy grins."

And nobody at our table doubts his sincerity. He's watching two busty blondes gently relieve each other of their lacy, skimpy outfits, much to the delight of every other pervert in the joint. Our table in the balcony—the Crow's Nest, as Lars calls it—overlooks the proceedings. The place is packed and despite the heat, everyone's having a sweaty good time. Drinks are going down like water (which they very nearly are) and Def Leppard's *Pour Some Sugar On Me* blasts out at a volume slightly quieter than a plane crashing into a Motorhead concert. Somewhere, Lars is working the room and laughing all the way to the bank. Carol grips the arm of her leather club chair and sips a Cosmo, trying not to bite the glass. Mike, meanwhile, is threatening to tumble over the railing if he doesn't get a grip, either on the railing or himself.

"You're going to want to be careful there," I say.

Mike looks down and shrugs. "It's a make-able jump."

"If you're The Green Lantern. Just be careful."

"Yes, mother."

I turn to Carol and raise my gin-and-tonic. "Congratulations."

"Yes," she says, "I feel like quite the winner right now."

I chuckle and look over the crowd. Some of the usual suspects are in attendance. Lars's friend and business partner, Chuck. Timmy, the drippy guy from 3B who acts as Lars's sidekick. Steve Andria, an employee of The Glacier who, I suspect, has at least one solicitation charge in his past. A who's who of neighborhood degenerates.

The person whose appearance most surprises me—but should not—is Brian. He must not have known a friend of mine owns this club. Not long ago, Brian looked up and saw me. It didn't seem to kill his enjoyment of the naked chicks, but it definitely cramped his style. I keep an eye on him from the Crow's Nest.

"He hasn't killed anyone so far, has he?" Carol asks.

I slide over to her side of the table so we can talk without risk of laryngitis. "So far, so good. Then again, looking at the crowd, I'm not certain it would be such a big loss."

Carol slugs me on the arm. "By the way, you and Captain Dipwad over there are forgiven."

"For messing up your date?"

"No, for selling arms to Iran. Yes, for messing up my date."

"Thanks. And sorry. Ted seemed like a nice guy."

"He was. But I met someone at the bar the other night. We're going out for drinks at that place by Fletcher Island this weekend."

"He know you're an investor in this place?"

"No. And no one I know is going to tell him, right?" She emphasizes this by placing a hand on my knee and giving it a squeeze that a boa constrictor would consider cruel and unusual.

"I will most definitely keep it on the down-low," I say.

"Good for you."

Carol releases my leg just as Lars bursts into the Crow's Nest. He throws his arms wide, a scotch-and-soda in one hand, an unlit cigar in the other, and gives us a little cry of "Hey-hey!" It earns him a round of applause, sincere and otherwise, from the people at our table. After a quick bow, he flops into a chair, draping a gangly leg over the arm.

"Did I tell you or did I tell you?" he says, exuding an air of self-satisfaction that even Tom Cruise would find annoying, "Chuck is a genius. When he comes to you with an idea, you just hop in the saddle and ride that pony all the way to the bank."

I place my hands together, prayer-like, and bow toward him. He returns the bow, adding a little flourish with his cigar hand.

"I wish you'd taken the opportunity to invest, Joe," Lars says, shouting over the din, "You could have been in on the ground floor of this."

"Guess I'm just going to have to live with that."

Lars bounds out of the chair and takes a Monty Python-esque Silly Walk over the table, plopping into the chair next to me. "By the way, now that the club opening is out of the way, I'm concentrating full-time on getting the guy who broke into your apartment."

"You really don't have—"

"Yes, I do. Everyone's safety is on the line."

"What the hell are you talking about?"

Lars leans close and shouts over the music, making sure his voice is heard only by the two of us and Guam. "There's more to this story. I've done my looking around. It's not as simple as what you think."

"No, but—"

"I've seen things my eyes can't un-see, Joe. And I'm telling you this goes deeper than you can imagine. It's a conspiracy and I wouldn't be surprised to see Old Man Albertson right in the middle, spinning the entire web. Mark my words. This isn't nearly over."

Before I can call off this particular hound, he bounds out of his chair, gives a final bow to the Crow's Nest and disappears down the winding staircase to the main floor. I'm getting a headache in one eye that probably has nothing to do with the gin-and-tonic. Carol leans toward me, a strand of hair falling across her face.

"Lars is still on the case?" she asks.

"Unfortunately for me and the rest of humanity, yes."

She smiles and sips her Cosmo. "So, how are things going with *your* case?"

"Not great. My dead-people-to-any-idea-who-might-have-killed-them ratio is a little lacking."

"Did you just make that up?"

"No, I've been working on it. Sounded fresh, though, didn't it?"

"Yeah. Just a little wordy. Tell me about the case."

I bring her up to speed on what Brian said, the deal with the cabin, the correspondence case, Fran Mahoney and Tess imploring me to drop the whole thing. Carol rests her chin on her glass.

"Don't take this wrong," she says, "But you realize the person who dragged you into this benefits from both murders, right?"

"So the Minneapolis Police keep telling me. Thing is, if Tess is behind all of this, why would she drag me into it? Where do I fit in? I'm not an accomplice. What use would I be?"

Carol has no immediate answer to that. While she takes a second to think, Mike interjects himself into the conversation. He leans back from the railing and says, "You're her alibi."

"What do you mean?" I ask.

Mike's eyes linger on the floor for another second, then he backs away from the railing. "Okay, this chick's overweight. I got a minute." He sweeps into the seat next to me. "All right, let's imagine something's going on and Tess is part of it. Her boss needs to be taken out, so she goes to you and makes up this stuff about Nancy. When the boss gets killed, she's got you to vouch for her and the suspicion goes to Nancy."

"What about when Nancy gets killed?"

"Well, that's a more dicey situation because suspicion's bound to fall on her. So, *that's* when she tells you it's time to back off." He leans back and pops an olive from his martini into his mouth. "Did I leave anything out?"

"Yeah. What's going on? Why is Tess supposedly involved with it? Why was Tom killed? Why was Nancy killed? Why do hot dogs come in packs of eight and hot dog buns come in packs of twelve? Stuff like that."

Mike slides off the chair. "You can work out the details. I'm a big picture guy. Thinking on a higher plain. The philosophical—oh, we have achieved bazooms! Ba-zooms!" He bounds back over to the railing.

Carol watches him go, then turns to me. "I hate to say it, or even much think it, but Captain Bazooms might be on to something."

I set my drink on the table. "Yeah, but all the questions I just hit him with still apply. If there's something going on, what is it? And who else is involved? Besides, it's Mike saying this. You think he's some kind of idiot savant?"

"You're half-right."

Mike peers over his shoulder. "I think better when there's sex around. You should see how I think during actual sex."

"I'll take your word on it."

Carol shakes her head. "He's not exactly Stephen Hawking."

Mike shoots her a look. "Stephen Hawking doesn't have sex."

"Okay, enough with the sex," I say, "And Stephen Hawking. Drink your drinks and watch your naked chicks and let's all have a good time, dammit!"

But the ship's pretty much sailed on that, at least for me. Mike paints an interesting picture with Tess. Maybe she's up to something, maybe she isn't. Maybe it was Professor Plum in the library with a lead pipe. The possibilities are endless.

Lars, as he is wont to do, interrupts my thoughts, charging into the Crow's Nest. "Joe! Mike! I need your help. Somebody's been beaten up."

Before we can ask, Lars is hustling down the stairs. Mike and I are right behind him with Carol only a few steps back. He leads us down a long hallway on the far side of the bar.

"It's the way to the Pudding Pit," Mike says.

Swell. I can just picture it. Some joker got out of line, one of the ladies laid him out and now we have to get his pudding-covered carcass out of the building. But as we come up on the scene, it's clear the victim never made it as far as the Pudding Pit. He's lying just outside the door, face down. Various cuts are visible around his large head. His clothes are partially torn. A pool of blood is forming on the floor.

"We called 9-1-1," Lars says, "Chuck didn't want to, but I think it's the right thing to do. I need you to keep an eye on him."

Lars runs back to the bar. Mike stands with his back to the victim, arms folded, assuming a *Nothing to see here* attitude. I squat next to the guy and get a good look at him.

And discover it's Brian.

CHAPTER EIGHTEEN

I don't think about my own death too often. I'll find out eventually so there's no point being too curious about it. When asked how I'd like to go, my standard answer is, "I wouldn't."

There is one addendum, however: I don't want to go in a hospital. If I'm in a horrible car wreck and hemorrhaging internally, just leave me at the roadside and let me check out right there. I don't want blank walls, glaring lights and antiseptic smell to be the last things to hit my senses. It's not worse than, say, getting burned at the stake, but it's not too far down the list.

All this comes to mind in the waiting room of the Hennepin County Medical Center emergency room. The harsh fluorescent lights give it the washed out look of a cheap indie film. It's populated by the usual assortment of shady characters: gangbangers with jeans hanging just below their shoes, homeless guys in rags and the occasional uninsured mother clutching her child. And there's the usual banter.

"Yeah, he was just cleaning his gun. Six times."

"I don't know. His penis was still attached when he went to bed. Musta got up and tripped over something real bad."

Lars is back at the club and Mike can't be blasted out of there, so it's up to me and Carol to deal with Les Bos' first (though probably not last) brutal beating victim.

"Is it possible to get raped in an emergency room waiting area?" Carol asks, clutching her seat, "I mean, has that ever happened?"

"Why? You got your eye on somebody?"

"I was more concerned about you."

"Me?"

"Yeah, you got that clean and handsome thing going. Guy who's been in prison for a while? You're right up his alley."

"It's not *his* alley I'm worried about."

She gives that mock applause and we drop the banter. Brian came in a while ago with a boatload of cuts and contusions, but nothing more serious than that. Hopefully, he can tell me a thing or two about what happened.

"Did the police say anything?" Carol asks.

"They got a crapload of statements, but from what Lars told me, nobody really saw anything."

Carol folds her hands around a soda she got from a machine. "You think it's part of this thing you're investigating?"

"Maybe. It's also possible Brian got mouthy with some other HGH case and got his bell rung. I don't know for sure, though. That doesn't feel right."

"Feel right? You've investigated all of one thing in your life and you know whether or not something feels right?"

Nothing I can say to that. Still, Brian may be next in a line that now includes Tom, Nancy and, to a slightly lesser degree, Tess. If that's the deal, the *best* case scenario is that he was beaten up by a complete stranger. A short time later, a doctor comes out and tells us Brian is resting comfortably and will be fine.

"Is he awake?" I ask.

The doctor, a sour-looking dude who probably figures he could have been a TV doctor if his honker wasn't so friggin' big, gives us his patented Grim Face. "He is, but he's pretty zonked out. Are you family?"

"Yes. He's my brother." I throw an arm around Carol. "This is my wife." Carol flashes a smile without missing a beat.

The doctor makes a show of thinking about it. "I can let you see him for a minute, but that's it."

He leads us out of the lobby and down a row of screened-off beds, filled with those who've been violated in one capacity or another. He stops at one and draws back the curtain.

"Just a couple of minutes, remember," the doctor says.

We step into the cubicle. Brian's head is largely a mass of bandages and what isn't bandaged is turning an interesting shade of purple. His eyes are heavy-lidded. It takes a few seconds for him to realize anyone's there. I step toward the bed while Carol hangs back.

"Brian? It's me. Joe Davis."

The eyes slowly move toward me, taking a few seconds to focus. "Shit. You again?"

"A friend of mine owns the club. I came to make sure you're okay."

"I look okay?"

I hold up a hand. "Sorry. You're right."

"No, no. I'm serious. How bad do I look?"

"Um..."

"Give it to me straight."

Huh. What's a good frame of reference here? "You remember how Foghorn Leghorn looked after playing with Eggbert?"

"That bad?"

"Worse."

He closes his eyes and mumbles, "Fuck."

I lean closer to Brian and lower my voice. "Did you see who did this?"

"Why are you leaning so close? You coming on to me?"

"No. I just didn't want anyone to hear us."

"They can listen all they want. I didn't see who got me. I was trying to find the shitter, walked down this hallway, saw a sign that said *Pudding Pit* and thought, 'Hey, this might be interesting.' Next thing I know, someone cracks me on the back of the head and starts beating the shit out of me. That's all I got."

"You don't remember anything about him? What the guy looked like? How big he was? If he said anything?"

Brian shakes his head, gingerly. "He was big and he hit like a fuckin' mule kicking. Kicked like one, too." His eyes open wider. "Wait. I *do* remember something. There were two of them. Had to be."

"How do you know that?"

"The way the kicks were coming. I was getting it on my left side and my right side. Both at the same time. No way one guy was doing that."

"But you don't remember anything about the guys?"

His eyes cloud over again. "No. That's it."

It's frustrating, but what should I expect from a guy who's been beaten about the head and shoulders? "You think this has anything to do with Nancy?"

His face twitches as a spasm of pain runs through him. "I have no idea, man."

Carol puts a cautioning hand on my shoulder. "You think maybe we should let him rest?"

I'm forced to agree. Brian's had a hard enough night. I tap the bed railing and back off. "If you think of anything, you know how to get a hold of me."

Brian chuckles, softly and without humor. "All I got to do is walk around. You'll show up sooner or later."

Carol leads me out of the room and back to the hallway leading to the lobby. I take a casual glance to my left and stop in my tracks. Someone's at the end of the hallway, leaning against the wall, passively watching the door. It's a thin dude with a full head of gray hair. Mr. Gray-Haired Man, one of Barry Preston's henchmen.

"What's going on?" Carol asks.

"Bad dude. Nine o'clock."

Gray-Haired Man spots me and casually pushes off the wall. I tense up, waiting for him to come after me. Instead, he turns on his heel and walks the other way. I take off after him, anger overriding my common sense. Carol stumbles after me.

"Is that the guy from the restaurant?" she asks, "*That* bad dude?"

"Yeah. One of Barry's goons."

She grabs at my arm, trying to slow me down. "So why are we chasing him?"

"Because he's here! That can't be a coincidence."

Gray-Haired Guy keeps a brisk pace, not bothering to glance back. I'd guess he's a power-walker, but it's hard to picture him dork-walking around a lake with a big ass set of headphones. He's got a decent lead when he reaches the emergency room lobby and makes a beeline to the automatic double-doors. Once out, he climbs into a waiting car. Carol and I reach the sidewalk in time to watch the taillights disappear down Sixth Street.

"That was interesting," she says.

"Yeah. Just wish I knew what the hell it meant." Like most everything else that's happened lately.

***

I don't like waking up with an icky feeling and, sorry to say, it's largely due to being at Les Bos. Now, don't mistake me for a prude. I'm as perverted as the next guy and since the next guy is usually Mike or Lars, I'm pretty perverted. But there is something about making money from perversion that leaves me cold. It's terrific in the privacy of your own home, but once it's out in there in the world and someone's making money off it, well, that's just sad. Still, if the internet—and everything I saw last night—is any kind of cultural barometer, my sadness doesn't appear to be slowing the industry down at all.

I'm sitting at the breakfast bar with both a cup of coffee and a yellow notepad in front of me. I've scribbled down several names: Tess, Nancy, Brian, Barry and Deena. I've drawn lines between them, trying to find a combination that works, some pattern that causes all these loose ends to fit together. Below all that, I've written: "Duluth," "Fran Mahoney" and "Family Cabin." I tap the pen on the paper. It's all here in front of me. But nothing adds up or helps my headache go away. After a little more stewing, I decide to head over to Glacier's to work on the column. Get back to something I'm good at, channel some of this frustration.

The laptop bag and I are just out the front door of the building when I spot Barry Preston at the end of the front walk. He leans on a black Cutlass, arms folded, resplendent in a charcoal gray suit. City Block is near the back of the car, Gray-Haired Guy near the front. Barry makes no move, expecting me to come to him. I get the feeling he's not the sort of guy who swats flies or mosquitoes, he just stares them down. It's a surprisingly quiet morning. Not even a jogger in sight. Maybe he had the whole neighborhood whacked.

"Good morning," I say, for lack of a better greeting.

"Good morning, Mr. Davis. I thought we should talk. Would you care to go for a ride?"

"No. I'm okay right here."

Both City Block and Gray-Haired Guy tense up. Barry grins. "You realize I'm doing you a courtesy by asking?"

"Try anything and I'll fight like hell."

"You'll lose."

"I know. But it'll make a hell of a scene. There's a goodly number of windows behind me. Somebody will see something, probably get a license number before they call the cops. But by all means, do the rough stuff if that's how you get your jollies."

The goons look to Barry. Barry brushes some lint off his sleeve.

"Fine. If that's what you wish. I wanted to discuss the incident last night."

"The one where Frick and Frack beat the hell out of one of your employees? That incident?"

"You have no proof."

"No, but it's a fuck of a coincidence, isn't it?"

Barry pushes off from the car and steps toward me. The goons start to follow him, but he holds up a hand, backing them off. "What do you think you know?"

"Thought you were concerned with what Tess knows."

"I have my eye on Miss Lashley. And at the moment, I also have my eye on you. You're still digging around my company. May I ask why?"

"Two of your employees are dead. One's been getting threatened and one had the crap kicked out of him. You see a pattern?"

"Yes. You were at all of those events."

Holy crap, he's right. So much for getting up on my high horse. "I hate to tell you this, but something's going on in your company."

"And what would that be?"

"That, well, there I don't have quite as many, uh, concrete answers."

Barry narrows his eyes, scrutinizing. "I can't tell if you're stalling or just a complete idiot."

"I have the same trouble."

He smiles, in spite of himself. "I'm actually here to give you a piece of advice, Mr. Davis."

"Oh, goody."

"I assume you're on your way to a coffee shop. To write your, um, column or whatever it is you do."

"You would be right."

"I would suggest you keep at it. Enjoy your success and whatever other fulfillment comes with it. Make that the only focus in your life. Nothing involving my company would be nearly as...rewarding. Do you follow me?"

"You know 'Back the fuck off' is much more concise."

"Still, the message comes through, doesn't it?"

"Loud and clear."

"Good. And I would suggest keeping your distance from Miss Lashley as well."

"Why?"

He gives me an enigmatic smile. "It would safer for you. Let's leave it at that."

Barry walks to the car and climbs in the back. City Block moves around to the passenger door. Gray-Haired Guy still has his eyes locked on me. His fingers curl into a make-shift gun, using his thumb to drop the hammer. He nearly grins as he climbs in the car and slams the door.

Well, they don't get points for subtlety. But if that weak feeling in my legs means anything, they definitely get points for effectiveness.

***

"Okay, I've got to ask," Mike says, drumming his fingers on the dash of my Saturn, "Why is it you haul me along on every one of these deals? This shit gets dangerous. Why can't you call Carol or Lars?"

"I screwed up Carol's date the other night, so I can't ask her any favors. And Lars takes any situation to DEFCON Five. You think I'm going to bring him along if there might be trouble? Besides, I may need your bullshitting skills."

"Okay, there. That last part. That makes sense."

We're heading over the Third Avenue Bridge, aiming toward Tess's apartment building. In the rearview mirror, the sun is dropping behind the Minneapolis skyline. I've been calling Tess most of the afternoon, trying her cell, home and office numbers. So far, I've left three messages and a string of hang-ups.

"If she won't answer your phone calls, why do you think she'll let you upstairs to see her?" Mike asks.

"I don't. You may have to bullshit our way past the doorman."

Mike tries cracking his knuckles. I wish to God he'd either break that habit or a finger. Anything to get him to stop. "You're really worried about Tess?" he asks.

"Something about that chat with Barry. Didn't exactly leave me reassured. And it's not like her to be out of communication for an entire day. I want to make sure she's all right."

"You're getting a little obsessed here."

"Yeah. But at some point, you have to quit fighting it and say, 'Fuck it, I'm obsessed.'"

A few minutes later, I ditch the car in front of Tess's building and lead Mike inside. The Doorman gives me the usual disgusted look.

"I need to get into Tess Lashley's apartment," I say.

The Doorman shakes his head in disgust. "Nice. No 'Hello', no 'How ya doin'?' No nothin'. Just 'Let me into Tess Lashley's place.' Nice manners you got."

"I'm sorry. Hi. How are you?"

"Go fuck yourself."

Oy. "Look, this is kind of an emergency."

"And if I let in everybody with that sob story, I'd have people running amok. Get lost."

Mike elbows me aside and throws a forearm on the desk. "Here are your options: you can let us up there or you can find yourself in a world of hurt. Your choice."

The Doorman doesn't seem fazed. "And who the hell are you?"

"My name is Benjamin Franklin Pierce and I am this man's attorney. Now, are you going to let my client up there or do I have to get a writ?"

"A writ?"

"A writ. Indeed. You realize what a writ would mean?"

"Trouble?"

"Have you ever seen a writ that wasn't?" A slight hesitation by the Doorman and Mike, adopting his best weasely, arrogant demeanor, moves in for the kill. "Now, I suggest you let my client into Miss Lashley's apartment or there is going to be a serious Writ of Kiss Your Ass Goodbye coming down on you. Understood?"

"Understood. But—"

"*But* is not what I want to hear right now, my friend."

"I need to check with building management and—"

Mike slams his palms down on the counter, the smack echoing through the lobby. "Did you miss my client telling you this is an emergency? Are we expected to dick around—more than we already have—while you waste time calling building management? But if that's what you need to do, fine. Go ahead. I'll just get that writ started."

Mike takes out his cell phone and starts dialing. I have no idea who he's actually calling. The Doorman practically dives across the counter to stop him.

"Okay, okay, let's go up! I don't want any trouble."

Mike makes a show of slipping the phone back into his pocket. "You bet your ass you don't."

Three minutes later, the Doorman is leading us into Tess's apartment. I bump into Mike on the way in and from habit I say, "Excuse me, Mike."

The Doorman, of course, catches this. "Wait a minute, did you call him 'Mike'? I thought his name was Benjamin or something."

Mike gets right in the Doorman's face. "My name is for my friends."

The Doorman raises both hands and backs away. "Got it. Got it. Do what you need to do." I've got to give Mike credit. Alternately sly and bullying, complete commitment and quick thinking. One of his finest performances.

It takes only a second to realize Tess isn't in the apartment. The place is, as always, neat as a Mormon shitter. (Don't ask me what a Mormon shitter is. I heard that expression once and it made me laugh.) No sign of a struggle, a home invasion, anything of that variety. But the place is still empty. Where could Tess be on a Saturday night? While I'm checking out the study, I find something of interest on the nearly empty desktop. On a scratchpad near the phone are the words: Fletcher Island, 10 pm, 8/25, bring letter.

I pick up the scratch pad and stare at it. Fletcher Island isn't far from here. 8/25 is today's date. 10 pm is about ninety minutes from now. No idea what the letter is. Looks like Tess has a meeting tonight.

Time to crash it.

CHAPTER NINETEEN

"You ever think how murder is entirely preventable?" Mike says, slipping his cell phone back into his pocket and propping his feet up on my dash (even though I've told him a thousand times not to do that), "Y'know, you hear the stories and you think, 'Get it together, asshole. Leave the husband. Let the argument with the co-worker go. Don't tell your brother he's a worthless drunken fuck after he's had a bottle-and-a-half of tequila and he's cleaning his shotgun.' Y'know, a simple ounce of prevention."

"That's kind of hard to realize at the time, though, isn't it?"

"But that's what I'm saying. I mean, if one of us ever found ourselves in that position, would we be smart enough to walk away or get a restraining order or have the other person killed? Y'know, a sensible solution? Or would we just think no one's going to kill us and wind up pissed off when we wake up with our brains next to us on the pillow?"

Mike's mood has taken a turn for the morose. He just had a cell phone chat with Jeannette. Either the conversation didn't go well or he watched *Se7en* this afternoon and he's having flashbacks.

"Something up with Jeannette?" I ask.

"No. I thought we should have a little breathing room, so I broke off our date for tonight."

"To be here?"

"I didn't say it was an upgrade. It's just a convenient excuse. Told her you were having some trouble and needed to talk to someone."

"How did she take that?"

"She asked me about a hundred times if I was seeing Carol tonight. I kept telling her no. I mean, she seemed alright at the end, but I don't know. She talks about Carol and me and she gets this crazy look in her eyes. I'm starting to worry about my safety."

"As opposed to Carol's."

"Oh, well, hers, too. I guess."

Mike glances at the clock on his cell phone. We're in a fairly secluded spot near Fletcher Island, an inaccurately named peninsula across from downtown Minneapolis. It's a strange spot for a meeting. Great for 5Ks and picnics. But meetings after dark? Not so much.

"You sure Tess is going to be here?" he asks, "I mean, the note could have been wrong. What do we do if she doesn't show?"

"We go to The Tav, get drunk and drive home."

Mike nods. "Right in our wheelhouse."

I scan the island again, barely visible through the shrubs sheltering us. We're near the parking lot at the entrance to the island. Beyond the lot is a lawn strewn with picnic tables and benches. Beyond that is a trail leading to a small parking lot on the other side of the island. We've been waiting here half-an-hour, just in case Tess came early. As usual, she's maddeningly punctual. Her car pulls into the main lot at ten-thirty on the dot. She climbs out and makes a beeline to one of the benches, perching on it and keeping her head on a swivel.

"Okay, she's here," Mike says, "Any sign of who she's meeting?"

"Not yet. Probably be along—wait a minute—"

I see a tall, skinny figure slinking along the edge of the park. He's dressed all in black and has a stocking cap pulled down on his head. He moves into a grove of trees not far from my car. Tess is about twenty feet away and has her back to the guy. He sits and watches her.

"Who is this guy?" Mike asks.

"I don't know," I say, "But it doesn't look like he's meeting with Tess."

"Set up?"

"That's what I'm thinking."

"What are you going—"

Before Mike can finish, I'm out of the car, heading right for this guy. He doesn't hear me coming. In fact, he doesn't move until I'm right up on him. He half-turns just before I grab him, pinning his arms in a bear hug. The guy tries to squirm free, but I've got a good hold on him.

"What the hell do you think you're doing?" I say.

"Take it easy, take it easy," the guy says, his voice sounding a bit familiar, "My wallet's in my back pocket. There must be five hundred dollars in there. I…Joe?"

I get a good look at him in the thin glow from the streetlights. I can only roll my eyes and let him loose. "Lars, what the hell are you doing here?"

Lars straightens his clothes and brushes himself off. "I'm following Tess."

"Why?"

"As a favor to you. You took Brian to the emergency room the other night. I owe you one."

In his own completely stupid way, Lars is actually very sweet. And typical of him, he pays back a favor with a completely useless gesture that's more trouble than it's actually worth. I take a glance toward Tess, who has, thankfully, been oblivious to all this. I pull Lars back toward the car.

"What are *you* doing here?" Lars asks.

"Strangely, the same thing you are. Tess is supposed to be meeting with someone. Now, more importantly, how the hell did you get five hundred dollars in your wallet?"

"My take home from the club. I told you, you should have invested."

"And you really would've handed the whole five hundred over to me if I was a mugger?"

"Yeah. Then I would've hit you with my binoculars, taken the money back and run like hell. So, I'm glad we got things cleared up."

We reach the car and Lars plunks down into the back, tossing a pair of binoculars just smaller than the Hubble Telescope on to the seat beside him. Mike glances back.

"You look like either a bird-watcher or a low-life," he says.

"I used to be a bird-watcher," Lars says.

I slip behind the wheel. "Now he just concentrates on being a low-life." I turn back to Lars. "You've really been following her around all day?"

"Mostly the last few hours."

"Where did she go before this?"

"Nowhere special. Bought a bottle of wine, grabbed some groceries, swung by her office and then came here."

We keep an eye on Tess for another minute or so. Finally, she sees someone emerging from the path to the other parking lot. She bounces up and gives her ensemble a once-over. A jolt goes through my stomach when I see who's joining her.

Barry Preston.

"What the fuck?" I say, "Barry's supposed to hate Tess. What the hell's he doing here?"

Mike shrugs. "Well, she *does* have a habit of sleeping with her bosses."

Before anyone can stop me, I'm out of the car and running toward them. They must be engrossed in their conversation since neither of them notices me until I've joined them. Tess quickly sticks something behind her back. Barry puts his hands in his pockets and smirks at me.

"Mr. Davis," Barry says, "How nice of you to come by."

Tess lowers her voice. "Joe, what are you doing here?"

"Funny, I was going to ask you the same thing," I say.

"We are having a business meeting."

"At ten o'clock on a Saturday night? At Rape/Mugging Central? What's it about? Human resources?"

Tess looks to Barry, her hands still behind her back. Barry shrugs, taking an easy step away.

"Perhaps we can do this another time," he says, walking back to the path between the parking lots.

I move to follow him. "Where are you going? What's going on? Don't ignore me!" But I'm like a dog chasing a car here. I have absolutely no idea what to do if I catch it.

Tess blocks my path and shoves me backward. "Joe! Back off! This isn't any of your business!"

I'm right back in her face, royally pissed. "Since when do you decide what is or isn't my business?"

"When it concerns my boss, it's my business!"

I make another move to get past her—Barry's now disappeared down the path—but Tess blocks me again. We wind up in a struggle that's really a glorified slap-fight. After a few seconds, someone pulls us apart.

"Why don't you guys break it up?" Lars says, "We can call all this hostility to a halt and maybe go get some frosty chocolate milk shakes."

Lars has Tess by the shoulders, leaving himself wide open for an elbow to the sternum. Thankfully, she doesn't seem inclined to throw it. Yet. Mike's got me around the chest, pinning my arms at my side. Tess pulls herself free of Lars's grasp and sticks a finger in my face.

"I don't care what you think, Joe," she says, through gritted teeth, "You stay the hell away from me!" Then her face softens for just a moment, "Just...just stay away." She picks up her purse and stalks after Barry.

"She's up to something," I say, "No fucking idea what, but she's up to something."

Mike slaps a piece of paper against my chest. "Probably has something to do with this. It's what she was hiding behind her back."

"How did you get it?"

"She dropped it when you two were scuffling. I don't think she noticed me pick it up."

I unfold the paper. It's written in shaky, loopy cursive, but it's still readable. A letter from someone regarding the balance in their variable insurance policy, which is much lower than expected. The client notes that they've had similar balance issues with their other accounts. They've tried contacting their financial advisor, but haven't had a lot of luck. They're hoping Insurance Service will be able to provide them with some answers.

And it's signed, "Fran Mahoney."

I step back, practically ready to throw up. "This is the letter Nancy used to open the correspondence case. Tess has it."

"Why?" Mike asks.

I look to the path between the two parking lots. "Maybe I can still ask Barry."

A second later, I'm off at a full run, Mike and Lars trying to keep pace. Mike, however, is a smoker and Lars is lazy, so they fall back quickly. The path snakes an uneven course over various rocks and twigs until coming out at the small gravel lot. There's a couple sitting on a bench at the end of the path. It's dark, but I can see the guy is tall and gray-haired and the woman has long, dark hair. I'm glad Barry and Tess didn't go far. If he won't talk, I'm certainly in the mood to beat some answers out of him. Even if there's a distinct possibility he won't talk and will, in fact, beat the crap out of me.

I haul ass over to the bench, grab the son of a bitch and yank him to his feet. I brandish the letter from Fran Mahoney.

"What the fuck is all this about?" I scream.

And then I realize this isn't Barry.

This is a good-looking guy whose hair now looks more blonde than gray. In fact, he sort of reminds me of William Katt in *The Last American Hero*. Well, a William Katt who may be shitting his pants as we speak. He looks from me to Lars to Mike and before any of us can say a word, he takes off running.

Carol looks up from the bench. She has what can best be described as contained murderous intentions on her face. "So, Joe, when your testicles come down somewhere around Milwaukee, remember that I warned you."

***

I have a game I play with every new girl Mike dates. It's called Find-The-Flaw. See, all of Mike's new girlfriends give a positive first impression because they all more or less fall into the same categories: physically attractive (and I'm not talking pleasant or passable, I'm talking *knockouts*) and very personable. The goal of Find-The-Flaw is to spot the girl's eventual deal-breaking trait in the shortest amount of time possible. So far, the all-time winner is a girl named Jen Spradley. She went from saying her first hello to me to bitching out

212

the waiter without pausing for breath. The all-time loser (if loser's the word I'm looking for) is Carol.

From the first, I found Carol to be personable and attractive. But she was also witty, intelligent, worldly, open-hearted, politically aware and ambitious. By the end of our first meeting, the only flaw I could find in her was a willingness to date Mike. (Then again, she might have been playing her own game of Find-The-Flaw.) It's telling that Carol remains the only one of Mike's exes with whom I've remained friends.

And that's why it's so disappointing that she wants to kill me right now.

I'm careful to keep the breakfast bar, Mike and the cats between Carol and me as she stalks around my place like a caged animal. Of course, push comes to shove, the breakfast bar is the only one I can count on to remain in place. Mike stares at the floor with the same hangdog look he gets when parents, girlfriends or bosses yell at him. Lenny and Squiggy jockey for position at the edge of the hallway, ready to desert me like the treacherous bastards they are. Lars is hiding out in his apartment. Personally, I'm hoping Carol doesn't destroy my belongings. I just got the place in order again.

"I don't believe you assholes," she says, flicking out a hand and nearly knocking over my bowling trophy, "I manage to get another date, hot on the heels of my last debacle, and you screw it up again! What did I ever do to you?" Mike clears his throat but she stops him with a fierce look. "Just don't go there."

"Yes, ma'am."

I clutch the cordless phone, wondering if I'll have to use it as a weapon. "It was a mistake. I'm sorry. I totally forgot you were going to be down by Fletcher Island."

"Do I need to constantly remind you idiots of my schedule?"

Mike ventures a look. "Y'know, it might not be a bad idea. I mean—"

"Shut up before I open that window and throw you out of it."

The cats scurry into the bedroom. Mike eases backward. Yep. Me and the breakfast bar against certain doom. What's worse, I'm not even giving Carol's homicidal rage my undivided attention. I've been trying to get a hold of Tess, who has apparently resumed radio silence.

"If it's any consolation," Mike says, "The guy looked like a real dweeb."

Carol turns slowly toward him. "How is that any consolation?"

"I found it consoling," he says.

"Not that it's any of your business, but he was a nice guy. And a hell of a kisser."

"Better than me?"

"Non-smoker and doesn't use his tongue like an invading force. What do you think?"

I set the phone down on the breakfast bar and, taking my life into my own hands, step between them. "It was an accident," I say, "I'm sorry. It won't happen again."

"It wasn't supposed to happen last time either."

"I know. All I can tell you is I'm sorry."

"No. You can tell me you'll drop this nonsense and go back to writing about *Gilligan's Island* or the time Margie Hanson pantsed you in home room or whatever the hell makes people think you're clever."

Ooo, capping on the column. She *is* pissed. Mike and I stay quiet, letting Carol pace the room and work out her anger. Finally, she settles into the chair at the end of the breakfast bar.

"Please tell me you found out something interesting," she says, "I'd hate to think you messed up my date for nothing."

I toss the letter on the breakfast bar. "I think Barry and Tess are up to something. Fran Mahoney wrote that letter to NewCo Mutual, saying she was concerned about the balances in her accounts. Nancy must have gotten the letter and opened a case. There was no sign of the letter at the office, but I think Tess was trying to show it to Barry tonight."

"What does it prove?" Carol asks.

I sigh. "That two people are dead and I have a letter from an old lady in Duluth. I got nothing."

Mike stretches out on the futon. "I still say Tess is setting you up. That's my theory. And Lars was right. Cherchez La Femme."

I walk over to the futon. "I told you, that whole theory is too elaborate."

Mike shrugs. "I don't know. I once arranged a stalking to get a girl back."

Carol spins toward him. "You stalked a girl?"

"No, no. It was a pretend stalking. You remember Andrea Huffnal? Chick I dated a while back? She dumped me for no good reason, so I hired Lars's friend Chuck to write her some threatening notes, make a few sick phone calls. And who do you think she called to protect her?"

"Oh my God," Carol says, looking ready to throw something at Mike's head, "You terrorized a girl?"

"What terror? It was just Chuck. She was never in danger. Only problem was, once we got back together, she was a little clingy. Wound up having to break things off with her."

Carol shakes her head. "You have any idea how many times I look at you and think about the bullet I dodged?"

"What do you mean?"

I walk back to the breakfast bar. "If you two don't mind, I'm going to get back to something relevant."

Carol sits on the back of the futon, propping her chin on her fist. "You said something about Tom's family cabin? Up on the North Shore? And this Fran Mahoney, she lives in Duluth, right?"

"Yeah."

"So, it looks like you need to go to Duluth. Track down Fran Mahoney. Check out the family cabin."

She's right, of course. It's the only place that might not lead me to a dead end. Frankly, the thought makes me a little nervous. It sounds like the sort of thing real detectives do.

"Okay, sounds like a plan," I say, "Who's coming with me?"

"I'm out," Mike says, holding up his hands, "I don't take road trips to Duluth anymore."

"That's fine. You think I need another six hours of you screaming and crying?"

"That wasn't my fault. Stoner laced that pot with something. I'd swear on a stack of Bibles."

Rather than bicker with Mike, I turn to Carol. "Okay, what about you? You want to come along?"

"I have a day job."

"You're an ad writer. You can take that on the road for a few days, can't you?"

She lets out a breath through her nose. "What about Lars? Can't you bring him?"

"I would, but I'd be lucky if Duluth was still standing by the time we left."

As if on cue, the T-and-A entrepreneur himself charges into my apartment and perches on the arm of my futon.

"Okay, this is how we deal with Old Man Albertson," he says, "I've got a plan for getting him out of that apartment."

"I suppose knocking on his door is out?" I ask.

"I've tried that. He won't answer."

I'm going to regret this, but: "What's your plan?"

Lars draws us into a huddle. "Okay, the only thing that's gotten him out of his apartment, as far as we know, is the note he left for Joe."

"I don't *know* that he left that for me."

"But we're going with that theory. So, we re-enact the break into your apartment."

"Re-enact?"

"The whole thing. Right down to the trashing. Remind him of the circumstances. Get his synapses firing. See if he'll react the same way again."

Bile burns its way up my esophagus. "You want to trash my place again? I just finished cleaning the damn thing up."

"We need to be authentic. This can't be half-assed."

"It's going to be no-assed because I'm not doing it."

Lars waves his hands. "You are standing in the way of this man's life."

"Really? I thought I was standing in the way of some moron trashing my place for no good reason."

"After everything I've done for you—"

"What have you done for me? Other than leave my door open so my apartment could get trashed in the first place? Other than bother me with crackpot schemes and conspiracy theories? Other than put a serious, consistent dent into my booze supply? What have you done for me?"

Lars stiffens, practically clicking his heels together, and offers a slight bow. "I'm sorry you feel that way. Good day, sir."

Summoning what dignity can be stuffed into a frame that goofy, Lars marches out, slamming the door behind him. Mike and Carol look at me, disapproving.

"A little hard on The Beav, weren't you?" Mike says.

"Wait 'til I lose my shit with you two."

Carol puts a hand on her hip, her lecturing pose. "I hope you're more pleasant when we go up to Duluth."

My eyebrows go up. "So you're in?"

"Yes, I'm in. Just try and hold this trip to two days and promise you won't get pissy with me."

"I can promise at least half of those things."

She shakes her head. "Typical guy."

Mike hops up from the futon. "I got to tell you guys: I'm not comfortable with this."

I lean toward him. "Well, maybe you could visit another sick aunt. Take your mind off it."

Carol narrows her eyes and snaps a look at Mike. "Yes, Michael. I've been meaning to ask you about that."

Mike backs away, hands raised. "You know what? We're all friends here. Have a good time in Duluth." Mike swallows some beer, his hand positioned on the bottle so he's giving me the finger.

***

If my car could speak, right now it wouldn't be speaking to me. It's an urban vehicle, accustomed to cruising parkways plotting to throw open a door and take out some bicycle-riding clown holding up traffic. Highways are a brief, necessary evil, designed to quickly cover the distance between the city and the suburbs. They certainly aren't meant to be used for several hour-long trips. My car would sip white wine if it could.

So, it's certainly not pleased to be making its second trip to Northfield in only a few weeks, particularly when the weather is slightly hotter than Hades and there's not a tree in sight. The car expresses itself with an occasional shiver, the kind that makes me listen for Scotty shouting from the engine room. ("She canna take much moore, cap'n. She's about tah blew!") I respond as I always do to car-related crises: I turn up the stereo.

I should be making tracks up north, but Carol needs a day or so to get her affairs in order. So, rather than sit around and do nothing, I decide to talk to Deena Reilly, get her take on Tess and her father. Assuming she even knows.

I try the house first, but no dice. An overly helpful neighbor, a prim woman with the sheen of a porcelain doll, tells me Deena's at the gym. She even gives me directions. Got to love those trusting souls. They keep bounty hunters and serial killers in business. The gym is in a strip mall about ten minutes away, one of those hole-in-the-wall, let-yourself-in-after-hours gyms that are all the rage. (Because, y'know, so many times I'm awake at four a.m. thinking: "You know what I could go for right now? A hard twenty minutes on the exercise bike followed by a good ass-raping in the parking lot.") I wait all of about two minutes before Deena strolls out, towel around her neck, workout bag in hand. She's a pair of legwarmers away from being a retro Jane Fonda. I hustle over before she can reach her car.

"Deena! Good to see you again."

She reacts by snapping into a modified karate stance. I quickly back up. Once Deena recognizes me, she relaxes, but doesn't quite lose the stance.

"Guess it was your turn to ambush me," she says, "Something on your mind?"

"Okay if we talk?"

"I'm not sure I've got—"

"You heard what happened to Nancy, right?"

Deena hangs her head. After a second, she tosses her bag into the car and nods toward another part of the strip mall. "There's a coffee shop over there. I've only got twenty minutes."

"Fine by me."

We spend five of those minutes looking for a table. I would have preferred something indoors, wrapped in a cool cocoon of air-conditioning but everyone in town is thinking the same thing. We wind up at an uneven wrought-iron table next to the sunbaked parking lot. The air is fragrant with exhaust fumes and we get a beautiful view of the speed bump. Deena stirs her dark-roast-two-sugars with a cheap wooden stir stick.

"I suppose you're going to tell me Tess had nothing to do with what happened to Nancy?"

"No, I think she might have."

Deena pauses in her stirring. "Sounds like you and Tess had a falling out."

"More like the end of a truce. But, yeah."

She tries not to look amused. "Well, I can't tell you much about Tess—"

"Is anything going on with her and your father?"

The first reaction is classic shock: mouth open, eyes bugged out, hands on the table, causing it to lurch and nearly spill our drinks. Second reaction quickly follows, as Deena screams (and I mean *screams*) with laughter. I try to ignore the curious looks from the people inside the coffee shop.

"You are fucking kidding me," she says, "Why would my father have anything to do with...that woman?"

I tell her about the meeting on Fletcher Island, leaving out the part about messing up Carol's date. As Deena listens, her face darkens and she slumps back in her chair. I try not to stumble through the finish, but it's not easy since she looks like she's ready to come over the table and strangle me.

"Sorry about all this," I say, "I hate to be the bearer of bad tidings, but—"

"Okay. Fine. Do you think they're—"

"I have no idea. I was hoping you could tell me."

Deena slams her fist on the table, forcing me to steady it. "How fucking dare he? How could he possibly—"

I'm scrambling to defuse this, lest this conversation become more of a sideshow for the patrons. "I don't know that they're doing anything. I just know they met and that seems strange, given everything that's happened. I was hoping you'd know what it was about."

"Sorry. I only have a clue when people bother to fucking tell me something."

Well, great. I've already created one hell of a scene for the next Preston family dinner. "If it's not, um, y'know, a—"

"Sex thing?"

"Or a romantic thing. Romance could be involved. But probably sex. But if it's not either of those, is there any reason your father would want to talk to Tess? Something at the office he might be concerned about?"

"You mean, other than the two murders?"

Y'know, when she says it like that, it *does* sound pretty stupid. "Yeah, I guess something like that."

Deena dismisses it with a small shake of her head. "My father doesn't talk with me about his business. And I'm not all that interested anyway. Tom tried talking to me about the office, but he eventually gave up. You know what I mean?"

Absolutely. I can practically hear the humming in my head now. I glance at my watch. My twenty minutes is running low. "Did Tom ever mention the name Fran Mahoney?"

"No. Who's she?"

"Nobody. Just a business thing. What about Wayne Donovan? He's a financial advisor. You know anything about him?"

"No. Never met him. Never heard of him." Deena slides out from the table. "That's all I've got time for. I have to pick up the kids."

We start toward our cars. Deena stops and looks at me. "Do you really think my father is up to something?"

"I don't know. But something's going on. Tom and Nancy weren't killed for no reason."

Deena shakes her head, sadly. "Good luck. If you're going up against my father, you're going to need it."

I watch her walk away. She didn't have to remind me about Barry, but the chill rolls up my spine nonetheless. Now I know why Han Solo never wanted to know the odds.

CHAPTER TWENTY

Going on a road trip with your friends is like an experiment in opposites that a professor of mine once conducted. One day in class, he gave us a fact and asked us to remember it until tomorrow. The success rate among the class was about fifty-fifty. Then he gave us another fact and asked us to forget it by tomorrow. Of course, nearly everybody in the class remembered it. Humans are nothing if not contradictory.

A road trip with friends is similar. We can spend every waking hour hanging around our friends as long as we have the option of leaving or throwing them out at some point. When that option is removed during a road trip, we become aware of their stifling, constant proximity. And all those little proclivities we ignore in everyday life come crashing in like a radioactive boulder. We want to maintain friendly relations with this person, but there's no way out of this claustrophobic trap we're in. If the trip goes on too long, we risk a complete meltdown and a situation in which the guys in the movie Alive came out with friendlier relationships.

I glance over the rest of the column by using the wireless internet connection on my phone. Normally, I love reading my stuff in print, but this occasion is taking the edge off. Carol doesn't appear to be any more excited than I am. I'm at her place, watching her pack. She's not exactly setting a land-speed record filling the suitcase she's got open on the bed. I'm left with an inordinate amount of time to study the various paintings of various female nudes in various states of recline.

"You ever notice you have a lot of pictures of naked women around here?" I ask.

Carol casually tosses a folded pair of jeans in her suitcase. "Nothing wrong with it. The female body is beautiful."

"What about the male body?"

"Oh please, it's disgusting. It's all hair and crevices and protuberances. Ick."

"And yet you say this as a heterosexual female."

"It's just an aesthetic thing. A guy's body serves a purpose. It's like a garage door opener. Perfectly functional but you don't take pictures of it and say, 'Wow. What a beautiful garage door opener!'"

"Garage door opener? That's the metaphor you're going with?"

"I stand by it."

Carol keeps packing while I try to ignore the paintings. This trip already has an uncomfortable level of intimacy to it. I don't need to be oddly aroused before it even begins. Carol half-heartedly rummages through her bureau drawers.

"Really, how long do you think we'll be up there?" she asks.

"Probably just overnight. I want to check out Fran Mahoney, maybe talk to the advisor then check out the cabin."

"Do we have a hotel reservation?"

"Yeah, I found a place up the hill, over by the Miller Hill Mall."

Carol pauses in folding a sweater. "Do we have one room or two?"

"Um, well, the blog doesn't pay me a lot for travel expenses—"

"At least tell me there'll be two beds."

"Yes. I've got you covered there."

She tosses the sweater into the suitcase. "This better just be overnight. Or you're going to be sleeping in the car."

"Understood."

Fortunately, my cell phone interrupts this nice little moment. It's Mike. I step into the main room to grab it.

"Are you on the road yet?" he asks.

"Not just yet. If you remember, Carol packs like she's taking the Queen Mary from Liverpool."

There's a chuckle at the other end, but Mike's voice quickly grows serious. "Listen, I got a problem with Jeannette."

"Hang on a second." I step out into the hallway, getting as big a buffer zone as possible between Carol and this conversation. "Okay, what's the deal? She still jealous of Carol?"

"No. She isn't jealous of Carol. She wants to *be* Carol."

Okay. As if my life wasn't already deep in the Bizarro World. "She wants to *be* Carol? What gives you that idea?"

"I was over at Jeannette's place last night. She's got a shrine built to Carol in her bedroom closet. Said she'd been waiting to show it to me. There's a collage of about a hundred pictures of Carol in the back of her walk-in. It was the creepiest—and most strangely arousing—thing I'd ever seen."

"Holy shit."

"She said she liked me more than any of Carol's other boyfriends and that Carol never should have broken up with me. She wants to make up for all of that."

"Oh, geez."

"I know. And on top of that, she wants to get her hair dyed and cut the same way as Carol's. Wants me to steal some of Carol's clothes."

"You've done that before."

"Yeah, but that was just underwear. This is really sick!"

I pace the floor, hoping Carol's not eavesdropping. "Okay. You got to break up with Jeannette. That's a no-brainer."

"I know. But how? The woman's crazy. I try to break it off now and she might cut off my wang while I'm sleeping."

"If you break it off, how does she get access to your wang?"

"She's nuts and my building security is a bunch of morons. Do the math."

I don't have nearly the time or energy to deal with this now. I search for a way to comfort Mike and get myself, however temporarily, out of this conversation. "Look, when do you see her again?"

"Not for a few days. I'm pretending I'm busy at work."

"Much like when you're actually at work."

"Joe!"

"Okay, calm down. You got a couple of days? Cool. I'll be back from Duluth by then and we'll figure something out."

"I'm scared, man. I'm really scared."

"Well, it's not the worst thing that could happen to you."

"What could be worse?"

"Carol could still find out."

Mike lets out something between a gasp and a sob and I hang up on him. Carol and her suitcase meet me in the main room when I return.

"What was that?" Carol asks.

"Mike, just…Mike."

And for one of the few times in my life, I'm glad I have a friend so f'ed up that that simple explanation is enough.

***

Duluth is a port city, nestled between a collection of bluffs and Lake Superior. It's part of the Twin Ports, along with Superior, Wisconsin, a dumpy little nothing of a town on the other side of the bay. Really, they're twins in name only. It's as if one twin got all the good looks, charm and brains and the other got all the strip clubs.

The drive up salves my concern about a road trip with Carol. We chat the entire way, easily flipping from one subject to the next. Not an awkward moment to be had. I forget that Carol can be one of the less self-involved conversationalists I know. And by *one of*, I mean pretty much the only one. Our hotel isn't much above the level of a Motel 6. It's up the hill from the main part of the city, on a stretch called the Miller Trunk, near the Miller Hill Mall. (I have no idea who the hell Miller was and no desire to find out. I have enough on my plate at the moment.) We're at the hotel only long enough to dump our stuff in the cramped and barely-cleaned room before setting out in search of Fran Mahoney.

I only have an address to go on, but in a world of Google Maps and Android Phones, that doesn't present much of a problem. Fran Mahoney's place is in a neighborhood called Pine Hill. The neighborhood is a mix of elderly lifers and rental units. My guess is that the rental units will eventually take over. Fran Mahoney's home is an older, two-level house—probably built in the twenties—with a cute little front porch. It's seen better days, though. The white paint and the black trim are peeling. The lawn has grown shaggy. A pair of torn curtains cover the picture window at the front. I park across the steep street (like practically everything else in Duluth, the house is on a hill) and crank the emergency brake.

"Think we should have called first?" Carol asks.

"I've tried calling. Now we take the direct approach."

We amble across the street, trying to look inconspicuous. I get the feeling the elderly set still pays attention to who comes and goes. We pass the front gate—part of the chain-link fence surrounding the yard—and up to the porch. I give the oak door a quick rap. Nothing.

"Doesn't feel like anybody's home, does it?" I ask.

Carol shakes her head. "Doesn't feel like anybody's been home for a while."

This restless feeling buzzes through me, like bumblebees under my skin. Maybe it's what a couple hours in the car will get you. Maybe it's what happens when you've been stonewalled at pretty much every turn. But I want some answers about Fran Mahoney and I want them now. I step off the porch and give a look around the neighborhood.

"Think anybody's watching?" I say.

"Doesn't look like it. Why?"

"Follow me around back."

I've got an advantage here. I'm the sort of clean-cut, fastidious young man who, from a distance at least, can be confused for a cop or a bill collector. Or on occasion, a Jehovah's Witness, but I don't like to talk about those occasions. Carol follows me to the backyard, which is screened off by a wooden privacy fence. The backdoor is thin and slightly dilapidated. Flimsy enough for my purposes. Carol grabs my arm.

"You're thinking about breaking in?" she says.

"Absolutely."

"This is ridiculous. She could be out at the grocery store."

"Bullshit. Look at this place. The yard's a wreck. The outside hasn't been tended to in God knows how long. This neighborhood is all old people. They still take pride in their houses. If they can't keep up their yards, they get someone to do it for them. Believe me, if the place looks like this, Fran Mahoney hasn't been here in a while. I want to know why."

"And how are you going to get in?"

"Going to use a little brute force."

I square myself, hoist my right leg and thrust all said brute force right at the door. I hit it perfectly. Right above the doorknob, right where the door is most vulnerable. So, it comes as a bit of a shock when the door doesn't move, and my leg suddenly hurts like hell. I collapse to the ground, holding my knee and swearing.

Carol kneels next to me. "Brute force is a bitch."

"Specially the way I use it."

"Yeah. Meantime, you don't suppose that basement window over there would do the trick, do you?"

She points to a small window a few feet from the backdoor. It opens out and is held shut by a single teeny nail.

"Well, if you want to take shortcuts, sure," I say, painfully getting to my feet.

Carol helps me over to the window. The nail comes out easily and the window swings open. The room below may have once been a bedroom, but has since been converted to a storage room for piles of neatly-split logs, either for a fireplace or a wood-burning stove. It's about a six foot drop to the tile floor. I go first, feeling a few electric shocks of pain rolling up my now-bad leg. I try to help Carol down, but we wind up tumbling into the wood pile.

"Well, this is lovely," she says, feeling around for splinters.

"Sorry. Guess I'm not as strong as I look."

"Actually, you're *exactly* as strong as you look."

The basement is undistinguished, unkempt and older than the hills it's built on. The rest of the house is more of the same. A layer of dust covers everything. The doors are either stuck or creaky. Nothing looks as if it's been moved in a good long while. We make our way to the center of the large living room. I look around, trying to figure out why my Spidey Sense is tingling.

"What do we do now?" Carol asks.

I'm quiet for a second then the something hits me. "The cable box is on."

"What do you mean?"

I point to the little rectangular box, resting just above the finest twenty-seven-inch TV 1985 could produce. "The box is on."

"So?"

"So, it's August. If the cable box is on, the electricity works. Do me a favor: go in the kitchen and see if the water's running."

Carol does so and calls out an affirmative. "So, what does all this mean?"

"The only time the electric company won't allow the power to be turned off is during the winter. Same for the water. And did you notice there's no mail piled up in the front? But you look around and the inside of this place is as ragged as the outside. I stand by what I said: no one's lived here for, well, months at least."

It's dawning on Carol, but she throws me the mental alley-oop anyway. "Then what's the deal?"

"The deal is, someone's still paying the bills and collecting the mail. But nobody lives here."

Carol joins me in the living room. "Maybe she's out of town. Has a place in Arizona. Something like that."

"It's August. What the hell kind of snowbird goes to Arizona in August? And wouldn't there be something about an alternate address in NewCo Mutual's computers?"

"Maybe the advisor has it."

We're quiet for a second, awash in the same creepy feeling. Carol looks around; at the dust covering the knick-knacks and family pictures, swirling on the hardwood floors, settling into the crevices of the ancient furniture.

"Okay, let's say what we're both thinking," she says, "Fran Mahoney is dead."

I take in a breath through my nose, amazed it doesn't bring on a sneezing fit. "Then why keep the power on? And the cable? If she's got life insurance, why didn't somebody call in a claim?"

"Maybe the advisor knows."

Clearly, Carol's anxious to get out of here. I don't blame her. The place is feeling more and more like a haunted house. This time, we leave via the backdoor, seeing no point in another struggle with the basement window. We're nearly out the front gate when an older man, anywhere between seventy and three-hundred-and-fifty, materializes on the other side. His mouth holds a wad of chewing tobacco the size of a bocce ball and his beady green eyes stare out from below gray eyebrows that haven't been trimmed since Jack Benny was all the rage.

"I help you?" he says, in a voice like ground glass.

Time to channel my inner Mike. "Hi, I'm Warren Webber, with Pfister Developments. This is my partner, Jennifer Piccolo. We were hoping to talk with Ms. Mahoney. Do you know her?"

He doesn't look convinced. "Know *of* her."

"Well, we wanted to talk to her about a development opportunity we're putting together in the neighborhood. Do you know if she's going to be home any time soon?"

"Don't know. She ain't been around for a while."

"Oh. Don't suppose you have any idea where we can reach her?"

"No." He turns to walk away, but hesitates. "Someone said she's in Phoenix. Staying with relatives."

I try to keep it casual. "I see, I see. Who was the someone who told you that?"

"I don't know. Tall, skinny kid. Probably just out of college. Business suit. Had a scar on his jaw. Real nasty. Couple inches long and had them—what do you call 'em—suture marks. That's all I remember."

I give him an appreciative wave. "Thanks for the help."

"Don't fuck up the house. Some of us gotta live around here."

He gives us the stink eye as he walks away. I'm wondering if our grizzled friend might call the police anyway. Not willing to give him the chance, Carol and I hustle back to the car, off to a meeting with the I'm-guessing-late-Ms. Mahoney's financial advisor, Wayne Donovan.

***

Wayne Donovan's office is in a high rise downtown. (High rise by Duluth standards being about twelve floors.) I ditch my long-suffering Saturn on the street and lead the way into the refurbished marble and glass lobby. Carol drags her feet a little.

"What's up?" I ask, glancing over my shoulder.

"We're in really deep here. I mean, we're not cops. How are we going to get this guy to talk to us?"

"I'm going to run a massive bluff. Just follow my lead."

"Mike says you're lousy at bluffing."

"Compared to Mike, Ted Bundy was lousy at bluffing."

The NewCo Mutual Financial Advisors' office, Duluth branch, occupies a corner of the tenth floor. It's got the same tan-and-beige color scheme that dominates the home office. A pleasant-looking blonde receptionist greets us as we walk in.

"Good morning. How may I help you?" And she really seems to mean it.

I shrug off the nerves and lean on the counter, looking put out. "Is Wayne Donovan in?"

"Do you have an appointment?"

"I do not. But I need to speak to him about one of his clients. Fran Mahoney."

"Are you a relative?"

"Yes. Indeed. My name is Warren. I'm Fran's nephew. Grand-nephew. In-Law. And if you don't mind, ma'am, I'm hopping mad and I want to talk to Mr. Donovan."

236

The receptionist rises, uncertainly. Probably hasn't been at this job all that long, probably hasn't had anything difficult come her way. And here I am, blowing that right to hell.

"I'll be back in just a moment," she says, scurrying off.

Carol and I drop into plush green seats in the waiting area. She looks at me. "You really think he'll buy you as a relative?"

"I'm the black sheep of the family. They don't talk about me much."

A few minutes later, Miss Perky returns and asks us to follow her to Mr. Donovan's office. We head down a long hallway to a manly-man sort of lair decorated with hunting trophies and pictures of Wayne Donovan in his younger, more athletic days. Through the picture window, there's a beautiful view of the harbor and the Blatnik Bridge; an imposing suspension bridge that's Duluth's version of a High Bridge. Donovan himself is a barrel-chested, barrel-stomached guy who clearly has some football in his history. When we walk in, he's straightening his mop of graying dark hair. He gets up from the desk and greets us with a smile full of white teeth.

"Carrie said you're a nephew—of sorts—of Fran's," he says, tilting his head back slightly, looking down his nose at me, "What can I do for you?"

"Wondering where Fran is these days," I say, "She's kind of the last family I got. Came up here and didn't find her."

Donovan sits on a corner of the desk, folds his arms and looks at me with a curiosity that borders on suspicion. "So, why come to me? Why not a neighbor or something?"

"We talked to the neighbors, but they don't seem to know anything. One of them *did* know she had a financial advisor and mentioned you by name. So, we thought we'd check here. You're kind of our last resort."

"I see. Well, I'm sorry, Warren, but I'm not sure I can tell you anything about your aunt. I haven't talked to Fran in quite a while."

"When was the last time?"

He looks toward the window. "Y'know, I'm really not certain. It's been that long."

"Is there another address for her? Something out of town?"

"I'd have to research that. It would be in our computers if there was."

I lean on the desk. "Here's what I don't get. Fran has no other family or friends. There's no sign someone's lived in her house in a couple of months. But somebody's making withdrawals from her accounts. Who could that be?"

Donovan fumbles with his tie. "Well, that's, that's an excellent question. And I've got to tell you, I'm just as confused as you are."

"I'm sure."

"Here's, here's the deal. I'll talk to my advisor's assistants. Get some research done on this and find out what's going on. We'll, we'll get to the bottom of it."

"So, if I'm hearing you correctly, you, a financial advisor, have no idea what's going on with your client's accounts and need to have some assistants research it?"

He tries to laugh. Fails. "Sounds pretty bad, doesn't it?"

"It does."

"But I can assure you, we're, we're going to get—"

"To the bottom of this. Good. I mean, I don't want to name drop, but I've got connections at this company. I'm personal friends with Barry Preston's daughter, Deena."

"Deena. Yes. Tell her I said hi. Been a couple years since I've seen her."

In my short experience trying to get answers out of people, I've discovered you reach a brick wall where you're not getting further information without the use of thumbscrews. And the longer I stay here and the harder I push this, the more likely it is my bluff will get called. I scribble down my phone number and let Donovan usher us out of his office.

"We will get to the bottom of this," he says, waving the paper with my number, "Kevin! Kevin, I think we have something for you."

At this point, a tall, pale kid with red hair and freckles, sort of like Danny Bonaduce if he hadn't grown up twisted, crosses our path. Donovan clamps a beefy mitt on the kid's shoulder.

"Kevin will be able to help us out," Donovan says, "Great with the research, he is."

Kevin looks up from the file folder he's carrying and stares stupidly at Donovan. Then I notice the scar on his jaw. A big, angry thing with suture marks across it. Before either Kevin or I can say anything, Donovan shoves the kid toward his office and hands us over to Miss Perky. Donovan wishes us a good day and issues his eightieth vow in the last three minutes to get to the bottom of this Fran Mahoney thing. Somehow, I'm not holding my breath. More annoying, there's this strange buzzing in the back of my head. I used to get this when I was studying in college and felt like I was overlooking a major piece of information. Carol and I stay quiet until we're on the elevator.

"Whatever's going on with Fran Mahoney," Carol says, "That guy is definitely in on it. What do we do next?"

"Grab some dinner. Maybe head back to the hotel. It's going to be dark soon. I don't want to deal with the cabin until tomorrow."

We track down my car and make plans to find a restaurant. I negotiate my way toward Superior Street and naturally make a wrong turn. I wind up going around the block a few times until I get myself situated. It's on the second trip around that I realize something's wrong.

"There's a tan Buick behind us," I say, staring into the rearview mirror.

"So?"

"It's been following me for two blocks."

Carol looks back. "You don't know it's following you, do you? I mean, it's only been two blocks."

"Yeah, but they've been the same two blocks."

"So we're being followed?"

My hands have gone a little clammy on the wheel. "We're being followed."

CHAPTER TWENTY-ONE

The only car chase I've had to date took place both in high school and in my mind. I had just left the latest James Bond flick and was driving my crappy Dodge Omni home over twisting rain-slicked roads. I was deep into the Bond fantasy, driving away from armed henchmen while my best friend Andy screamed his head off. Personally, I thought Andy was being a baby. Yes, I did overcook one turn and briefly went off the road and destroyed Mrs. Dondelinger's chicken coop. But I got away with it and kept the world safe for democracy. Nothing to it.

Of course, back then I was seventeen and was going to live forever. Right now, I'm thirty-three and might not survive the next ten minutes.

"What are we going to do?" Carol asks, throwing her head back and forth, keeping the Buick in her sights.

"Run."

"Well, duh. *Where* are we going to run?"

I don't have an answer for that. The Saturn's fighting its way up a hill, heading for the bluffs over Duluth. Where the hell is Steve McQueen and that '68 Mustang when you need them? Okay, what are the options? Hop on to Highway 53 and head for the Iron Range. Double back and head for Highway 35 and the Cities. Go north and head for the Canadian border. Of course, I've got a quarter tank of gas and pit stops aren't allowed in car chases.

"Maybe I can lose them," I say.

"How?"

"I'll think up an idea."

"Stop!"

Carol screams this because the traffic up ahead has come to a standstill, likely due to a stoplight. I throw the car left, cut across the other lane and wind up in the parking lot of a mall. Probably left a collection of middle fingers back there. There's a road circumnavigating the mall. Not a lot of traffic at mid-day.

"They coming after us?" I ask, afraid to look back.

"Just made the turn. You got about twenty feet."

I slam on the gas, hoping like hell no one pulls out without looking. I need to lose these guys. The parking lot has only so many options. Beyond pulling into the actually mall and trying to recreate *The Blues Brothers*, I'm not sure what I can do.

"Who are these guys?" Carol asks, still looking back.

Good question. This had to come out of the little interview we just had with Donovan. If someone had been watching us, they never would have let us walk into that office. And this is a fairly clumsy pursuit (befitting its fairly clumsy get-away attempt). It *had* to be thrown together after our visit.

Circling around the mall, I spot a frontage road preciously close, separated from the mall road by only a small patch of grass. Beyond the frontage road are the four lanes of Highway 53.

"Hold on," I say.

"Like I'm not already."

I jerk the wheel to the right. The Saturn slides across the patch of grass. We find ourselves on the frontage road. Again, I mash the gas pedal down.

"They following?" I say.

"Yep. Just cleared the grass."

Dammit. That was about the trickiest move I've got. I need to get to Highway 53 and head north. Up ahead, there's a bend in the frontage road. No way to see if there's an intersection for Highway 53 or if the frontage road even stays parallel with the highway. Just have to keep running.

Carol grips the dash, despite having her seatbelt fastened. "Joe? All the signs are turned around backwards."

"So?"

"So, wouldn't that mean this road is—"

Before she can say anything else, a big-ass white truck comes around the bend, heading straight at us. The road isn't wide enough to accommodate us both.

Carol and I scream. I yank the wheel a bit to the left, hoping the truck will do the opposite. It does, climbing the embankment slightly. We shoot past.

"You were about to say: one way?" I say.

Carol just grips the dash and winces, preparing for death to come at any moment. Behind me, there's a horn honk and probably more obscene gestures. A glance in the rearview mirror tells me the Buick has made it past the truck.

"We're going to jail," Carol says, "Someone's going to call the cops."

Duh. "Shit! Why don't *we* call the cops? You got your cell phone?"

"Left it back at the hotel."

Before I get too pissed, I realize that's where I've left mine. Just what I need: technology proving what a complete moron I am.

The frontage road winds down slightly. There's no entrance to the highway in sight. There are a few streets leading away, but for all I know, they're cul-de-sacs. Best to take my chances on Le Road of Death.

I skirt a few cars backing out of driveways. But the Buick does as well. We follow the roll of the road, dropping down and shooting up again. The Buick puts on a burst of speed, nearly reaching my back bumper. When we come up over the top of the small rise, a Mini Cooper has materialized in front of us.

"Fuck!" Carol screams, closing her eyes.

No time to think. All I can do is react, pulling the wheel to the left. Fortunately, the Mini Cooper makes no movement. There's just enough room for me to pass, unmolested. The same can't be said for the Buick.

It goes right, launching itself up the embankment. It gets by the Mini Cooper and tries to get back to the road, but the rear quarter panel clips the pole of a highway light. The rear of the car is thrown back toward the frontage road. As soon as it hits the pavement, the Buick goes into a roll. It flips three times before finishing right side up, hanging on the embankment. I slam on my brakes.

Carol looks back. "Do you think they're all right?"

"One way to find out."

I swing the car around and race past the Buick and the Mini Cooper. A soccer mom-type stands, goggle-eyed, next to the Cooper. I'm hoping she's too rattled to remember a hell of a lot about my car or bother to get my license plate number. I give the Buick a look-see as we pass. Wayne Donovan has managed to open the passenger door and stumble out. If I'm not mistaken, the driver is Kevin-With-The-Scar. That answers that. I cruise along the frontage road. Carol sweeps back her hair with one hand, shaking her head as she stares out the front window.

"You think the cops will come after us?" she asks.

"We'll find out soon enough, I guess."

"What do we do now?"

I glance at her, trying to summon up my best James Bond. "I believe we have a dinner date."

***

No longer feeling safe in Duluth, we set a land speed record getting back to the hotel and checking out (Too bad. I was really looking forward to the dried-up roll and pulpy orange juice that probably makes up the continental breakfast.) Minutes later, we're on Highway 61 and heading up the North Shore for Denton. We're at least twenty minutes out of Duluth before either of us feels like speaking.

"On the bright side," Carol says, "This wasn't a wasted trip."

"Just hope we don't get wasted *on* the trip."

"You're saying 'wasted' in the death sense, right?"

"Right."

245

"Good. Because there's that other wasted that means having a cocktail or seven. That's pretty much my evening plan."

That's enough to break the ice. During the hour-long drive, we slowly come down from the adrenaline rush. The scenery is spectacular; the road winding past the endless expanse of the lake, delivering up seascape after seascape, interrupted only by the occasional charming Podunk town. Denton is one such town, a typical North Shore tourist trap: gas station, hotel, restaurant, twenty-seven antique stores. The locals work overtime keeping the place at the most inviting variety of rustic. Once we hit town, our first option for dinner is a place called Sven's Café.

I ditch the Saturn next to the Viking ship-style sign that's probably adorned the place for several decades. Sven's itself has just enough decoration to rise above the level of a dive. Yes, the carpeting's a bit threadbare, the paneled walls have seen better days and the warped-to-not-warped-tables ratio could be a bit more even. But there are Monet prints on the wall and knick-knacks on the shelves and I'm guessing the burgers are pretty damned good. The hostess sets up with a booth and a couple waters.

Carol waits for the hostess to walk off and lowers her voice. "Okay, clear enough: this Wayne Donovan guy was stealing money from Fran Mahoney's accounts. Right?"

"Looks like it. And since Fran couldn't get a satisfactory answer out of Mr. Donovan, she wrote to the home office and asked someone to look into it. Nancy grabbed the letter and opened the case."

"And that's as much as we know for sure. I mean, Nancy was killed and Fran Mahoney's disappeared. Obvious thing is that Donovan must be behind it."

I drum my fingers on the table. "Yeah. Problem is, how does Tom's murder figure in?"

Carol taps a straw on her hand. "Maybe we'll find out at this cabin. Do we know where it is?"

"Just outside out of Denton. That's all I got so far."

"That's not a hell of a lot to go on."

"And that's what brings us here."

Carol gives me a quizzical glance, but fate does my dirty work and brings our waitress over to the table.

"Welcome to Sven's. My name's Ella. The special today is the meatloaf with mashed potatoes and mushroom gravy. Can I get you anything to start with?"

Ella's slim, small and wrinkled. Her graying hair is done up in a bun and there's a bit of smoker's gravel to her voice. Still, she's got kind eyes and a welcoming smile. She's probably delivered the spiel on the daily special about a hundred-and-six-thousand times over the years but doesn't seem bored by it. We order burgers, fries and sodas and I strike my most charming pose.

"Ella, huh?" I say, "I think you know a friend of ours."

She props an elbow against the back of the booth. "Really? Who would that be?"

"Tom Reilly."

Ella barks out a laugh. "Tom, yes. He comes through all the time. Haven't seen him lately. How's he doing?"

Apparently, word of Tom's demise hasn't gotten around Denton. "He's hanging in there. Just been busy, I guess."

"Yeah, he's usually up here every weekend in the summer. Stays at his father-in-law's cabin. Never see the father-in-law, though. Typical rich guy. Builds that big old damn cabin and never uses the thing."

"Yeah." I slide the salt shaker around the table, trying to look casual. "Cabin must be close by?"

"Oh yeah. Just up the road. You know the Lakeview Motel, the place on the right just as you're leaving town?" Well, now that she's given me the location, I do. "It's right past there. Driveway's just past the Lakeview's parking lot."

"Wow. That is close."

Carol glances toward the exit. We'd both like to bolt out of here, but we play it cool. Ella glances back at the rest of her section.

"Got to run," she says, "If you see Tom, tell him not to be a stranger, okay?"

That gives me a little shiver, but I nod and smile. "I definitely will. Might not see him for a while, though."

When the food arrives, we try not to rush through the meal. The day's been aggravating enough without adding heartburn to the mix. We finish as fast as proper digestion will allow and haul ass to the car.

"There's still enough daylight for a quick look around the cabin," I say.

A smile plays on Carol's face. "You knew Ella would give you the info, didn't you?"

"Absolutely. I grew up around here. Every one of these towns has a Sven's Café and every Sven's Café has an Ella. She could tell you the family histories, shoe sizes and sexual hang ups of every person that walks in there more than twice. And she never keeps that stuff to herself."

Carol gives me a golf clap. "Well done."

"Let's hope I live to gloat."

As expected, Ella's directions are flawless. The Lakeview Motel is, in fact, on the right just as you're leaving town. Just past the motel parking lot, a tiny driveway, nearly concealed by brush, winds away from the road. I pass it and park behind a gas station kitty corner from the motel.

"What are we doing?" Carol asks.

"I want to keep the car out of sight. We'll walk up to the cabin. If somebody's there, I don't want them spotting the car."

"Who would be there?"

"I don't know. One thing I've learned so far: if you're not expecting something, expect something."

We hike across the road and start up the driveway. It's clear after not too many feet that the cabin is *way* back from the road. The driveway winds and rolls through the jack pines. I keep an eye out for the cabin while Carol looks for any sign of cars, people or furry woodland creatures. After ten minutes and a lot of huffing and puffing, the cabin looms into view. I use the term *cabin* in its loosest possible sense because this thing is a freakin' mansion. Two-plus stories, with a wing extending away from the main house and a wrap-around porch providing a view of the lake. We stop cold.

"Clearly, we went into the wrong line of work," Carol says.

The driveway still does the dippy-windy thing for a little way. We take the more direct route, climbing over a small, brush-strewn hill that leads to a manicured lawn in front of the cabin. I look down as we dart around the lawn furniture, heading for the side of the place.

"This lawn is like a golf course," I say, "And not a crappy public course, I mean a country club."

"You've been in a lot of country clubs?"

"Been thrown out of a few."

My number one concern, developed only as I was coming up the driveway, is that the place might have an alarm system. I'm betting against it, given that no one could case this joint without one of the townies spotting them. And even if the system was tripped, the only semi-competent police force in the area is about an hour south. Still, it's a concern. As we circle the place, I peek in the window, trying to see a motion detector or anything that would trip us up. There's nothing in sight, but that doesn't mean it isn't there. Just have to hope for the best. We stop at a side door just off the kitchen. It's screened both from the driveway and the lake. Perfect spot to break in. Just one problem…

"Don't take this wrong way," I say, staring at the doorknob, "But I wish Mike was here."

"To help you break in?"

"Yeah."

Back in college, Mike had a sideline business as a cat burglar. He generally did it only when he was short on cash and usually only for food or small ticket items he could pawn. He claims he hasn't done it since then, but I'm sure he hasn't lost the touch.

Carol folds her arms and rubs her chin as she stares at the doorknob. "Do you know anything about breaking into a house?"

I slip my hand inside in my coat sleeve and punch out one of the small windows in the door. "Absolutely nothing."

Carol rolls her eyes as I reach through the broken window and unlock the door. It opens on to a thin kitchen containing the requisite adorable breakfast nook.

"They're going to find out someone broke in," Carol says, "Then they're going to dust for fingerprints and we're going to be screwed."

"Okay, number one, there's no alarm and nobody comes up here all that often, so it's going to be a crap-long time before anyone finds out we broke in. Number two, you really think the local Gomer-and-Barney-Fife show is going to have fingerprinting equipment? They'll just ask around, see if somebody saw something."

"And if someone did?"

"Yeah, an average-looking man and an average-looking woman were seen strolling around. I'm sure they'll be at our front door in minutes."

We move from the kitchen to the living room; a huge room with wood-beamed ceilings and a picture window looking out over Lake Superior. Everything is plush and faux-rustic; the sort of place where rich people wear flannel shirts and sip Perrier. There's a television and game room off the living room. A wide staircase leads upstairs. I'm guessing the bedrooms are up there.

Carol shakes her head. "This is a cabin? No, a cabin is a rustic little place in the woods. I would have killed to grow up in a *house* this nice."

"Easy. Your class envy is showing. Leave that unchecked and they'll call you a socialist."

"Yeah, when *they* don't even know what socialism is. Okay, shake it off." She closes her eyes and shakes her hands. "Fine. What are we looking for?"

"Good question. Nancy said there's something up here. If Tom was hiding anything, this is where it would be."

"Great. Nothing like breaking-and-entering for the vaguest of reasons."

"Let's look around. You take the downstairs, I'll take the upstairs. And try not to watch TV or play with the pool table."

"I'll at least stay away from the pool table."

The carpeted stairs lead to a corridor with about six doors. I discover three largely-empty guest rooms and two bathrooms. The last room in the corridor has been converted to a study. Guessing it's either Barry's or Tom's. I'm wagering there's something interesting to find in there.

The study is barren of decoration, leading me to think its Tom's. No way Barry misses an opportunity to wave his metaphorical dick. There's a simple desk next to the window and a couple filing cabinets along one wall. The filing cabinets are unlocked, but only contain bills and personal papers. I pull the drawers out of the desk and meticulously empty them on the floor, going through the contents as thoroughly as possible. I'm about to put one of the drawers back in the desk when something catches my eye. A flat, black rectangular box, barely bigger than my middle finger, taped to the back of the drawer. I pull it free and heft it in my hand. It's a USB drive and I'm guessing a valuable one since they're not usually taped to the back of a drawer. I stuff it in my pocket and finish looking through the desk. But it renders nothing else of interest. I'm halfway down the corridor when Carol's voice comes from the bottom of the stairs.

"Joe! Someone's coming up the driveway."

CHAPTER TWENTY-TWO

We like to think we're inherently good. Until we get caught doing something we shouldn't. Then we realize there's no such thing as inherent good, just the fear of being busted. All those parents, teachers, bosses, cops and Gods we've run across are the only things keeping us from turning into baboons. Then again, that's how the Nazis think, so maybe I should reconsider that whole viewpoint.

At the moment, all I know is that I'm about to be busted. Big time.

I make a headlong dash down the stairs, somehow managing not to go ass-over-teakettle. I slip along the wall, avoiding the picture windows. Carol is already hiding in the kitchen. A blue Toyota winds its way up driveway and is nearly at the house.

Carol drops into an impression of me. "Number whatever, nobody's coming up here for a crap-long time." It's actually not an impression of me. It's one of those all-purpose-guy-voices that sounds like a Cro-Magnon crossed with the Frankenstein Monster. It actually sounds more like Mike.

"I didn't think Barry or Deena would come up here in the middle of the week," I say.

"You think Donovan might have tipped Barry off?"

I shake my head. "It's been two hours since we left Duluth. No way Barry could get up here that quickly from the Cities."

"So who is it?"

A second later, through the tunnel of the house and the picture window beyond, we see Wayne Donovan and Kevin-With-The-Scar getting out of the Toyota.

"They recover quick," I say.

Carol smacks me on the back of my arm. "You didn't think they'd follow us up here?"

"Right into Barry's backyard? No, I didn't think they'd do that."

"Bad time for a grave tactical error."

"And an even worse time to bicker. Now, get moving."

We slip out the kitchen door, carefully closing it behind us. Immediately, a problem presents itself. There's no way we can get around the house without Donovan or Kevin-With-The-Scar spotting us. We could duck back into the woods, but it's not much of an escape route. We're just as likely to get lost as anything.

"What do we do?" Carol asks.

There's a woodshed just beyond the kitchen door. I nod toward it. "We hide behind that. When they go in the house, we make a break for it."

"A break for it? Have you been watching *Magnum P.I.* repeats again?"

"Would you shut up and move!"

We rush around the side of the shed and find a hiding space below a small window. I wait to hear the sound of a door. The air is still enough to hear any kind of moderate noise and I'm wondering if Donovan and the kid heard us talking. But the sound of the door doesn't come. Did I miss it? Or did they hear us and are sneaking up right now? Would I even be able to hear them? Do we stay here and take our chances or do we make a break for it?

Turns out not to be an issue. The next time I see Donovan and the kid, they're not going into the house, but walking down a path toward the lake. They seem to have recovered from the crash, but Donovan is not having a particularly lovely day. Kevin-With-The-Scar is working overtime to placate him.

"I really don't think they'd know to look here," he says, struggling to keep up with Donovan.

"They knew to come to my fucking office. There's no way that guy's Fran Mahoney's nephew. He's either a cop or a private eye or something. But he's not what he seems, I'll tell you that much."

"Yeah, but you really think they'd dig it up?"

"We're going to find out, aren't we?"

They disappear down the path. Our opportunity to run is right here, but suddenly I don't feel like taking it. Donovan and the kid are looking for something and it's not the USB drive in my jacket pocket. There's something else to find here. I turn to Carol, who's standing on a cut log and peering through the window above us.

"Oh my God," she mutters.

"What?"

"I thought this was a woodshed. It's a fucking sauna!"

"For God's sake, would you get over it?" Although, frankly, I'm also a little disgusted.

Carol steps down. "Are we clear to make a run for it?"

"Let's wait a second."

"Are you high? These guys find us, they will *kill* us. For starters!"

"They're looking for something. I want to find out what it is."

A second later, Donovan and the kid come back up from the lake. Carol and I fall silent. Thankfully, they show no sign of heading our direction. Donovan puts his hands on his hips.

"Okay, fine," he says, "Doesn't look like they were here."

Kevin-With-The-Scar looks relieved to the point of being smug. "I didn't think they would be."

"But that guy is up to something. Trust me. He's not going away."

"They don't know anything."

"You willing to put your life on it? Because that's more or less what we'd be doing." He points down the path, using his middle finger. "Anybody finds that down there, this whole fucking thing falls apart. And I'll give you three guesses who's going in the shithole first."

The kid looks more pale than usual. "Me."

"Yes. And the guy coming right in behind you will be me."

Donovan wanders a few feet away, head down. Kevin-With-The-Scar follows him.

"If it comes down to it," Kevin says, "Maybe we could talk. Y'know. To the cops."

"Are you out of your mind? Tom was going to talk. You saw how that turned out."

Kevin lets out a breath. "How can I forget?"

Donovan pinches the bridge of his nose. "Look, we got things covered. I'm going to go call the Cities, let 'em know we're in the clear. For now."

They walk across the lawn, thankfully, heading out of our lives. Then I hear a fucking twig snap behind me. I spin around and see Carol looking like she's about to throw up. She stares at the offending twig, lying under her foot. Maybe Donovan and the kid didn't hear it.

"What was that?" Donovan says.

Snake-eyes.

Footsteps approach the shed. We fade over to our right, to the opposite side from the footsteps. If worse comes to worse, we can circle the shed and run like hell. After all, we're on foot and they have a car. What could possibly go wrong? For the moment, though, we're able to stay out of sight.

"Could have been an animal or something," Kevin says.

"Yeah. Or it could be those two from the office."

Running, of course, would be a complete mistake. They'd spot us and kill us. End of story. We need a place to hide and off-hand, I can only think of one. We continue to circle the sauna until we reach the screen door.

Donovan and Kevin-With-The-Scar tromp around the corner to the front of the sauna. They pop their heads inside, see the covered hot tub in the first room and check out the sauna room. Both being empty, they head out and walk around the grounds for a minute, failing to notice the punched out frame on the kitchen door. At this point, Donovan figures it must have been an animal or his imagination or something. He and the kid march to the car, hop in and head back down the driveway.

Only after the sound of the car has faded away do Carol and I push away the cover of the hot tub and look out.

"Thank God the hot tub's drained." Carol says, color finally coming back into her face.

"Pretty much our only chance," I said, "The other option was the hotbox in the sauna and I don't think there's room in there for both of us."

This is probably the first time I've ever climbed out of a hot tub with some girl, knowing I wasn't going to get any, and been glad about it. The grounds are thankfully quiet again. I stare at the path Donovan and the kid had checked out.

"What do you think is down there?" Carol asks.

"Only one way to find out."

The path winds downward, heading for a little creek in the distance. It would be a charming enough nature walk if we weren't scared shitless. The trail gets thinner and more brush-intensive as it descends. We're near the creek when I stop.

"They couldn't have come much further than this," I say, "They weren't gone all that long."

"So, what were they checking out?"

I peer into the brush, trying to picture what they were looking for. Then I spot it. And the sight of it sends a chill through me.

"That's got to be it," I say, pointing to a spot a few feet into the brush.

Carol gasps when she sees it. It's a rectangular mound of dirt, maybe five feet long, undistinguished but for the freshly carved path leading over to it. If you didn't know to look for it, you wouldn't think much of it.

"Is that…?" Carol asks, not really wanting to finish.

"Yeah," I say, fighting off the willies, "I would bet you cash money we've found Fran Mahoney."

***

We don't say a hell of a lot until we've found a room at the Lakeview Motel. I waste no time getting out my laptop and setting it up on the bed. Carol locks the door and pulls the curtains, keeping a furtive eye out. We keep our voices down, fearing someone will hear us. If the noise from the other room means anything, it's not an irrational fear. I take the USB drive out of my pocket and hold it up.

"I found this in Tom's study," I say, "No idea what's on it."

"Tom still had a USB drive? I thought everyone was storing paperwork online these days."

"Don't ask me. I'd still keep stuff on disc if it was socially acceptable."

Carol lets out a groan, frustrated at being trapped with a Cro-Magnon Man. I don't blame her for being cranky. She's probably jonesing for a bag of red licorice. "If you want to know what's on it, I suggest you put it into your laptop."

"What if it's got a virus?"

"Then a generation will lose your thoughts on kung fu movies and jelly bellies and we'll just have to muddle through."

Yep, she's getting cranky. Best to get down to business. I pop the USB drive into the laptop and wait. Carol glances anxiously through the tobacco-stained curtains. The accommodations haven't provided us a non-smoking room. Or, come to think of it now, two beds.

"Your computer always run this slow?" Carol asks.

"The computer's got a lot of stuff on it."

"Large quantities of internet porn?"

"No. Mainly, my columns. And a lot of internet porn."

The drive finally comes up. Not surprisingly, it holds a series of documents. As I crack them open, Carol peers over my shoulder.

"You recognize anything?" she asks.

"They're screen prints from NewCo Mutual's systems," I say, "Saw a bunch like them when I broke into Nancy's office."

Carol points to a series of columns. "Then I would guess these are account histories. Those are deposits. And those would be withdrawals."

"A hell of a lot of withdrawals. And all from different accounts."

"And look at the dates of birth. Nobody here is under the age of seventy."

I flick through the rest of the documents, but they're all the same. The clients are all elderly and all live in the Duluth area. "Decent amount of money, all told," I say.

"Yeah, but why? What's the purpose of stealing all this?"

I don't get a clear answer on that until I get to the last few documents. There are a couple screen shots of an accounting program. It's the balance sheet for a company called Bartlett Developments. They've been receiving a steady flow of cash over the last several months. Flicking through the other documents, we match withdrawals from the NewCo Mutual client accounts to the money coming into Bartlett.

"Looks like these people are investing in this Bartlett Developments," Carol says.

"Yeah. You think they know that?"

I close the laptop and shove it aside. For a long time, neither of say anything. I get up and pace the room.

"Okay, let's try this," I say, "Wayne Donovan is bilking his elderly clients out of money, funneling it all into something called Bartlett Developments. Fran Mahoney tries contacting Donovan, gets nowhere, tries contacting the home office. Donovan finds out about it, he and Kevin-With-The-Scar kill her. They ditch the body and keep paying her bills in order to cover their own tracks."

Carol nods. "Sounds fine. How does all the stuff in the Cities tie into it?"

"Well, first off, because Fran contacted the home office, Donovan's going to need somebody there to cover for him. And that somebody would have to be uniquely positioned to keep an eye on *all* departments."

"Tom."

"Exactly. Once he became vice-president, he wasn't just overseeing insurance. He could keep track of all the other accounts. Quash anything that might come up."

"Then why did Tom get killed?"

"He was going to talk. Maybe what happened to Fran Mahoney wasn't Tom's idea. Maybe he freaked out and decided to blow the whistle on everything. So he put what he knew on a USB drive, but got killed before he could use it."

"And Nancy was killed because she knew something."

"Exactly."

"How did Nancy know anything about it, though?"

"They talked at the party, before Tom was killed. Tom told her a little something, trying to get her help. Intended to tell her more later. Except he didn't have a later."

"But why'd he let Nancy in on it? Why not Tess?"

"I don't know. Maybe he knew Nancy had gotten the letter from Fran Mahoney. Maybe he was trying to protect Tess."

"Or maybe Tess is on it."

I stop pacing and rub my face. Cripe, I don't want to believe that about Tess. But the lines in my head are starting to connect. I sit down on the bed. "Thing is, there's somebody else we've got to be looking for. Tom and Wayne Donovan aren't running this show."

Carol cocks her head. "How do you know that?"

"Tom can't be running it or he wouldn't be expendable enough to kill. And you heard Donovan and the kid over at the cabin. They were afraid the same thing was going to happen to them. Which means someone else is calling the shots."

Carol slides over next to me and stares at the laptop. She slowly nods her head. "Barry. I'll bet you it's Barry."

"The guy running the company? How do figure?"

"Who promoted Tom to Service VP? Tom could keep an eye on everything, but Barry could keep an eye on Tom. Besides, who owns the property Fran Mahoney's buried on? Who gets the bends whenever someone starts looking around his company?"

Who did I see hanging out with Tess the other night? Shit, those lines are looking more and more solid. "I should talk to her about it," I say.

Carol lightly smacks me on the back of the head. "Are you out of your mind? You let her know what you know and you're in deep trouble."

"After what I pulled today, I don't think I can get much deeper. And if she's up to something, I need to hear it directly from her."

Carol shakes her head. "Your funeral. And I hope I don't mean that literally. Meantime, we should call the police. Let them know where they can find Fran Mahoney."

"Not yet."

"Excuse me?"

"The police go up there, they're going to haul Barry in for questioning. He's going to lawyer himself up and be completely inaccessible to me. Everything I've found out will be completely worthless. Barry will skate in this whole deal."

"Joe, a woman's dead body is lying in a hole in the woods."

"Look, not to sound hard-hearted, but she's not getting any more dead. It's really not an emergency."

"What part of that wasn't supposed to sound hard-hearted?"

We debate it a little, but Carol finally agrees not to take unilateral action. We could both use a stiff drink, but don't feel secure in leaving the motel room. We wind up aimlessly staring at the TV until the long-delayed subject of sleeping arrangements comes up.

"So, how do we do this?" I ask.

"We keep one foot on the floor and a space between us on the bed."

"How wide does this space need to be?"

"About a foot."

I sit up. "A foot? The bed is only about two feet wide."

"Then sleep thin. What are you wearing to bed?"

"Pajama bottoms and a sweatshirt. How about you?"

"A flannel nightie."

"Great. Bunking with my grandma."

Carol narrows her eyes. "Keep it up. You'll need to sleep with one eye open."

"Like I won't be doing that anyway."

Contrary to that statement, I pass out not long after my head hits the pillow. A day's worth of abject terror really takes it out of you. My dreams are indistinct, but there's a lot of movement and yelling involved. I briefly slide out of sleep, as I'm wont to do in the middle of the night. My foot is no longer on the floor. Neither is Carol's. We're nose to nose and I've got an arm around her. I should move, but I don't want to. Carol's eyes open and she gives me a sleepy smile.

"You think this is what Mike was worried about?" she asks.

There's a fluttering in my stomach and I know what my next move should be. But I hesitate. The smile disappears from Carol's face. We're on the precipice of something new and immensely weird. What can you do at a moment like this but turn and run like hell the other direction?

"I should put my foot back on the floor," I say.

"Good idea."

"In fact, I should put the rest of me on the floor."

"Grab a pillow."

I slide off the bed, trying not to think how bacteria-ridden the carpet must be. My mission here is clear: spend the night on the floor, work out the kinks in my neck come morning and never speak of this again. If Mike dating Jeannette is a violation of the rules, I don't even want to think about what this is.

Life's complicated enough at the moment, thank you very much.

CHAPTER TWENTY-THREE

Relationships, both short- and long-term—and granted, I have more experience with the former than the latter—are about overcoming things. Usually small things. He's disgusting when he eats, she talks all through the movie. He doesn't do laundry until his pile of dirty clothes resembles Kilimanjaro, she can never finish a soda, thus littering the countryside—and his apartment—with half-empty soda cans. If those little things remain just that, the relationship progresses along just fine. If though, those little things overwhelm the participants' willingness to overcome them, the relationship goes away. Most relationships don't die by gunshot wounds. They die by paper cuts.

For me and Tess, communication was the big paper cut. The small talk always ran out fairly quickly. I was never comfortable asking her anything deeper than, "How's it going?" So, you can imagine how awkward it feels to ask, "Are you in on criminal conspiracy?"

My heart threatens to batter its way out of my rib cage as I wait for Tess at The Tav. If I'm going to confront her, I want it to be on my home turf. And if she does lose it, nobody in the place will pay much attention, focused as they are on the big screens and the booze. My second pint of Hefeweizen arrives just as Tess walks in. She tosses her purse on the table, folds her arms in front of her and arches an eyebrow at me. I've gotten friendlier greetings from high school principals.

"Why am I here?" is how she greets me.

"And a friendly 'Good evening' to you, too, madam."

"After what you pulled the other night, did you expect a hero's welcome? You're lucky I'm even here."

"Yeah, I feel really, really lucky at the moment."

Tess claws the tabletop. "Joe, this can't go on any longer, okay? I asked you to help me out because Nancy was threatening me. She's gone. The threats have stopped. There's no reason for you to keep looking into this."

"No reason? Two people have died pretty much right in front of me. My place has been trashed. I've been threatened a couple of times over. I've been chased and muscled around by goons. You think I'm just going to suddenly say, 'Well, that was fun. Wonder who's on Fallon tonight?'"

"Then you should leave it to the police."

"Would these be the same police who haven't found anything worth noting? The same police that you don't trust?"

She lets out a weary sigh. "Fine. What do you want from me?"

I take a deep breath and dive into what I uncovered in Duluth: the disappearance of Fran Mahoney, getting chased by Wayne Donovan and Kevin-With-The-Scar, even the discovery at the family cabin. Tess's mouth hangs open a bit more with every detail. By the time I'm done her initial hostility has pretty well melted.

"You're sure of all this?" she asks.

"I got it on a USB drive from Tom's office. I'm thinking this is the information he wanted to share before he got killed."

Tess grabs a waiter and orders a white wine. "You're wrong about one thing, though," she tells me, "Barry isn't involved."

"How do you know that?"

"I just do. I can't explain it, but I know he's not involved. Trust me." I can't disguise the chuckle that gives me. Tess cocks her head to one side. "You do trust me, don't you?" she asks.

"Should I? Because you've got Tom's old job and you insist the most obvious guy to be behind all this isn't behind all this. How do I know you don't have a good reason for that?"

Tess takes a big slug of her white wine and throws a few dollars on the table. "You can go to hell."

'That's not an answer."

"Well, that's the answer you're getting."

She glares at me. One of my hands goes to my sternum while the other snakes toward her glass of wine, trying to cut off the two most obvious points of assault. Tess, however, shakes her head, looking sad.

"It's too bad," she says, "I thought we were friends."

Tess turns on her heel and walks out. The entire thing was short and not particularly sweet. And for some reason, I feel guilty. Why should I? Yes, Tess wants a friend. But she may be a criminal.

And between Mike and Lars, I have enough criminal friends in my life.

***

There are times—frequent times—when I wonder how I've reached age thirty-three without really growing up. Yes, I have a job and an apartment and I pay all my bills on time. But it's an easy job, a small apartment and only a few bills. It's a lifestyle that gives me plenty of time to goof off. In fact—and I'm completely serious here—when asked if I'd like to own a house someday, the main appeal is the thought of building a Batcave in the basement.

But for the moment, let's consider the case of my friend Mike. He's got a good job, made his fair share of money, lives in a nice apartment and drives a cool car. And as I walk into my place, he's crouched in a ball, hiding near the arch windows. Why, oh why, did I trust him with my spare key?

"What's going on?" seems to be the appropriate question to ask him.

"I broke up with Jeannette."

"Uh-oh."

"Yeah, she took it like an uh-oh. Kept asking what she was doing wrong, said she'd make it better, said she'd kill herself."

"You really think she will?"

"No. She's batshit crazy, but she's not suicidal. She'll process the whole thing and realize she actually wants to kill me. And if she does that, Carol will figure out I was dating her and then I'll be in *real* trouble." After a second of contemplating his own mortality, he asks, "You got any grape soda?"

"In the fridge."

"You mind getting it for me? I don't want to give away my position."

"You drink the grape soda, you might have to take a whiz and then give away your position anyway."

"No, my body is a finely-tuned machine. All I have to do is— ah, cramp! Cramp!"

Mike flops on the floor, clutching his hamstring. I trudge over to the fridge to fetch the soda.

"I don't know what you're afraid of," I say, "You've wanted Carol back for a few years—"

"I have not!"

"And now someone is willing to be Carol for you. Sounds like a win-win deal to me."

"You're not funny, Joe."

"My readership would disagree."

"Your readership's never kissed a girl. What do they know?"

I bring the soda into the living room. To protect Mike's position, I have to sink to the floor and slide the bottle toward him, hoping like hell it doesn't tip over. Mike's hand shoots out and cleanly grabs the soda. I drop heavily on to the futon and flip through the channels, looking for something that isn't a prophecy of doom or an exposure of an alien conspiracy. Mike sips his soda and stretches out his hamstring.

"You okay?" he asks.

I shake my head. "Tried talking to Tess, see if she'd tell me what she's up to. About the meeting with Barry and everything. No dice."

"I see you're not having any luck with women, either."

"Oh, just these last thirty-three years or so."

Mike peeks through the window and drops down quickly. His breathing picks up. "Someone's coming."

"Jeannette?"

"I didn't get a clear look."

"Mike, you realize I live in an apartment building, right? It might be someone who, y'know, actually lives here."

He ventures another look. "Two guys. Both wearing suits. One of them is pretty big."

A flash of horror rolls through me. "Big like a city block?"

"Yeah."

"The other guy have gray hair?"

"Yeah. I need to worry about these guys?"

"No, you're going to be fine." I, on the other hand, am completely fucked.

CHAPTER TWENTY-FOUR

According to dream interpretation, dreams in which we're being chased mean we've got a nagging problem. I'm going out on limb here, but I think the nagging problem is The Boogie Man trying to chase you down in your dreams. There you go: analysis of your subconscious, didn't cost you a dime. Buy my book.

I'm sure this little episode's got a future playing out in my own dreams. Assuming I *have* a future. Mike, meanwhile, has banished all thoughts of his own demise and is now focused on mine.

"Those guys disappeared at the front," he says, craning his neck for a view out the arch windows, "You think they're in the building?"

"Probably. If they want to come in, that security door isn't going to stop them."

"What are you going to do?"

"Clear out the back. You stay here. Don't let anybody in."

"What if they kick the door down?"

"Well, *then* let them in."

I charge down the back hallway and step lightly across the deck. The problem with the whole erector set of decks and stairs is that, while they're lovely, they're not indigenous to the building. They get maintenance work only when the creaks and yawns are so loud that the tenants fear the thing is about to step away from the building and go into business for itself.

I think light thoughts as I slip down the stairs. There's no sign of Barry's goons. Hopefully, they're out front, with no thoughts of me escaping out the back. If I can make it to the car, I can go for help. It takes forever to get down the stairs, but neither City Block nor Gray-Haired Guy appears. A bird caws here, a car whizzes past there, each noise like a bomb going off in the cool darkness. I sprint down the back walk.

And Gray-Haired Guy steps out of the shadows.

"Come here, fucko, we need to talk."

Well, I'm certainly not going to talk when the invitation involves calling me *fucko*. Gray-Haired Guy's cut off the route to my car, so I run back toward the building. There's a backdoor on the ground floor. If City Block's gone up to my apartment, I've got a clear path through the building and out the front. I negotiate the lock smoothly, a small miracle in itself, and slam the door shut in Gray-Haired Guy's face.

And I run right into City Block.

He's casually holding Mike in a headlock, permitting no one and nothing to pass by. Gray-Haired Guy bangs at the back door.

"Let him in," City Block says, "Fucko."

I open the door and Gray-Haired Guy throws me up against the wall. City Block does the same for Mike. Gray-Haired Guy does the talking, through gritted teeth.

"You're going to go upstairs and get the USB drive—"

"What USB drive?" I say.

Gray-Haired Guy grabs me by the throat. "Go ahead. Play fucking dumb. But we know you have it, fucko. And we're here to get it. And then we're all going to go for a ride. You try anything, you're dead."

"Aren't we dead, anyway?"

"Shut up."

Behind them, the door to Old Man Albertson's place opens. He's probably checking out the commotion, not realizing how dangerous things are out here. If they see him, these guys might kill Old Man Albertson as a witness. Suddenly, a brown rifle butt appears in the doorway. It hovers a moment then crashes into the back of Gray-Haired Guy's head. He goes down like a shot. City Block spins around in time to have the barrel stuck under his nose.

"Okay, shitbag, get inside," Old Man Albertson growls. He barely flicks his narrow green eyes toward me and Mike. "You two can drag the other bag of shit in. Let's move."

I have to confess: much as he's a legend in the building, I've never actually seen Old Man Albertson before. I always pictured a wispy, decaying figure; sort of like Albert Einstein crossed with a bowl of mashed potatoes. The real Old Man Albertson, though, is anything but. He's tall and thin, with chiseled features and a diminishing buzzcut. His gravelly voice emerges from a barely-opened corner of his mouth. If this guy isn't an ex-Marine, I'm Gomer Pyle.

The apartment also comes as a surprise. Rather than being a collection of old newspapers, dirty dishes and food wrappers, maybe the skeletal corpse of a former beloved pet or two, it's as neat as a barracks. Spare bits of furniture. Neutral colors. A few old family photos on the bureau to add some warmth. And it hits me: Old Man

Albertson isn't afraid of the world, he's just disgusted by it. The place has nothing to offer him, so he'd rather hang out in his apartment.

Old Man Albertson's giving orders the second we walk in. Two straight-back kitchen chairs are brought into the living room. City Block sits in one while Mike and I struggle to get Gray-Haired Guy's carcass into the other. That done, Mike fetches some duct tape and we use a couple rolls securing the goons to the chairs. Old Man Albertson nods toward the green couch and Mike and I waste no time finding seats. He stands in front of the chairs, the shotgun loosely at his side. He and City Block stare each other down.

"You're going to pay for this," City Block says.

Old Man Albertson responds by casually flipping the shotgun around and driving the butt between City Block's eyes. Bit of a love tap, but enough to draw blood. He stands over City Block and gives him the junkyard dog growl.

"You mind your tone, fat boy. I've never taken shit from any goddamn kraut and I'm not going to start now."

Mike whispers, "Kraut?"

I hold my index finger to my lips.

Old Man Albertson goes on. "Here's the deal, sonny boy. You and your pansy friend are going to tell me why you're in enemy territory, messing with my men. And if you don't give me the answers I want, if you even look a little hinky, I'm blowing your heads right back to the goddamned Fuhrer."

Blood is trickling between City Block's eyes, which are, for the first time, betraying a bit of panic. "Fuhrer?"

"What did I tell you, jerry? Don't fuck with me! I mention Uncle Adolph, don't you pretend you don't know him! Bullshit me one more time, Nazi scum, and I will motherfuck you right back to the Fatherland."

Mike and I exchange a look, finally getting it. Old Man Albertson, our kindly neighbor and savior, is completely fucking insane. Then again, if you're going to be trapped in the apartment of a shotgun-toting loon, you want him on your side.

"Um, Sergeant?" I ask.

Old Man Albertson gives me a glance. "What is it, soldier?"

"Permission to question the prisoner?"

"Affirmative."

I step over to City Block, hoping to play some variety of Good Cop. City Block's clearly torn; not wanting to die but also wanting to rip my head off.

"Barry sent you?" I ask.

"Go to hell."

"Bartlett Developments, tell me about that."

"Go fuck your mother. Tell me about that."

Okay, that's rude. Kill me if you have to, but why drag my mother into this? "Fran Mahoney. Old lady up in Duluth. What do you know about that?"

"I know you can go fuck her and yourself."

"What about Tom Reilly?"

"What about you fucking a dog in the asshole?"

Yup, bestiality. We've gone that far down the food chain in a matter of seconds. I take a breath through my nose, trying to stay in Good Cop mode. "Look, I know this isn't the greatest of circumstances, but I could really use your help. And I think, deep down, you know this is the right thing to do."

"I think, deep down, is where you can go fuck your faggot ass."

Clearly, this guy needs to get either laid or a thesaurus. Old Man Albertson drops a hand on my shoulder, gently moving me aside.

"Let me handle this, soldier," he says.

City Block, though, is feeling his oats. "You think you're tough because you got that gun in your hands?"

Old Man Albertson calmly sets the rifle in a corner. In a flash, he's got his thumb and forefinger up City Block's right nostril, automatically doubling its size. The thumb and forefinger return a moment later with several nose hairs.

City Block's eyes flood. "Ah! Fuck, man! What the hell?"

"Listen, shitball, I don't think I'm tough because I got a gun. I think I'm tough because I survived two weeks in the Ardennes, separated from my unit, trapped behind enemy lines. I was cold as hell, starving like a bastard and so horny I could cut glass. But I didn't whine about it or run home to mama. I made my way back to my unit and got back to killing you Nazi bastards. I'm tough because I learned to survive against all odds. You want to know what that's like, you kraut shitpile? Let me give you a taste."

Old Man Albertson stalks into the bedroom. City Block looks to me for an explanation, but all I can do is shrug. When Old Man Albertson returns, he's carrying a service revolver.

"I'm going to teach you something about odds, jerry slime," he says, "Now, how the hell does Russian Roulette work again? One bullet in the chamber with five empties or five bullets in the chamber and one empty? Ah fuck, let's do one empty. I ain't got all night."

City Block's face flushes. He struggles against the duct tape, but he's in there securely. His head might explode before Old Man Albertson does it for him.

I look over at Mike. "We can't let him do this."

"Why not?"

"It's murder, you idiot."

"And what were they going to do to us? Buy us cigars?"

I hop off the couch. "Sergeant, I'm afraid I can't let you do this."

"Quiet, soldier. I'm trying to remember the rules here."

Give City Block another second and there'll be urine flowing down his pant leg. *This* is a guy ready to talk.

I snap to my imitation of standing at attention. "Permission to resume questioning the prisoner, Sergeant."

"You tried that. Didn't get us anywhere, boy."

"Sergeant, with all due respect, I believe the prisoner's more willing to talk." I hope this ends soon. I can't keep up this military shit for long.

Fortunately, Old Man Albertson's in a giving mood. He lowers the revolver to his side. "Fine, soldier. But this kraut better be in a chatty mood or we're right back to Russkie Roulette."

I draw City Block into a huddle. His eyes are wide and his voice is surprisingly gentle.

"This motherfucker's crazy," he says.

"Oh, stumbled on to that, have you?" I say.

"Get me the fuck out of here."

"I'll do my best. But you're going to have to tell me a few things."

City Block's sweating something fierce. He looks toward Gray-Haired Guy, who must be the brains of the outfit. Unfortunately, that brain is turned off at the moment. City Block hangs his head. "Yeah, Barry sent us. He said you have a USB drive and he wanted us to get it from you."

"How the hell does even know I have it?"

"I couldn't tell you. I just take orders."

The sinking feeling in the pit of my stomach, though, knows exactly who told Barry about the USB drive. The only person outside of Mike and Carol who knows I have it. Someone I thought I could trust. Tess.

I shake it off and keep the questioning going. "What about Bartlett Developments?"

A nervous look toward Old Man Albertson and City Block's voice drops to a whisper. "I don't know a damn thing about that. Charlie and me, y'know, we do odd jobs for Barry, but he don't let us on in on the business stuff. Fine by me. I wouldn't know what the hell he's talking about."

"Would your partner know?"

"No. I mean, Charlie's smart, but he's got his limits, too, y'know? We just handle the muscle stuff. That's all."

I study City Block's panicked face. I have no sense that he's lying to me. I give him a slight nod, just a bit of reassurance. "What about Tom Reilly? What do you know there?"

"He had a fight with Barry about something. That's all I know."

"And you and your partner killed Tom."

"No! That we did not do. If Barry handled that, he farmed it out to somebody else. Charlie and I had nothing to do with that."

"What about Nancy Balstrom?"

"I don't know who that is. She a friend of yours?"

Old Man Albertson steps in, still holding the service revolver. "This Nazi's bullshitting us."

City Block shakes his head, frantically. "I'm not."

"Go fuck your mother, you kraut-humping scum. Let's do this thing."

Old Man Albertson pops out the cylinder, spins it and slaps it back into place. City Block breaks down in tears.

"I don't know anything! I don't! Please don't do this! Please!"

Old Man Albertson turns to me. "You satisfied?"

I can only glance at the revolver. "Yeah, definitely. Very, very satisfied."

"Good."

He slips the revolver into the waistband of his slacks and nods toward the rotary phone on the end table. "Call the police. Get these guys out of here."

Mike is quick to do the honors. City Block sobs, quietly. Old Man Albertson and I drift toward the door. He glances at the goons.

"I still don't believe the big guy," he says, "Maybe they came for that USB drive or whatever the hell it is, but they came here to kill you, too."

Sobering thought, even from a loon. "It certainly would have been a, a war crime."

Old Man Albertson chuckles. "Drop that war crime nonsense. I know those guys aren't Nazis."

I snap him a look. "That was a sham?"

"Something I learned a long time ago. SOBs like that aren't afraid of someone who's tough. But they *are* afraid of someone who's crazy."

I can't help but return the wry smile. "Well, you had me fooled. What about the cops? Those guys are going to tell them everything we did."

He cocks his head, amused. "I'm a helpless old man. A recluse. They broke in here and tried to mess me up. Thank goodness, I was able to defend myself. And thank goodness I had a neighbor who was willing to come down and check on me and calm me down and corroborate my story."

If Old Man Albertson needs bullshitters, he's come to the right place. I offer him my hand. "I appreciate this. Any way I can pay you back, just let me know."

"Well, there is one thing. Can you get your friend Lars to leave me alone? I'm not leaving here and, frankly, he makes my ass tired."

***

We turn Frick and Frack over to the police, answer some basic questions and run back up to my apartment. I make a quick call to the Denton County Sheriff's Department, letting them know what they can find on Barry Preston's cabin property. When I'm off the phone, Mike's pacing around the apartment.

"We should have kicked their asses," Mike says, "I don't know why we let them intimidate us. They're not that tough. We could have—"

"Gotten killed if we tried anything stupid. And fighting those guys would have been the definition of stupid."

Mike shakes out his tension. "Okay, now what?"

"I don't know." I pick up the USB drive and heft it in my hand. "I don't have Barry's name on any of this information. But his company is on it, his son-in-law created it and he sent a couple goons to get it back. And he's got a body buried on his cabin property. You think that's enough to nail him?"

"You better hope so. 'Cause if Barry's not in deep shitting trouble, you're going to be."

Before I can contemplate that happy thought, my cell phone rings. It's Tess.

"Where are you?" is how she starts the conversation.

"I'm at home. Relaxing after your boss sent two goons over to rough me up."

There's a pause. "I take it they didn't get the USB drive."

My heart drops through my shoes. Much as the evidence was telling me otherwise, I wanted to believe Tess wasn't in on this thing. I close my eyes. "Nope. USB drive is right here with me."

"Fine. I want you to bring it to Barry's office."

"Well, we have a problem there, Tess. You see, I've got something you want and you don't have *anything* I want."

"I wouldn't go that far."

There's a shuffling on the other end of the line and a different voice comes on. "Joe? Joe, I'm sorry. I didn't think they'd—"

It's Carol.

CHAPTER TWENTY-FIVE

Despite the weirdness of the last few weeks, it has been a journey of discovery for me and my friends. For example, I've discovered I can really drive like a maniac. Mike has discovered this makes him extremely nervous.

"Truck coming up," Mike says, gripping the dash, "Might want to slow down. No, don't go around him! You are going to get us killed!"

I ignore him and focus on the road. We're shooting down Highway 94, heading for Minneapolis and Barry's office. Just before she rang off, Tess gave me fifteen minutes to get there.

"What are we going to do?" Mike says, "When—if—we get there?"

"I'm going to take them down."

"Take them down? Who the hell are you? Sonny Crockett?"

"Nobody was Sonny Crockett. Except Don Johnson." Say what you want about Don Johnson, but you show me another guy who could be tough while wearing pink. Yeah, didn't think so.

A few minutes later, we pull into the parking lot of Barry's office building. The lot is deserted. Orange lights throw weird shadows along the ground. Mike fidgets as he looks over the scene.

"You're really going in there by yourself?" he asks, "You're going to hand over that USB drive and let them kill you?"

"Of course not," I say, "You're coming with me."

"Bullshit."

"Bullshit. Or the last words Carol's going to hear from me are, 'Mike's dating Jeannette.'"

"Oh, you would do something that shitty, wouldn't you?"

I clench my fist but avoid punching the dash. "Look, they've got Carol, all right? Tess made it clear on the phone that Carol's only safe if I hand over the USB drive. I don't see that we have much choice."

Mike sighs and looks out the window. "You're right. But we're all dead the second you hand it over. You know that, right?"

"Yeah, I do. But I got to play along and hope that I see some opening to get us out of this mess."

"And if you don't?"

"Then we're fucked."

"Ah. Great. No pressure or anything."

I take out the cell phone and call Tess. She answers, quickly.

"Go to the front door," she says, "Someone will meet you."

"Someone? Who is—" And then I'm talking to a dial tone.

We trot over to the glass foyer. A few moments later, the heavy front door opens. Brian, gun in hand, steps out to greet us.

"Move," he says, nodding toward the corridor behind him.

Severely lacking firepower, we don't have much choice but to follow orders. Keeping our hands where Brian can see them, we're marched to the elevators.

"Carol's okay?" I say as we wait.

"Fuck you."

"I'm getting a lot of that tonight. So, you and Tess were in on this from the word go?"

"Pretty much."

"You trying to run her down was a show for me, huh?"

"Yep. By the way, you owe me for the repair on my back window, asshole."

"I sincerely hope you get the opportunity to collect."

We get off the elevator and are led down to Barry's corner office. Having been here only one time before, and most of that spent in abject terror, I've forgotten how much this place resembles an airport hangar. Barry's desk sits way on the far side of the room. Moonlight cascades through the picture window behind it, illuminating the place's austere whiteness. Shadows coagulate at every edge of the room. Carol and Tess stand on the Persian rug in front of the desk. Tess has a gun pointed at Carol's temple. Wayne Donovan lounges in the club chair across from the desk, watching Carol and Tess like he's at a ballgame or something. Kevin-With-The-Scar stands behind Donovan, all wiry; geeky intensity. Brian sticks the gun in the small of my back. Mike and I take a long walk across the room.

"Where's Barry?" I ask.

Tess's confidence is wavering, but she's trying to put up a good front. "That's not your concern. Did you bring the USB drive?"

"Yeah." But I make no move to get it. "So, you were suckering me the whole time. Why?"

She spits out the words. "Because I needed an alibi. For Tom's murder. For Nancy's. I figured you were so self-involved, you wouldn't care. Guess I called that one wrong."

"So, Nancy never was threatening you. It was you and Brian putting all that together."

"That's right."

I slip my hands into my jacket pockets. One hand closes around the USB drive. I look over at Donovan and Kevin-With-The-Scar. "And you guys killed Tom, huh?"

Donovan picks some lint off his pant leg. "No choice. Tom couldn't deal with the Fran Mahoney thing. If Tom didn't understand it could get rough, he shouldn't have gone along with this in the first place. Maybe it's my fault. I've known him long enough. I should've known he didn't have the stomach for this."

And suddenly, the buzzing in the back of my head goes away. It'll do that when I've figured things out. Tess clears her throat, trying to get my attention. Yeah, that looks bad, I admit. Carol is being held at gunpoint and that doesn't have my undivided attention.

"Do you have the USB drive or don't you?" Tess asks.

I hold it up. "Present and accounted for."

Tess puts out her hand. "Give it to me."

I take a step toward her, but make no move to give her the USB drive. "This isn't you, Tess."

"Joe, this isn't the time—"

Carol struggles a bit against Tess's grip. "Joe, be careful."

"No, I don't mean it in a Kumbaya sort of way," I say, "I mean, this isn't your idea, Tess."

Tess's grip on Carol slackens. "What are you talking about?"

Mike gives a fearful look around. "Yes, Joe, please don't keep the nice people and their guns in suspense."

I spin toward Donovan. "You're telling me Tess is behind this whole thing?"

Donovan squirms a little. "Yeah."

"Sorry, no. Tess is career-minded. Psychotically career-minded. No way she puts that at risk for a goofball scheme like this. I know her that well, at least." I look at Tess and see something pleading in her eyes. I'm on the right track. "And, sad as I am to say it, I don't think Barry's involved, either. He's got hired goons. He's got a reputation to keep up. He's not really going to let Archie and Jughead over there kill a woman and bury her on his property. So, who's running this show? Well, one little thing has been bothering me and I just figured it out."

"And what's that?" Donovan asks.

I step toward him. "You said you hadn't seen Deena Reilly for a few years. Thing is, when I talked to Deena, she said she'd *never* seen you before. Somebody's lying."

The tension in the room is jacked up, but I'm warming to my own theory. No stopping me now. I step toward Tess and Carol.

"So, now I ask myself," I say, "What if this thing doesn't need Barry's approval? What if there's someone close to Barry who can blind him to everything being done in his company? But she's got to keep that anonymity or she's screwed. Am I right, Deena?"

Then comes the sound of two hands clapping. Deena Reilly slowly emerges from the shadows. She walks across the office floor like a panther, ready to strike. She stops a few feet away from me.

"Well done, Mr. Davis," Deena says, "I was hoping you wouldn't figure it out. Actually, I was banking on it." She's still looking at me when she adds, "Tess, you can put the damn gun down."

Tess, relieved, lowers her arm down and deposits the gun on the desk. Immediately, Brian, Donovan and Kevin-With-The-Scar train their guns on Tess. Mike sidles up to me.

"What in the blue fuck is going on?" he says, out of the corner of his mouth.

I'm still looking at Deena as I say, "Up to the point where Deena walked in, this was all a show for us. We were supposed to think Tess has grabbed Carol to try to get the USB drive back. Then when we hand it over, they probably kill Tess, Carol, you, me, maybe a handful of other innocent civilians before continuing on their merry way." I stare at Deena. "Guess you and Nancy weren't as tight as she thought."

Deena shakes her head. "Not when she can't mind her own business."

"Car bomb was kind of a nasty way to do it."

"Didn't want to leave any traces. I farmed that out to someone who used to work for my father. Helps to know someone who knows explosives."

I look toward Tess. "Barry was wondering what was going on, wasn't he? That's why you were meeting with him."

"He wanted me to check things out," Tess says, "I couldn't tell you about it. I'm sorry."

"Barry suspected Brian was involved, though, right? That's why his goons beat Brian up at the club. To send a message."

Tess flicks a look to Brian. "Yeah. I didn't tell them to do that."

"You *did* tell Barry about the USB drive, though," I say.

"Yes. I'm sorry. He hated me after the affair and I thought I could get back in his good graces if I helped him out and—"

"Shut up!" It's the first time I've seen Deena lose her cool and it gets the attention of everyone in the room. She takes a deep breath, getting a hold of herself.

I turn to Deena. "That's where the urgency was, right?" I say, "If this whole thing blows up and the company's going to be dragged through the mud, Barry will move heaven and earth to find out who's behind it. And then you'd be in deep shitting trouble."

"He's not going to find out," Deena says, "We'll have the USB drive back. And the chain of evidence will be gone."

"You thought Tess had the USB drive. That was the whole point of threatening her, right? It wasn't Nancy and Brian. It was just Brian, right?"

"Well done."

"Brian broke into my place looking for it, thinking maybe Tess had passed it along to me. And I'm guessing you broke into Tess's place looking for it."

"You're on a roll. For all the good it will do you. Now quit fucking around and give me the USB drive."

"For all the good it will do you. I called the police up in Denton. They're probably digging up Fran Mahoney's body as we speak."

In one moment, the cool composition of Deena's face crumbles and a mask of snarling hate appears. She charges at me with raised hands. They hover as she tries to decide the best way to lash out. Then all at once, she drops them and nearly regains her composure.

"It doesn't matter," she says, "No USB drive. No evidence. Nobody can prove a damn thing. In fact, there's a room full of people who will say Tess and Tom were behind the whole thing." Deena backhands me across the face, putting what I'm certain is a pretty good welt on my jaw. "Oops. Looks like Tess slapped you right before she pulled the trigger. Now give me the damn thing."

I don't like these odds. Yes, there's four of them (Deena, Donovan, Brian, Kevin-With-The-Scar) and four of us (me, Mike, Carol and Tess). But they have three guns to our none. And while I have no doubt Carol and I would go down swinging, Mike and Tess might switch sides if there's half a chance of saving their own asses. A glimmer of an idea comes to me, but I'm not certain it will work.

Then again, I'm certain we'll be killed if I don't at least try. I roll the USB drive in my fingers and wander toward Mike, Carol and Tess. Deena lets me do it, safe in the knowledge I'm not going anywhere.

"Know what I'm going to miss the most?" I ask, "Touch football. The big tournament is coming up next month. What about you, Mike? Do you want to play touch football?"

Mike looks at me as if I've lost whatever's left of my mind. Then his eyes widen slightly as he joins my wavelength. "I was hoping Carol would join, too," Mike says, "I mean, she's seen me do the blindside hit enough times. I think she'd be good at it."

Carol looks at us, disgusted. "I cannot believe you guys are talking about—" And then *she* gets it. "Never mind. Team wouldn't be balanced, though, would it? Wouldn't you need at least one more girl?"

I shrug. "Chance we'd have to take."

Deena sticks her hand out, shaking it. "For the last fucking time, give me the USB drive."

"Sure," I say, "Catch."

It's a completely stupid plan, one with a Frosty-The-Snowman's-in-Hades chance of actually working. But when you're pretty much doomed, you're willing to try anything. I toss the USB drive toward Deena, the little thing arcing through the dim light. Deena watches it. And we move.

See, Mike and I play in a touch football league every fall. Mike is the key member of our team, The Pigs. Not because he possesses inordinate skill or superior knowledge of the game. It's because Mike has learned to get away with more cowardly blindside hits and cheap shots than the average football player will ever know. Hopefully, Carol has picked up on some of it from the days when Mike dragged her to all his games.

While the USB drive is in the air, Carol lowers her shoulder and plows into Deena, hitting her with a spearing tackle to the midsection. Brian watches, stunned, allowing me to further stun him with an elbow to his already-bruised face. His recoil and cry causes him to drop the gun. I kick it away and dive forward, stretching out to catch the USB drive (that's *my* touch football specialty). Meantime, Mike spins and throws a casual punch into Donovan's nuts, looking around all the while, as if something else has his attention (just like he does it on the field). Mike shoves Donovan into Kevin-With-The-Scar. They go down in a heap, causing Kevin-With-The Scar to accidentally shoot Donovan in the ass.

"Motherfuck!" Donovan screams, grabbing at his hind quarters.

The kid, in shock, drops the gun. Mike follows my lead and kicks it into the darkness. Carol rolls off of Deena and I stand over her.

"It's over, Deena."

Deena responds by booting me in the shin. As I limp away from that, she screams, "Get the fucking guns!"

Suddenly, we're faced with a choice: try to get the guns or make a break for it. Given that we're just as likely to shoot ourselves as anyone else, running seems like the best bet. Mike leads the way, grabbing a shell-shocked Tess as he goes. Carol grabs my arm and half-drags me out. I limp the whole way out of the office and down the hall.

"What do we do now?" Carol asks.

"Get out of here," I say, "Then we call the police. We give 'em the USB drive and everything we know."

We limp down the stairs and out of the building. Turns out Tess and Carol, having been grabbed by the bad guys, have no vehicle. We all pile into my Saturn. It's almost clear of the parking lot when the first shots ring out. Everyone drops their heads. I'm positive something just pinged against the car.

"Guess they found the guns," Mike says.

"Got to hand it to them," I say, "They're determined."

And, apparently, good shots. I'm no more than half a block from the office when the car stops responding to the accelerator. I pump it, but still nothing. Mike starts slapping me on the shoulder.

"Get moving, get moving!" he shouts, "What the hell are you doing?"

"They must have hit something," I say.

Sure enough, we're only another half-block before the car stops altogether. I look in the rearview mirror and see a pair of headlights charging out of the office parking lot. I scramble for the door handle.

"Got to move!" I say, "Follow me. Fast!"

In a flash, we're all out of the car and running for the next intersection. The shin is still bothering me, but the adrenaline helps with that. There's a glass door on the corner, probably a bar or something. It looks inviting enough. If we get among witnesses, maybe Deena won't try anything. As I whip open the door, I get a glimpse of the sign overhead. And I realize why the whole thing looks inviting.

Les Bos.

Are you fucking kidding me?

It's a mildly sleepy night in the bar. There's room to run. The patrons let us pass, unconcerned. Lars is coming down the circular staircase. He gives us a big wave. Deena leads Brian and Kevin-With-The-Scar through the front door. There's no hope I can shout to Lars, given that *Cherry Pie* is probably registering on the Richter scale. Immediately, I start with the hand signals. Much as I cap on my friends, there's a certain degree of ESP you get in knowing someone so well. It only takes a quick jerk of the thumb toward Deena and Co. for Lars to realize we're in trouble.

Lars grabs the railing and hurls his tangle of arms and legs down to the floor. In a single bound, he's blocking Deena's path. She takes a second to size up the situation and decks Lars, knocking him over a table. Nice try, Lars.

Mike tries to cut around the Stripatorium, but two things suddenly appear in front of him. One is Brian, clearly looking for payback for the atomic wedgie. The other is Jeannette.

"Mike! I thought you'd be here," she says, "I need to talk to you."

Mike's head is on a swivel, looking at Brian, looking at Jeannette, trying not to look at Carol. "This really isn't the time."

"Mike, you always say that."

"I know. And I'm usually full of shit. But believe me, this actually isn't the time."

Jeannette steps toward Mike, but Brian shoves her out of the way. Mike tries a roundhouse right. Brian blocks it and grabs him by the throat. And Jeannette brains Brian with a chair.

"I said I had to talk to Mike!" she screams.

For a second, nobody does anything. Kevin-With-The-Scar takes the initiative, turning and running like hell out of the bar, leaving Deena completely on her own. Deena shoves past me and runs up the stairs, heading for the Crow's Nest and higher ground. I charge after her. When I get up to the Crow's Nest, Deena's looking around, panicked. She probably hoped there was a back stairs or something, but no such luck. I've got her hemmed in.

"It's over, Deena," I say, "Just give it up."

But all sense of calm or smugness has been replaced by an animal's desperate will to survive. Deena picks up a highball glass and throws it at me. A quick duck to the right keeps my head out of the path. Yeah, I suppose it was kind of foolish to think she'd come quietly.

Deena backs toward the railing, her face contorted with rage and hatred. "Go fuck yourself, you smart ass piece of shit!"

"Now come on. You can tell me to go fuck myself or you can call me a smart ass *or* you can call me a piece of shit. Piling it all on? That's just not nice."

Deena's face goes bright red. Clearly, our bantering days are over. She bellows at me; a feral cry of pain. She grabs another highball glass (really, Lars, who the hell busses these tables?) and smashes it against the floor. I step back to avoid shrapnel. Deena squats down and comes up with a very large and very jagged shard of glass.

"Get out of my fucking way," she growls, stepping toward me.

Hopefully, somebody's called the cops. Hopefully, somebody's willing to step in and help me out. But I probably won't have a lot of luck with that. Guys frequenting titty bars don't generally go out of their way for others. I'm on my own against the Mad Glass Slasher Lady. I hold up my hands and back toward the stairway.

"Look," I say, "You don't want to do this."

"Bullshit. I've wanted to do this since I first laid eyes on your smug idiot face. Give me one good reason not to kill you right here."

And what am I going to say to that? Clearly, with my smug idiot face, I don't bring a lot to her table. And once you've started murdering people, the corpses get easier to deal with as you go.

The stairs are close now. "Yeah, I, I got nothing."

"I didn't think so."

Deena takes a slash at me. I jump back as it comes perilously close to my chest. She swings backhanded. Again, I jump back to avoid it. Deena raises the shard above her head and tries to bring it down on my jugular. I grab her arm, surprised at her strength. Guess she's not messing around at that health club.

"Die!" she screams, "Why don't you fucking die?"

"I'm working on it! Cut me some slack!"

Nice to know I'll have my sense of humor even unto death. While Deena's arm struggles to drive the glass into my neck, the rest of her goes into Tasmanian Devil mode. Her legs alternately kick at my shin and knee at my crotch. Her free hand gouges and scratches my face. Meantime, it's all I can do to keep the glass out of my person. And I'm weakening.

Then there's a blur and Deena's no longer on top of me.

I sit up, transfixed by the tangle of arms and legs that currently makes up Tess and Deena. They get to their feet, Deena no longer holding the shard of glass. Tess looks toward me.

"Joe, are you—?"

And that's as far as she gets before Deena cold-cocks her, sending Tess sprawling. But Deena no longer has the glass and Tess and I are blocking her only escape route. Deena retreats to the edge of the Crow's Nest.

"This isn't over," she says.

"Yes, it is. It's not—" is as far as I get before she rolls over the railing.

Tess and I run to the edge of the Crow's Nest. We get there in time to see Deena drop on to the runway, landing right in front two strippers in mid-strip. She lands on her heels and winds up on her ass. But she's in one piece. The music cuts out. The patrons stare at her. One of them breaks the silence.

"Take it off!"

This brings a round of similar cheers. Deena has no time for this, leaping off the stage and shoving her way through the crowd, heading for the back hallway. Lars staggers into her path, only to get knocked head first into the bar. Carol, however, cuts off her route. Deena screams and heads toward another hallway, Carol in hot pursuit. They disappear as Tess and I reach the main floor. Mike runs over to us.

"Told you it was a make-able jump," he says, "What the hell happened up there?"

I look at Tess and smile. "Tess saved my ass." I look toward the hallway where Carol and Deena have gone. "Isn't that the way to the Pudding Pit?"

Mike breaks into a smile of pure greed and lust. "Holy shit, it is. I gotta see this."

He takes off at a gallop, with Tess and me a step behind. We can hear the sounds of a struggle coming from the Pudding Pit. When we arrive, Carol is rolling around a hot-tub sized vat of pudding, beating the living hell out of Deena.

"I can die now," Mike says, "I mean, I thought I could die before, but this..." The man is on the verge of weeping.

Carol has the situation well in hand. All those hours of cardio are apparently paying off (if you can call winning a Pudding Pit fight a *pay off*). When it's done, Deena's slumped against the side of the Pit. Mike and I help Carol out of the gooey mess.

"That," Mike says, shaking his head, "That was amazing. I am so turned o—impressed. I'm very, very impressed."

Carol wipes some of the pudding off her face and tosses it back into the pit. She stares at Mike then looks at me. "The police are coming?" she asks.

Lars pokes his battered head into the Pudding Pit, his timing as impeccable as ever. "Police are on their way."

"Good." Carol looks down at her ruined clothes. "I'm not sure if I should try cleaning them or adding whipped cream."

"Add the whipped cream," Mike says, "Definitely. That would be amazing."

Carol stares at Mike again. "Just one thing I'm not clear on. Michael?"

"Yes?"

"When did you start dating Jeannette?"

EPILOGUE

I've always wondered why buzzers sound the way they do. Surely, as a people, we've progressed beyond an ear-splitting whine that sounds like Fran Drescher being fed to a wood-chipper. (Not that I'm opposed to Fran Drescher being fed to a wood-chipper.) But why not just a disembodied voice, a gentle female lilt perhaps, saying, "Excuse me? Sorry to bother you, but there's someone downstairs." If we can rig cell phones to play Run Runaway *as a ringtone, surely, this must be the next stage of our evolution.*

At any rate, I'm thoroughly annoyed that the buzzer is what gets me out of the bed. Yes, it's almost noon, but it's been an exhausting couple of weeks. I blink into the bright sunshine as I stumble down the hall.

"Yeah?" I grunt into the receiver.

"It's Carol. You got a minute?"

Ah nuts, why couldn't she have called first? I haven't showered, I'm unshaven and I'm wearing a pair of green boxers with little footballs all over them. I'm not exactly ready to hold court.

"Okay, I'm going to let you in," I say, "Just step inside, wait one minute and come on up."

"I take it you aren't decent."

"I am decent. I'm als—"

"You're also naked. I've heard this joke."

I use the minute to slip on a pair of shorts and a t-shirt, run a brush over my teeth and slap a Twins cap on my head. That's as close to presentable as I can get by the time Carol knocks on the door.

"You must have looked like holy hell a minute ago," she says as I open the door,

"Long night."

"In the sense it's almost the middle of the day?"

"The middle of your day, girlfriend, not mine."

Carol tosses her purse then herself on the futon. She declines an offer of coffee, probably knowing I'd serve her reheated stuff from the day before.

"Just wanted to see how you're doing," she says, "Are you relieved?"

"Relieved doesn't begin to cover it."

"Quite a coup you scored."

For a few days, the whole affair gained a round of media attention. Not the sort of publicity NewCo Mutual likes, what with the CEO's daughter bilking clients then killing them. Everyone was rounded up, and according to Sergeant Hara, they're all working overtime to cut deals and testify against each other.

"Has to be good for the web traffic," Carol says.

"Certainly hasn't hurt. Lance has been highlighting *Cup o' Joe.* Thinks I should try getting a book deal. Maybe the site can publish the serialized version."

"You should do it."

I wave it off. "By next month, people will have forgotten all about this."

"Suit yourself. Seems like a lot of work for nothing."

"I wouldn't say 'nothing.' I broke up a nice little conspiracy and took down the CEO of a major company."

"Barry's out, huh?"

"Yeah. Couldn't run the place with a hell of a lot of authority after this. But strangely, I don't feel sorry for him."

Carol playfully kicks my foot. "Barry wasn't the only one who lost something."

I wince. "Poor Lars."

The attention Les Bos received was a momentary boon to the business. However, it brought about further scrutiny and the realization the place had been operating without a liquor license. Apparently, neither Lars nor Chuck had bothered to follow through on that one.

"Were they able to pay the fine?" Carol asks.

"We'll see. For the moment, it sounds like they're going to be able to unload the place. A Mormon theatre group wants to buy it. They're willing to give Lars and Chuck about a third of what it's worth."

"Thirty cents on the dollar return? That's one of Lars's more successful investments."

"Yeah. He's pretty happy about it."

Carol shakes her head. "I suppose they'll get rid of the Pudding Pit."

"It'll always live in Mike's memory. Speaking of which, how's he making up the thing with Jeannette to you?"

Carol stifles a grin. "He's no longer allowed to talk to, look at or have any human interaction with my female friends. And he's going to be cleaning my car and changing the oil for the next six months."

"Sounds like he got off lucky."

"Oh no. I'm just getting warmed up."

It's enough to make me cross my legs for protection. "And what's the punishment for my part in the whole thing?"

She smiles. "Well, I'll give you a pass. You've had a productive couple of weeks."

"Couldn't have done it without you guys."

Still smiling, Carol drops her eyes to the floor. A voice comes from my bedroom, interrupting us.

"Joe, is there somebody here?"

Tess comes out of the bedroom, wearing a white t-shirt of mine. And only a white t-shirt of mine.

Carol is quickly on her feet. "I'm, I'm sorry. I didn't realize you had someone here—"

"Oh, uh, Tess was sleeping. I didn't—"

"It's okay. I have to go."

Tess holds up a hand. "Don't worry about it. You don't have to—"

But Carol already has the door open, practically shielding Tess from her view. "Yeah, yeah, I do. I've got something, uh, going on. Good, good to see you again, Tess."

Tess disappears into the kitchen while I follow Carol out into the hall.

"I'm sorry," I say, "You were only dropping by for a second and I thought she'd sleep through it and—"

Carol puts on a big smile, but there's something vacant in her eyes. "It's okay. Don't worry about it. You, uh, you two are back together?"

"I don't know. I doubt it. This is just kind of a, a heat of the moment thing. Nothing's really going to change—"

Carol's eyes slide away and she starts down the stairs. "It's okay. You don't have to explain. No big deal. I'll see you around." And she disappears around the corner.

I step back into the apartment and close the door. Tess comes out of the kitchen, holding a mug of reheated coffee.

"Was she okay?" Tess asks.

"I guess. She just...yeah, she's fine."

Tess cruises into the living room and plunks down on the futon, taking a look around. "We should go out for breakfast. I know a cute little place over in Minneapolis. Then I was thinking maybe we could go clothes shopping. I know a few things that would look great on you. And I've had some ideas about this room. I think you could rearrange it. Make it really Feng Shui."

Huh. Then again, I should really see what's bothering Carol...

THE END

Randall J. Funk is the writer of the Joe Davis Mystery series. He is also an actor, director, and playwright. His plays include *The Hound of the Baskervilles*, *The Mudslinger Party*, and *Bring Me The Head of Dominic Papatola*. He lives in St. Louis Park, MN with his son Ben.